Wolves of Cold Creek

Lily's

Tail

Brittany Putzer

Copyright © 2023 Brittany Putzer

Lily's Tail

Editing by: Kat Pagan, Pagan Proofreading

Cover designed by: Charles Putzer Jr.

Formatted by: Frankie Page

ISBN: **979-8-218-40184-9**

Published in the United States of America.

For those who struggle with their fucked-up pasts, your second chance is a page turn away...

Trigger Warning

Lily's Tail is a wolf-shifter romance that contains scenes that may be upsetting for some readers. The content includes triggers such as (but not limited to): murder, death, profanity, violence, graphic sexual activities, demanding alpha men, needy headstrong women, witchcraft, guardian angels, and sexual assault.

CONTENTS

Lily

Dancing

Past

*O*ne stroke at a time. Don't overthink it.

I dip the fragile bristles into the sunburst pigment. The vision in my mind fast-forwards in a flash of luminous imagery. I need to capture this moment before it fades away. My wrist flicks, striking layer after layer of the delicate hue onto the starkness of the white. The vibrant tone streaks across the once-dull backdrop, morphing into a snowy mountain sunset. My fingers cramp as they conclude their visual masterpiece.

My wolf stirs inside me, begging to hunt down this location, to seek out why Luna is showing it to us, as I take a moment to admire the painting.

Ever since I was young, this was the way I expressed myself. It set me apart from my twin brother. Not that it's a competition. I mean, how could it be? He's a *hero*, a Guardian. I snort at the thought. His magical abilities will always far surpass mine. His crooked smile flashes behind my eyes and causes me to smile. Even though I've always lived in my brother's shadow, I wouldn't change it for the world. I love the big brute.

My phone pings with an incoming message and my next thought is: *Well, most of the time I love him.* I know it's him without having to look. He's the only one who messages me. I read his text, asking me when I'm returning to our pack.

I rub my temples and scan my room. It may not be full of furry packmates, but it's mine... ever since I decided I wanted to do something more with my life. Be something *more* than the twin sister of a Guardian. I may be in my thirties, but you're never too old to learn. Because as it turns out, you *can* teach an old dog new tricks.

"I come bearing gifts!" a husky voice announces as it precedes the person who entered without knocking.

"See, when I gave you a *key*, it was for emergencies only. Like if I lost mine or I was too sick to let you in." I side-eye my soon-to-be dead friend.

Jake slaps a palm to his chest. "Ouch." Then he shakes the bag he's holding. "And here I thought you'd drop to your knees, overjoyed by what I brought you."

I sniff the air and water pools in my mouth. He holds the goods above my head.

"You were supposed to be showered and ready to go." He cranes his neck to glance at my latest project. "Oh, that's amazing, Lil!"

Once he's distracted, I jump and snatch the bag out of his hands. I rummage through the contents and squeal. My lips wrap around the straw I find inside and I inhale the chocolaty cream. My moan echoes around us before I tug the plastic from between my teeth and swallow my first mouthful.

"It's better than I remember it," I tell him.

"Double-chocolate cherry milkshake." He grins. "Like our first date."

I roll my eyes. "It wasn't a date."

I stretch my sore limbs. How long was I sitting here? I check the time and curse under my breath. Then I collect some clean clothes and stumble around to find a clean pair of underwear. I seriously need to get better at doing my laundry on a regular basis.

Jake flops onto my bed and watches me struggle. "What are you looking for?"

"Undergarments." I rustle through my dresser.

"You mean like these?" he calls out.

I pivot on my heel and narrow my eyes at him as he twirls a pink thong around one finger. "Where did you find those?"

"You don't remember?"

"Just give them to me." I hold out my palm.

He unfolds himself from my bed and stands. I bite the inside of my cheek as he towers over me. Damn that smoldering *grin*. Slickness coats my thighs before I clench them together. I met Jake during my first year at college. He was short and stocky and blended in as an average guy. I lick my lips. We had many study sessions over the years, which ended in mutual releases of pent-up sexual frustrations. Now he's grown into a well-sculpted piece of art.

"How badly do you want your underwear?" he whispers into my ear. His hot breath sends tingles down my spine. "If I remember correctly, you wore this particular pair last weekend to the art gallery." He kisses the quickening pulse on my neck as his hands slither to my ass. "You teased me the whole night until I slammed you against the bathroom stall and fucked you into oblivion."

I shiver as his words wash over me. I push away from his heated frame. "Was that before or after I sucked you dry?"

Jake hisses as the bulge in his jeans vibrates against his zipper. *Oh, yeah, he remembers.* His mouth clashes with mine and our tongues dance. Why does he have to taste so good? If only he were

3

a wolf shifter too. He grabs a fistful of my rear end and kneads it. It really is a shame he's just a human. His fingers dip into my pants. I moan as he tugs at my peach fuzz.

"Maybe you shouldn't wear any underwear tonight?" He teases my soaking entrance. "It'll be easier access."

"Who said I was going to let you touch me tonight?"

He swirls a finger in my juices, and I gasp at the delicious pressure. Then he pulls away before sucking his digits clean. "I'll give you fifteen minutes to get ready." He pecks my cheek. "Hurry up."

Then Jake leaves, closing my door behind him, and I melt onto my bed. He's a whirlwind of passion. I hum softly as my body still buzzes. And he's not even my mate. A shiver racks my frame. I can't wait to experience *that* pleasure.

The canvas catches my attention from across the room, almost as if it's calling to me, and I tilt my head. Maybe the vision I had will lead me to my future husband? I look forward to that day. Then I can leave my stuffy old pack and join his—whoever he is. Not that my family is bad. There's just too many memories. I swallow down the images as they try to rise to the surface.

A knock raps on my door again. "I don't hear you getting dressed. Get a move on, Lil."

I chug my shake and quickly change. Once I'm clothed, I assess myself in my full-length mirror. High heels, skintight dress, and no undergarments. I smirk while I apply lipstick.

Packs of Cold Creek, eat your furry little hearts out.

Lily is going to be returning as a hot and single artist. No longer living in the shadow of her brother. I cringe. Speaking of, I forgot to message him back. I shoot him a quick text, letting him know I'm alive and well. Then I grab my keys and swing open the door.

"Damn." Jake whistles. He twirls me in a circle. "I'm one lucky man to be able to say I ate that pussy."

4

I smack him. "Say that one more time, and I'll make sure you're never able to have the pleasure again."

"Don't cut off a starved man." His arm slips around my waist. "Now, let's go celebrate our big day."

"I can't believe we're graduating," I whisper to myself.

"Don't remind me," he growls.

We walk into the night air, and I let the silence envelop us. Poor Jake. His dad is super controlling. He *allowed* Jake to finish his degree, but the moment he gets his diploma, Jake's enlisting so he can keep up the family tradition. It's a sore subject for my friend. I squeeze his hand and he offers me a sad smile. But it'll be better this way and *easier* to call things off between us. Jake has no idea *what* I really am, and I'd like to keep it that way.

"Let's not think about what comes later," I declare as I wave down a taxi. "Tonight, we're getting drunk, dancing, and going home with complete strangers. Then regretting the hangover tomorrow."

The room is alive. Spinning with vibrations, strobing lights, and sweaty bodies. No shifters. No pack laws. My nails glide up a man's bicep, creep along his neck, and fist a handful of his hair. He bruises my hips between his palms and his erection rubs into my belly. He's a big boy. I lick my lips before slamming them against his. His mouth tastes like fire whiskey and creates a delicious burn as I swallow. I purr as my balance wavers.

How many drinks have I had? Just enough to experience a wonderful buzz.

The stranger pulls away so he can shout in my ear. "Let's take this to a dark corner." He gropes my aching pussy. "I promise I'll make it worth it."

I giggle and continue to gyrate against him to a rhythm that thrums through my blood.

"You can even bring your friend." He nods to Jake.

I tilt my head to see *my friend* squeezing through the crowded dance floor with bottles of water in hand. "My hero!" I wave to Jake. "How did you know I'd be thirsty?"

His boyish grin brightens his face. "How many years have we known each other? I can tell when you're getting dehydrated."

"You are such a good provider." I chug the liquid. Droplets slither over my overheated chest. When I finish, my hunky dancing partner is gone. "Where'd he go?"

"Who?" Jake questions.

Did I imagine the hottie? I bite my lip. Nope, I can still taste him. My girly bits tingle as I watch him grope another girl on the dance floor before licking her neck. Jake twirls me and dips me back. "You're incredible, you know that?"

I smirk up into his eyes. "Yes, I do. But thanks for the reminder."

His gaze eats me up. "I look forward to making you scream."

"Who said you'll be the one to do that?"

Jake lifts me in the air and I wrap my legs around his waist. Damn, his erection is begging to pierce me. I rub against it to the beat of the song. I drape my hands around his neck and suffocate him with my cleavage.

"Fuck," he mumbles into my flesh before he sucks on the exposed skin.

I arch my back. *Luna, help me.* He may be human but my body is singing as he strums me like a familiar instrument. I can already envision the painting I'd create for this moment. Simple strokes against a popping background. Blurs of unknown shapes with us centered amongst them. Bodies melting together.

"What do you say, Lil?" Jake growls in my ear.

Was he speaking? My eyes flutter open and I see that the club is closing. The customers are chugging their drinks and stumbling towards the exits.

"Did I miss something?" I pout.

"Don't worry, baby. The party doesn't have to end here."

"What did you have in mind?"

"Laying you on your back and devouring that glistening pussy of yours," he says, and I mew into his neck. "Then fuck you over and over again until we pass out."

"What's my other option?"

"I could drop you off at home and you could finger-fuck yourself." He nips my ear. "Either way, we can't stay here. They're closed." Jake sets me on my feet and wraps an arm around my waist before he guides me into the warm night air and hails us a taxi. "So, what'll it be?"

I tug him into the waiting car. "Let me paint you naked," I tell him more than ask, as I scan his angular cheekbones and strong jawline.

"Nope. These goods are for a very exclusive audience, and not to be displayed on your wall for everyone to ogle."

"Where to?" the driver demands from the front seat.

Jake ignores him. "I'm *not* modeling."

"You're no fun," I huff. "We should spend the night at your place because it's bigger and more private."

"But I love yours, especially when the entire floor can hear you shout my name." Jake kisses my cheek.

"I'm not *that* loud," I fire back, and he arches a brow. "I'll prove it!"

7

I won't admit he's right. But he is. I can't help it. With all the pack rules about meeting your mate and getting married for life, I didn't have much of a sex life before I came here. The alpha always said: *What's the point if someone isn't your forever wolf?*

But my alpha isn't here, and neither are any of the other judgmental wolves. I grin at Jake. "If you let me come home with you, I'll do that thing with my tongue you love so much."

His gaze darkens before he hollers at the driver, "Take us to Peach Street."

Jake's nails scrape my scalp as he devours my mouth. He tugs off his shirt and throws it across the room. His bedside lamp titters dangerously close to the edge as the next clothing item hits it dead-on. Jake rips off my gown, and I gasp as my heated frame meets the icy air-conditioning of his apartment. He pulls a nipple between his teeth and my back arches. Goose bumps cover my body.

"Touch me," he demands.

My lip twitches. "A little needy?"

His smoldering eyes meet mine and my body ignites. He strokes my swollen mouth with his thumb. "I'm going to miss this."

The pain laced in his words acts like a bucket of ice water to my libido. "Jake…"

He kisses my palm. "I'm sorry. I didn't mean to ruin the mood."

I sit up and tug him to my side. "Talk to me."

"I'd rather fuck you."

I smack his thigh and his smile returns. There's my bestie. I lay his head in my lap and stroke his hair.

"Thank you." He nuzzles into my stomach. "For always being here for me," he says, and my heart splinters.

What happened to his parents? I know his dad was a big military guy. But he's never mentioned his mother. Not that I can say much about my family. My parents passed away in a car accident when my brother and I turned eighteen. Everyone says we were lucky because we were adults when it happened, but I feel like I need them more now than I ever did when I was a child.

I massage Jake's scalp. "No thanks needed. You've done the same for me."

He draws circles over my leg. "You know, if things were different…"

"Stop. We knew what we were agreeing to when we first hooked up."

"I know." He swallows. "But I want you to know that you mean more to me than just a hookup."

For a military brat, Jake is one of the most sensitive guys I know. He's right, though. If things were different… like fur didn't poke through and shred my clothes…

I mean, what would he think of me then? If I shifted to four legs and barked?

It doesn't matter. We made a pact, and now that we're graduating this weekend, we'll go our separate ways. I'll return to my family to hunt down my predestined mate as expected, while Jake attends basic training like his dad requires of him.

Life goes on, no matter how much it sucks.

"Hey. We still have tonight, right? How about we make the best of it?" I peek down at him. "Jake?" I smirk at his even breathing. Of course, he fell asleep. It was probably the gallon of tequila he chugged before we got here. I lean into the pillows. Yup. It's going to be an *exhilarating* night. I tug the comforter over us. "Sweet dreams."

Bang. Bang. Bang.

I clutch my pounding forehead. Did I drink too much last night?

"What the…" Jake mumbles from beside me. "Do you *hear* that too?" He wipes the drool from his chin.

"Unfortunately, yes." I wiggle out of bed and stumble to his en-suite bathroom. "Please make it stop."

Jake shuffles towards the noise. "They're probably doing road work or something outside and informing the tenants that the water will be shut off. It wouldn't be the first time. I'll be right back."

I groan at my reflection. I hate when I forget to take off my makeup. I use a washcloth to scrub at my racoon eyes. You'd think I'd have learned my lesson after all these years.

The front door slams in the next room and yelling ensues. I use my keen hearing to eavesdrop.

"Dad?"

"Why's your stuff not packed?" a deep voice replies.

"Why are you here?" Jake demands.

"Because you haven't been answering my phone calls or text messages. Is your phone working?" More shuffling and then a growl. "So you're just *ignoring* me? After everything I've done for you. Grab your shit. We're leaving. *Now.*"

"But you said I could get my degree."

"And you have."

"The graduation ceremony is *Saturday*."

"I never agreed to a pointless ceremony. Let's go," his dad hisses.

"I have company. Can we do this later?"

I freeze, glad I'm hiding inside the bathroom and not pinned under his father's critical glare. Will the psycho barge in on me? Break down the door? Talons extend from my fingertips, preparing to attack in a desperate attempt for self-preservation.

"Do you need me to take out the *trash* for you?" his dad asks in an icy tone that sends chills down my spine.

Trash? I'll show him what this pile of *trash* can do! Fur pokes through my skin. But shifting into a wolf won't solve my problems. If anything, it'll give them heart attacks.

"She's a good friend, not some…"

"You have *five* minutes. If you're not in the car by then, I'll take care of your *friend* for you."

Once the raging lunatic leaves, I step out from my hiding spot and lean on the doorframe. "So, he's charming," I say, trying to lighten the mood.

Jake combs a hand through his hair. "He's an ass. I'm so sorry."

I wave him off. "Don't worry about it. You warned me plenty about him and his moods."

Jake pulls me to his chest. "I thought I had more time."

I wrap my arms around him. "You gave me all the time you could, and I value that more than you'll ever know."

He kisses my head. "You're amazing. You know that, right?"

"No, I'm not." I swallow down my tears. I knew we'd have to part ways. I just didn't realize it would hurt this much. "Are you sure we can't keep in touch?"

Jake tenses at the question. "My father is going to do everything in his power to mold me into the perfect soldier. That's not how I want you to see me." He sighs. "I wish things were different, Lil, but this is the hand life has dealt us." He lifts my chin so I'm forced to look at him. "Be careful. The world has a habit of seizing compassionate people and crushing them into shells of themselves. Don't let them. *Fight* back." He releases my face. "I better go before he stomps in here again." Jake grabs his wallet and strides towards the exit.

I shake my head as I watch him go. Jake is ordering me to fight back, but what about *him*? We've had this argument thousands of times over the years and I never get any definitive answers. I step forward, wanting to stop him from walking out. Instead, I blurt, "What about all of your stuff?" I nod to the place he's called home for the last four years.

"Take what you want. The rest will end up in the dumpster." He offers me a sad smile. "My old life is gone. Time to lace up my combat boots and enter hell."

The click of the closing door echoes around me. The silence buzzes in my ears. I lean against the wall and stare at the old-fashioned popcorn ceiling. "Goodbye," I whisper to the shadows.

Why is this ridiculous ceremony outside? I swipe at my brow as I scan the stands, finding no sign of my brother. I check my phone. No messages from him either. I clench my jaw, fighting back the tears threatening to escape.

The student in front of me moves forward, and the wooden platform seems to inch closer.

"Come on, Azure." I bite my trembling lip. "You *promised* me you'd be here."

I sneak a peek into the crowd one more time. Families are waiting to witness their students crossing the threshold in their caps and gowns. Just not mine. Disappointment radiates all around me. I thought my brother would at least make an effort to be here.

"Lilith Cassandra Pawson." The dean nods at me.

I straighten my back and close the distance.

Loneliness. That's what my life's comprised of now. Sure, I can fuck anyone I want. But past that, there's not much more to it until I find my mate.

I force a smile and shake the dean's hand. Then I climb down the steps and move from the stage. I tug off my cap seconds before my pocket vibrates with an incoming message. Azure had an emergency but promises to see me soon. No apologies or explanations.

I glance down just as a butterfly flutters around my ankles, then returns to the clear sky. What I wouldn't give to have *that* freedom. My thoughts drift to my friend. I wonder what Jake is doing right now? I mentally send him all the positive vibes I can conjure up in my own despair. I chew my bottom lip as I count down the minutes until I can leave, grab a drink, and dance the night away.

Snowcapped Mountains

"**S**top fussing, Azure." I tug my suitcase out of the apartment. "I'll be fine."

I take one last sweeping glance at my home away from home for the last four years. I'll miss it. I narrow my eyes at my brother. Especially the *privacy*.

"Just make sure you call me often," he insists.

"I'm traveling deep into the mountains. I doubt they'll have great cell phone service there."

My brother couldn't lift a paw to help me pack my entire life into a bunch of little boxes or fill the moving van. But he's here now, trying to take back the present he gave me. Okay, well, it wasn't exactly a gift of his choosing. He slipped some cash onto a card and I booked everything online.

"Maybe you shouldn't go alone if you won't be reachable. Oh, I know! I can go with you." His frown deepens. "I just need some time to—"

I pivot and meet my twin's gaze. "Don't take this the wrong way, but you are *not* invited to stay with me at the cabin. Besides, it only has one-bedroom." I hold up a hand to stop his retort. "I need to do this, *alone,* to cure this artistic block."

It's not a lie. Ever since Jake left, my creative juices haven't been flowing. When I saw pictures of the snowcapped mountains, they reminded me of the vision I had a few weeks ago and I scheduled the outing. What I didn't expect was for Azure to actually show up to see me off like he said he would.

"Can't you get inspiration elsewhere? Like a sunny beach? Or maybe at Willow Creek?"

I huff out a breath and remind myself to be patient. Azure has been blessed with powers beyond my understanding, and if he is having a tough time letting me leave, he must have a bad feeling.

"Did you have a vision or something?" I ask him.

He pinches the bridge of his nose and squeezes his eyes as if trying to summon his abilities. "No. I just want you to be careful."

The air is thick around us. He's hiding something.

"Is everything okay with you?"

He opens and closes his mouth, then shakes his head. "Yeah, I'm fine."

Okay, something is definitely off but I can't put my paw on it. Maybe I should stay and talk things out with him?

Azure collects me into a hug, breaking me from my internal struggle. "If you aren't home in a month, I'm coming after you."

Home. That's one word for it. My parents had us when they were older, and our pack isn't exactly the largest. Azure and I are the youngest members. Every year, we lose at least one shifter to old age. Plus, with my schoolwork, I've been away for a while.

I pinch my brother's cheek when his frown doesn't ease up. "Can't you just be happy for me, Azure? I graduated at the top of my class, and this trip is my treat for all of my hard work." I poke him in the chest. "Do not ruin it for me."

A car pulls up a moment later, and I wave them down.

I know Azure doesn't approve of my art degree. But he doesn't have to approve of anything. This was my choice. And when I return, I'll open up an art gallery and teach kids art classes on the side.

"Are you ready, miss?" The cab driver reaches for my bag.

"More than you know," I address the man as I smirk at my sibling. "I'll text when I can. Don't give me that look. The cabin is secluded but there's still a reception desk within walking distance. I mean, they offer room service for Luna's sake!" I give the driver my suitcase. "Please be careful with those. There's paint inside that can bust open and make a mess all over my clothes."

Azure slips a wad of cash into my pocket. "Happy graduation, sis."

I embrace him again. "Thank you. Now go save the world, *Guardian*."

"Mom and Dad would be proud of you," he tells me.

"Of *us*," I correct as my eyes water. "I'll see you soon."

I clutch my parka as I follow the housekeeper. She unlocks the cabin and waves me through. I breathe in the earthy scent of the oak logs burning in the fireplace as I scan the small living area, kitchenette, desk, and another door that leads to the bedroom and bathroom.

"If you need more wood, just ring the front desk. We'll clean and refresh your towels every other day but let us know if you need anything sooner. Oh, and if you don't want anyone bugging you, hang the *do not disturb* sign on the knob."

"Thank you." I peruse the room service menu and write down a few items. "Can you have this delivered in an hour?"

"No problem." She walks me through the house. "The last occupants complained of a stray dog wandering around outside. But we never could locate it. So just be aware. And if it comes by, give us a call."

I grin internally. I'm a shifter. I can handle a little *dog*. "I doubt it'll give me any problems."

"Well, enjoy your stay and I'll have the cook get started on this." She waves my list in one hand before making her way to the front door. "Good night."

I lock it behind her and let out a breath. I can finally unload. I blare my music while the bass thrums around me, and shake my hips to the tempo as the lyrics wash over my frame. I skip around, setting up my paints and canvas.

My hand trembles. The blank space looms in front of me, daring me to conquer its colorless surface. Insisting that I acquire my focal point, choose a color palette, and make this creation meaningful. Why is this suddenly so hard to do?

I nibble on the handle of my paintbrush. Images of Jake's smile flash behind my eyes. Then his laughter warms my heart. I miss him. I swipe the canvas to the floor and hug my knees.

"What's the point?"

The setting sun shimmers through the window, creating a prism at my feet. The light beckons me with its rainbow tendrils. I shuffle to the glass pane.

"I can't believe it," I whisper. "It's just like my vision."

My breath fogs the picturesque landscape. I wipe it away and excitement bubbles from deep inside my chest. I can do this. With my resolve renewed, I tackle the once-intimidating empty space, eager to see what magic erupts when my mind connects with my nimble fingers.

I wipe my brow, smearing crimson on my cheek. The sunset's soft rays dance over the snow, creating a twinkling effect. I never realized how much I love capturing landscapes. There's something about the way the earth can look so different yet similar in other areas of the world. I admire my work. It's not my best, but it's progress. A step in the right direction.

Yes, this is exactly what I needed to do. My back spasms and I stand to stretch my cramping muscles.

I sip the crisp wine that the busboy delivered with my food. Another apology gift from my brother. Its fruity melody dances along my tongue. He has good taste—I'll give him that. When I look up again, I spot a shadow darting across the yard.

Am I seeing things?

I turn off my music and shove my arms into my jacket. Maybe it's the stray dog the housekeeper was talking about? I snatch the steak bone off my discarded plate and step onto the front porch. No movement. I shiver as the wind causes my eyes to water.

That's it. My next vacation I'm traveling somewhere warm. Like the beach.

"Hello?" I yell against the breeze. There it is again! A black blur, and I definitely saw a tail. "I'm not going to hurt you. I've got a bone if you're hungry."

Why am I talking to a domestic canine? What if it thinks I'm offering another kind of bone?

I smirk. It's been too long since I've been laid, and my immaturity is shining through.

A pair of ears pokes out from the top of the bushes. *Aw. Look at those tiny things.* Then yellow eyes meet mine and something stirs in my chest. It's not a pup! It's a wolf! I backpedal towards the cabin. Azure and I made sure I wasn't going to be trespassing on another pack's territory before I came up here. This area is no man's land.

The shaggy beast steps into my path, leaving massive paw prints in the snow. Poor thing. Its fur is matted with chunks missing. Scars line its paws and face. I tilt my head and get a gander of its private parts. *He's* been through tough times and probably suffered some sort of abuse.

Oh no. What if he thinks I'm looking to hurt him too?

"I'm not going to hurt you. I promise," I tell him aloud.

He growls and lowers his ears. I toss him the bone as a peace offering. He watches me as he sniffs the treat. His fangs clamp on to it, then he runs into the woods without a backwards glance. I rub my arms as his shadow is swallowed by the tree line.

I wonder where he lives. There're no fur families for miles.

The wind picks up and I shiver. I hope he can find shelter. I pivot and reenter the warm cabin, thanking my lucky stars that I don't have to live outside.

I rub my palms together, but even the fire can't remove the chill. I dash to the bathroom and begin filling the tub. Soon my toes burn as I slip my feet into the hot water. I push a button and the jets activate, hitting all the knots in my shoulders.

"Yes," I moan.

I scrub the paint from under my fingernails and my mind wanders. Images of the strange wolf flash behind my eyelids.

How did he get those wounds? Maybe he needs assistance. Could he not sense I was a shifter? Should I ask Azure to ...

I shake my head, disrupting the floating bubbles lining the tub's surface. My brother has his own missions to handle. Plus, he might tell me to leave early. Nope. I sip my wine glass with finality. I paid for the next few weeks. I'm staying.

And that's exactly what I do. I settle into a routine of painting, reading romance novels, and feeding the fur pest my table scraps. I mean, I was going to throw them away anyway, so they might as well aid a fellow furry, right?

My first week comes and goes in a blur.

I jab my chin as I stare at yet another blank canvas. But I have no desire to paint it. My wolf has cabin fever. She's not used to staying in human form this long. Even in college, I'd exercise in the woods behind my apartment. I rub the back of my neck to find fur sticking out.

"Fine. One quick walk, then we are going back to work," I grumble to her.

I open the door and double-check to see if the coast is clear. Then black fur breaks through my pores and I bullet into the forest. The crisp air fuels my muscles. The rainbow of color blurring past inspires my next project. I'll call it a kaleidoscope of destiny. I skid to a stop, and white flurries dance in the air before decorating my frame. I chomp at the ice pieces, enjoying how they melt on my tongue. This is fun. I prance when the cold seeps through my claws. They crunch into the powder, leaving a trail of snowy paw prints.

When was the last time I played outside?

With all of my adult responsibilities, it's been ages. Plus, after losing our parents, I had to grow up fast while Azure was away all the time.

A twig snaps in the distance. My ears pivot to its location. *Something* is watching me from the bushes. My hackles rise. I sniff the breeze, but the cold causes my nose to burn. A black shadow leaps over the shrubs. I tumble head over tail, wrestling with a powerful beast. It pins me to the ground and snarls at my exposed neck.

I transform into my human form. "Wait! Please don't hurt me!"

It inhales my scent, then tilts its head and assesses my appearance. Luna, please let it remember I'm a *friend*, because my ass is numb from the cold. My teeth chatter but he doesn't move.

"I'm going to put my fur back on," I warn before embracing the warmth of my heavy pelt.

He moves off me and shakes the dead leaves from his tuft. I tiptoe towards the cabin, eager to return to the blazing fire. The snow crunches behind me. He's *following* me. Why? I mean, I have been giving him table scraps. He could be hungry again.

Once I get to the door, I shift to two legs and tug my room key from around my wrist. Should I leave him out here to freeze? He didn't eat me, so I guess I owe him one.

"Do you want to warm yourself up by the fireplace?"

He responds by padding past me and flopping down on the worn rug. The embers twirl behind his golden orbs.

"I'm going to order dinner. Do you want anything in particular? They have a wonderful selection of roasts and fish entrees."

His figure remains motionless. Did he fall asleep?

I shrug and call the front desk. They're surprised when I request two of everything, but I tell them I've been out hiking and that I'm starving. I settle in the recliner and wrap a blanket around my shoulders. I tilt my head as I eye the wolf's body.

I don't want the resort to attempt to catch the beast, especially if they don't know he's a shifter. Well, I *assume* he's a shifter by his scent, but he's only showed me his fur side. I take in the rise and fall of his chest. He's definitely sleeping. I power on my Kindle, swipe to my dirty romance, and settle into the comfy fabric of the chair.

The creature growls, and I leap in my seat, dropping my e-reader to the floor. I bend to pick it up as his neck snaps to the entrance before a knock sounds.

"Easy. It's just our dinner." I brush past him to collect the goods from the delivery boy. Then I set the dishes on the table.

The beast meets my gaze but makes no attempt to shift to skin. Is he embarrassed to be naked in front of people?

I position his plate at his feet and step away. He chomps on the juicy pork chop. I cringe at the sound of bone snapping under his fangs. Food bits drip from his drool.

Well, he doesn't have great table manners—that's for sure.

After we eat, I clean up and make my way to the bedroom. A claw scratches on the front door and I pivot. He's waiting to be let outside.

"You can stay here for the night, if you want. I even have a bathtub if you'd like to clean up a bit. It's not very big, but it has to be better than nothing." I assess his matted fur and do not point out the smell lingering around him. I wonder when he showered last.

Slowly, the wolf morphs into a two-legged man. My gaze runs over his muscled frame. He has abs for days. I pause. But there're scars littering his body from head to toe. His elbow juts out at an unnatural angle, and I wonder if it was broken at one time and never set right.

Good Luna. What happened to him?

He opens and closes his mouth. Then he clears his throat. "Thank you." The words tumble out, almost like he hasn't spoken in a long time.

I throw my thumb over my shoulder. "You can bathe first."

His long strides bring him to me quicker than I thought possible. I backpedal a step. His fingertips graze my jaw, and rough callouses scrape my skin. "You haunt my dreams."

What an odd thing to say. I've never seen him before my arrival here.

Am I dreaming or...?

Yup, his face is coming towards mine. I attempt to take another step back but I hit the wall. His chapped mouth meets my pillowy lips. I gag. If it's been a while since his last shower, I bet his oral hygiene isn't any better.

A *zing* shoots to my toes. My body melts. How can this be?

I wrap my arms around his neck. This mountain man is my *mate*. His palm grazes my ass before squeezing it. He lifts me up and I enfold my legs around him.

"Let's bathe, mate," he demands against my swollen lips.

Mate! My brain is still having a hard time accepting this.

He sets me on the floor long enough to turn on the faucet. Then he tugs me into the scalding tub water. I can't help but watch him as he scrubs the grime from his sculpted frame. He's a mystery, yet I'm supposed to spend the rest of my life with him.

The water is black as it drains.

"Are you homeless?" I ask him. "Or on the run from something?" When he remains silent, I tug a hand through his wet locks. I guess he isn't much for small talk. "What's your name?" I try an easier question.

"Brock."

"I'm Lily."

He runs his tongue over my neck and his chest rumbles. He clutches my hips and rubs his erection over my stomach. Well, at least that body part is functioning. My core ignites and begs to make the bond with its counterpart. But my conscience reminds me that we know nothing about each other. Although I don't have any qualms about having the occasional one-night stand, this is my soon-to-be husband and my soul craves answers.

"What pack do you belong to?"

"No pack." He tempts my opening with his shaft.

I arch my back as he nibbles my shoulder. *Why are words escaping me?*

I need to put some distance between us. He slams into my core. The sudden, urgent pressure steals my breath from my lungs. I whimper and push his chest away. I'm all for rough sex, but at least give me some foreplay or lube first!

He ignores my feeble attempts to stop him as his hips mercilessly slam against me. His strokes are urgent. I bite my lip, wishing the pain would disappear.

Once he roars his release, he collapses beside me and snarls a singular word. *"Mine."*

Lily

End of the Line

Brock spends hours claiming and reclaiming me, even after I attempt to explain that I can't handle his abuse anymore. My vagina begs for a rest as she bleeds from overuse. When he finally passes out from exhaustion, I sneak out from under his arm and tiptoe to the bathroom.

"Shit," I whisper at my reflection.

Bite marks and scratches mar my skin. Is this *normal* for mates?

I never thought it would be this intense. Or painful. I slide my hair over the injuries to cover them as my mind tries to make sense of what I'm feeling right now.

Maybe this is a temporary phase until the bond is established?

I face-palm myself. Azure is not going to be happy with this mistreatment. My brother and mate are going to butt heads. I throw on a t-shirt and trudge to the fridge. I squat and instantly regret it as the motion makes my thighs scream. I snatch ice from the freezer and rub it over my swollen folds. I yelp as the cold burns, then quickly soothes the fire between my legs.

Leave it to Luna to give me a sex-crazed beast as a mate. I mean, I love to fuck but this is borderline rape… with not much *borderline* about it. I mean, where is the line drawn?

He is technically my spouse…

I clutch my head to stop the hundreds of questions popping up. I'll worry about them later. First I need sustenance. I call down to room service and order food. I don't even bother to create a lie for why I'm ordering enough for two. Then I stretch by my easel and wait for our entrees.

What should I paint next? I swirl my brush in the shimmering gold pigment. An ethereal forest with fairies and gnomes? My gaze trails to the window. A snow-covered cage against a backdrop of twinkling stars?

I yelp as my wrist is jerked. My supplies tumble to the floor, splashing my toes with a rainbow of spilled paint.

"Did I say you could leave?" Brock grinds out.

"I didn't realize I had to ask your permission to walk around my own cabin." I attempt to free my hand but he only squeezes harder. "I ordered food, then I decided to paint while I waited for them to deliver it."

His neck tilts to one side as he assesses my work space. "No more."

Anger boils my blood. After everything he's put me through, he doesn't even apologize. He just keeps making more demands. *Fuck him.*

"*Excuse* me? I'm a grown-ass adult! I don't need your permission to do anything or go anywhere."

"You are *mine*."

"We may be mates, but that doesn't automatically mean you own me," I growl as my fangs elongate. "Let me go!"

He ignores me and snarls, "We will live out there." He tugs his thumb towards the frost-covered landscape.

Is this brute serious? Not everyone wants to live the nomadic lifestyle he seems to prefer. I take a steadying breath. I just need to make him see it my way and explain what I *want*. Then his innate instincts will activate, and he will be forced to take care of his future wife.

"What about my *family*? That's not the way packs work. We stick together through thick and thin. And now that we're mates, you can join our group. It's sort of small and filled with elder wolves, but they are kind and—"

"*I'm* your family now," he interjects.

"But my brother…" I try again.

Brock tugs me to his chest. "Mine."

I swallow the bile rising in my throat. Azure will find a way to rescue me from this mess, right? Maybe he can request that Luna give me another partner? Because she royally fucked up with this one. He's insane.

"Room service." A knock echoes off the walls of my now prison.

Brock snarls and stomps to the entrance. He tugs it open. "*What?*"

"I have two steak dinners for Miss Pawson," the busboy stammers, looking past the beast to meet my gaze. "Are you okay, miss?"

I force a smile and nod. "Yes, thank you. You can just leave the food."

The man steps into the room to place the silver-domed plates on the table. He assesses my shaking frame again. He opens his mouth, but before he can question me, the door slams shut and Brock shoves the kid against the wall. "She's mine."

"Of course, sir." The young man shivers. The smell of urine stings my nose before I notice his stained uniform.

My mate clutches the busboy's neck and squeezes. I tug on his elbow. "Brock!" I scream. "You're hurting him!"

His palm slaps across my cheek, knocking me down to his feet. "Don't tell me what to do."

The other man's face turns blue. He kicks and squirms under Brock's hold. This can't be happening. There's something seriously wrong with this beast.

I plead on my knees. "I don't know who's hurt you to make you act like this. But, please, don't kill an innocent human."

"Humans aren't *innocent*," Brock snarls.

Shit. This is news to me. I've never had a bad experience with them. The poor delivery boy gurgles and draws my attention back to the situation at hand.

"Stop! Your mate isn't happy!" I pull on his arm.

"Your happiness isn't *required*." Brock watches me as he flexes his fingers, and the man's neck snaps. His limp body crumbles to the floor. The busboy's glazed eyes stare at me, unforgiving for the sins I wasn't able to stop.

My scream echoes around the room. I've seen dead animals before but never humans. "I'm so sorry," I whimper to the man who can no longer hear me, then sob as I close his unseeing eyes.

The moment I touch the boy, my mate snatches his body from my grip, before tearing it limb from limb. Splattering the walls with flesh and blood. Shock riddles my frame as I witness Brock destroy the corpse with his bare hands.

When he has no more bones to splinter or skin to peel back, he approaches me, red liquid splashing with each step he takes. He snatches my chin between his thumb and forefinger. "No one touches you but me." Then his hands drop to my shoulders as he shakes me out of my stupor. "Say it!"

A tear warms my blood-crusted cheek, and I whisper his mantra, "I am yours."

Without another word, Brock collects me into his arms and carries me to bed.

When I wake up, I can't help but pray that it's all been a nightmare. I scan the room and hope rises in my chest when I notice there's no sign of Brock. I tiptoe out of the bedroom and skid to a stop. The carnage in the living area reminds me I'm not so lucky. The busboy's blood paints every surface, including my beautiful art pieces. Then I notice the dismembered limbs are missing. I retch at the thought of my mate eating them, and the contents of my stomach add to the mess.

I swipe at my mouth and suck in air. This is not happening. I run to my purse. Thank Luna that monster didn't hide my cell phone. I dial Azure and wait. If he can't get here soon, surely the resort will send out a search party for their missing employee.

Come on, answer! It rings until it goes to voicemail. Of course, my brother's never there when I need him.

"Azure. It's me. Please…"

The sound of approaching footsteps echoes outside. I hang up, toss the phone out of sight, and leap under the covers where Brock left me. My breathing hitches as the door slams open before the sheets are tugged off me.

"We're leaving. Now."

I cringe at the blood dripping from his chin. Did he kill something else or was this leftover from last night?

31

Brock's gaze smolders as it trails over my body. He pounces on top of me and growls before rubbing his nose over my folds and breathing in my scent. He purrs as he drags his tongue over my opening. He pushes my thighs farther apart and devours my nectar.

"Please stop. I'm really sore," I beg him. "Shouldn't we focus on our next steps? You said we needed to leave, right? Why? Is someone after you?"

Again, he ignores me. "You're in heat."

My jaw drops. *Luna, no. I can't have this maniac's child!*

"Shouldn't we leave while it's still light outside?" I squeak past the terror building in the back of my throat.

"Fuck first."

I squeeze my eyes shut. I can't conceive a child like this. Surrounded by carnage. "I can't handle any more sex."

Brock holds my wrists above my head. "Rest later." His knee creates a path for him before he slams into me with a grunt. "I'm alpha. You're mine."

My sanity snaps. Those *words*. How I wish I could erase them from my vocabulary. He's a caveman. Maybe even illiterate.

"Get off me right now! I told you no!" I kick and claw at him. "I belong to no one!"

His dick twitches inside me. The sick fuck likes me fighting him. "We're bound together, forever." He finishes himself off, then snatches my chin with his hand. "Never question me. I know best." I cower under his glare until he moves off me. "Lie flat. I'll pack," he barks over his shoulder.

I do as I'm told while my hopes and dreams slide down my cheeks.

Brock and I trek through the snowbanks, sticking to the shadows. Our telepathic wolf connection is silent, except for a few short, clipped directions. I shake off the white flecks decorating my coat. One disadvantage to traveling in this winter wonderland is I stand out like a sore thumb. My dark bushy fur basically puts a target on my back.

"Why don't you trust humans?"

He snorts out a flurry of icicles. *"They are vile."*

"Not all of them." The silence thickens. *"Did they cause those scars?"*

He trips over a stump but quickly recovers. *"What else could?"*

"Other shifters."

"No. They just ignore what's happening."

"My brother isn't like that. He can protect us..."

"No." Brock bares his teeth, and my wolf cowers at his paws. His fangs sink into my scruff, and he tugs me up as if I'm a naughty pup. I fold into the fetal position while he carries me away. He strides a few feet, then drops me inside a damp cave. *"We rest."* He shimmies the snow flecks off of his fur until the moisture decorates the stone walls. Then he returns to his human form before examining our supplies.

I curl my tail over my face and pray he leaves me be. I can't handle another session of rough sex. Warmth floods me as a blanket is tucked around my curled-up form. His fingertip grazes my face. I meet his piercing stare, shocked by the kindness I see there.

"You're all I need." He lays my head in his human lap. "Rest. I'll keep watch."

His soft caresses soothe my fur soul. I wish he extended this compassion more often. I drift into a deep sleep until my head shoots up. I blink at my surroundings. Night blankets the world in a sea of stars. My gaze falls on my mate's figure. He's in wolf form, guarding the cave's entrance. His hackles are raised and he's watching a dot moving in the distance.

"What is it?" I ask him.

His ear pivots but he remains motionless. *"Them."*

"The ones who hurt you?"

"They want me back." His silhouette tenses, and I question whether his paranoia is justified or if his nomadic lifestyle merely drove him to madness. *"I won't let them."* A beam of light swishes in our direction and his chest rumbles with a growl. He backpedals. *"Follow."*

I gaze into the forest, then towards the back of the cave. Should I make a mad dash and gain my freedom? I squint into the tree line. What if these people are what he says they are? Is it worth the risk?

Brock snaps at my ear. His fangs scratch the tip. *"I said follow."* I whimper as blood trickles over my fur. *"Now,"* he snarls.

I take one last look at the shadows before I stride farther from my escape and closer to the big bad wolf in my midst.

We move throughout the night, only stopping to drink water. Brock's steps are sluggish and clumsy. I can't imagine how exhausted he is, considering he has yet to rest. It's been hours since we saw any humans. I wonder if they've given up their search or maybe they're just calling in reinforcements.

I huff out a steamy breath. *When will Azure get my message and come to my rescue?*

A yawn rips through me and causes my eyes to water. *"We should rest."*

"No." Brock stumbles over a root. It seems to be happening frequently now that fatigue has taken over his limbs.

"Where are we going?"

He ignores me and focuses his energy on moving forward. My paws become heavy. How much longer can he go? I'm so out of shape. I sit in classrooms, paint, and party. Not exercise.

Unless you consider sex exercise?

My eyes burn as the sun peeks over the horizon. Birds begin their symphony as they flutter overhead. *"We can't stay out in the open. They'll see us more easily during the day. Look. There's a cavern. Maybe we can rest until it gets dark?"*

He trudges towards the location to sniff it out. Once his paranoid ass is satisfied, he guides me into the back corner. I shiver at the icy stone floor. We left our supplies at the other cave so we could make a quick getaway, which means there are no blankets to snuggle with now.

I stretch out my aching limbs. At least we can sleep for a few hours. My heavy lids begin to droop as I worry about where we're going next. Does Brock have a plan? Or is his strategy to keep running until we both die? I can't do this for the rest of my life.

I whimper. I miss my brother and Jake. They are nothing like Brock. If only Luna allowed exchanges for mates, because mine sucks.

I yelp as a wet nose skims my ass. What the fuck! I scurry away from the unwanted intrusion. Brock growls, warning me to stay put, then he continues his investigation of my back end. He rubs my sensitive area and I can't stop my tail from rising, giving my mate full access. The beast's tongue strokes my center, and I quiver with need as my hormones go crazy and heat trails to my toes. His wolf latches on to my scruff and desperately humps the air until he slams into me. The soreness from earlier intensifies in this position. I beg him to stop, but he never misses a beat.

"It's almost over," he grunts.

Think of anything else, Lily. Like my home. My tiny pack. My sibling.

Brock's snarl vibrates across the cavern walls. His paw slashes my shoulder. I howl and curl into myself. His dick hangs like a third foot as he stomps towards me with his teeth bared. "Who was *that*?"

My body aches but I try to keep up with his train of thought. Did our wolf connection show him Azure? Maybe I said his name without thinking?

"Answer me!"

My wound throbs as I attempt to make my body as small as I can. *"I don't know what you're talking about."*

He snaps at my muzzle, tearing into flesh.

"Please stop. You're hurting me!" I cry out.

"Pain teaches lessons," he tells me, and my eyes grow wide.

Who taught him this morbid shit?

"Who was it?" He threatens to injure me again with his fanged scowl.

"My brother."

He narrows his gaze at me. *"You* love *him?"*

The question splinters my sanity. I don't think Brock knows what that word means. He's been neglected too long to know how to function in the real world. A tear dances over my fur. *"Yes, I love my brother."*

"No more."

My eyes snap to his. *"But he's your family now too. Won't you give him a chance?"*

"You have me. You don't need him."

"What does that even mean?" I screech down our bond. *"You're not making any sense!"*

"I'm alpha. *You're my* bitch.*"*

I shake my head. He's crazy. *"Azure is a kind shifter. He helps those in need and he always tries to be there for me. We love each other, and you can't take that away, even if you and I are mates."*

His eyes widen and gain a wild glaze to them. He leaps for me. His tired movements are slower than normal as we wrestle on the cold, unforgiving ground. We battle over dominance. I fight to keep in touch with those I love, and he rages for the right to be the only person in my life. My thick tuff splits open all over from his sharpened fangs. But I get a few good hits on him too. His jaw closes around my neck, waiting for me to submit. When I don't, he squeezes until my last ounce of rebellious attitude drains out of me and my body crumbles at his paws.

He nods with finality. *"You're mine."* Brock is a broken record. He curls up next to me and yawns, as if almost killing his mate is completely normal. *"Sleep."*

He wraps his paw over me and licks my wounds. I whimper as pain sears through me with every stroke.

How could this happen to me?

He releases another yawn before he drifts off to sleep. Once his breathing evens out, I glance around the cavern. There's not much in here except for a few boulders and twigs. Brock snores and kicks his leg, hitting my bruised shoulder. I yelp and pull away from him. I cringe, waiting for him to lash out. When nothing happens, I peek through my lashes. He's out cold. I tiptoe to the entrance of the cave. Every step is as agonizing as the next. I question if my ribs are broken as each breath feels like my last.

If I escape, I won't get far. I have two options. Continue to allow my mate to abuse me and live on the run. Or…

My wolf begs me to reconsider, but I've made up my mind. I morph into my human skin. My fingers wrap around an icy rock. I clench it in my fist.

This is breaking Luna's laws, my furry-conscious cries out.

I stumble towards my target, and my lip quivers. "I wanted to be loved, but not like this."

Luna created us to be cherished by our mates until *death* separates us. They are our furever partners.

Brock's words ring through my mind. "*I'm alpha. You're my bitch.*"

He has every intention of breeding with me too. I can't bring children into this mess! I raise the boulder with both hands. Fuck this. She can *have* him back. I'd rather die a lonely spinster than at the paws of this abusive beast.

My fur spirit whimpers, pleading with me to think about the consequences. But the cuts and bruises littering my frame remind me of what my future will look like if I don't take matters into my own hands. *Literally.*

The boulder slams between Brock's eyes. Again and again. His skull crunches under my adrenaline-fueled hammering. My limbs become gelatinous, and I collapse over his wolf form.

"I'm free," I croak out as my sanity splinters. My fingertips dance in the crimson, and I can't help but laugh at the irony. "Who's the bitch now?" I whisper into his ear before allowing darkness to swallow my existence.

Lily

Regrets

"**F**rom our initial examinations, we've concluded that Lily was raped and assaulted. Your sister has bruising spanning a third of her body and a few fractures that required strategic mending."

Where am I? Why do I feel like I got ran over by a semi-truck?

"How did this happen?"

Is that my brother? Does this mean I survived?

"We aren't sure yet. She's been heavily sedated and hasn't said much since her arrival. Considering what she's been through, it's to be expected."

I move to sit up but groan when pain radiates through my back.

Warmth covers my bandaged hand. "Easy, Lily. I'm right here."

I focus on my big brother as he stands at my bedside. "Azure?" My voice is hoarse and I have to force the words out.

"Yes, it's me." He kneels so that he's eye level and offers me water.

My lip quivers. "I thought I'd never see you again. He wasn't going to let me go."

Azure gently wraps his arms around me. "You're safe. I won't let anyone hurt you again. I promise."

Even if I'm damned for killing my mate, I have Azure back in my life now. Although our limited communication will probably be through text messages and phone calls, it's better than what Brock was offering me, which was no contact at all. I take in the sterile room and freeze.

Or was I captured by the same people who were after Brock?

"Where am I?" I stutter out.

"You're in the hospital," Azure assures me. "I received your voicemail and came as soon as I could." He kisses my palm. "While I was traveling towards your location, I called the reception desk and asked them to check on you in your cabin."

I cringe as images of gore flash behind my eyes. That poor kid Brock ripped to shreds... What my brother must think of his *weak* sister... I can't even go on a holiday without running into a deranged psychopath.

Azure sits on the edge of my bed, drawing my attention back to him. His fingertips graze my forehead before tucking my hair behind my ear. "Lil, what happened?"

I shake my head as tears spring from my eyes. Azure wouldn't understand why I did what I did. He's a Guardian. He punishes people like me. *Murderers.*

"Let me read your memories. Maybe..."

"No!" I shout louder than I intend. I know my sibling is only trying to understand what happened to me by using the powers Luna blessed him with, but I won't allow this event to taint his

42

image of his little sister.

"Just tell me this. Did that *monster* kill the missing delivery boy? The investigators found the kid's blood in your room, and he was last seen going to your cabin, but they haven't found a body yet."

All I can do is nod. The kid's screams still echo in my mind. Haunting me. The crunching of bone. The sound of shredding flesh...

"We'll inform the police so they can notify his next of kin," the other man in the room answers. I almost forgot he was here. "But before I leave, I need to talk to Lily about something. If you'll just step outside for a moment, sir."

"There's more to add to this nightmare?" Azure groans.

"I'm afraid so." The man frowns. He taps on his tablet before meeting my gaze. "Should I discuss this with you privately or is your brother allowed to stay?"

I gulp. *What more could he have to report? Shit. Did Brock give me an STD? He was pretty dirty. Fuck. I didn't even think about that...*

Azure rubs my arm, bringing me out of my despair. We lock eyes. He's worried about me. Hell, I'm worried about myself. I lean into the pillows and take a deep breath. I don't care what happens next. Brock is gone and he can't hurt me or anyone else anymore. Good riddance.

Whatever health issues I may have can be treated; they aren't going to be permanent. Not like my former mate's abuse would have been. Day in and day out, my life filled with endless rape, traveling in the dead of night, and never belonging to a pack again.

"You can tell him whatever it is you have to say."

The doctor takes a steadying breath before he shows us my lab report. I scan the numbers, but I'm not sure what any of them mean. Nothing is in bright red so that's a good sign, right?

I meet the other man's gaze with an arched brow.

"The bloodwork indicates that you are *pregnant*," he answers my silent question.

"What?" Azure pales and leans back, refusing to meet my shocked expression.

Shit. Guess I was wrong.

I'll never be able to get rid of Brock. His abuse will continue to haunt me because I'll have his pup to look after.

"You're not very far along, and the trauma you've experienced could possibly result in a miscarriage…" the doctor adds.

"How can she be carrying his child? He *raped* her!" Azure roars, fur prickling his arms and electricity sizzling the air around us.

The doctor clears his throat. "Shifter and human reproduction are very similar. If he didn't use protection, there's always a chance of conceiving a child. No matter the circumstances."

Azure runs his hands through his dark hair, tugging on the ends. "Why would Luna allow this to happen?" he asks himself. "This isn't right. I should have sensed that you were in danger. Or had a vision."

The agony in his voice breaks my already splintered heart. This isn't *his* fault. I had the vision of the mountains and thought it was a sign to travel there.

I pat his leg until he turns back to me. "Please don't blame yourself. This was an act of violence committed by a very sick man."

"Are you sure you're ready to be a mom?" he pushes out. "You wanted to open an art gallery and teach." The silence bears down on us as Azure rubs a bruise on my arm. "I'm sorry I couldn't protect you."

"No, it's my fault. I trusted that shifter. I was trying to help a wolf in need. Give him a hot meal and a warm place to rest."

My brother kisses the top of my head and sighs. "You have a heart of gold, Lily."

If only that were true…

I stare at my hands. The same ones that beat the life out of my mate. I'm the real monster, the one who should be caged and never allowed to see the light of day.

"Lil, I'll be here for you as much as I can, but you'll be raising this pup mostly on your own," Azure tells me what I already know. "It's not going to be easy."

He's right. I know he is. Our pack consists of older shifters. They'll help but not to the extent of a *father* figure. My vision blurs.

Brock wasn't all bad. Was he? He was just misguided and obviously abused. Maybe I can raise this pup to be better than its father? I clench my fist. But what if I can't? And I'm carrying a future killer? Either way, it should have the chance to *make* that decision. It is half mine after all.

"This pup may not have been conceived in love, but it'll be raised with it." I swallow the lump in my throat. "Luna gave this gift to me for a reason," I whisper more to myself than anyone else.

A gift or *punishment*? There's only one way to find out.

"Try not to worry too much." Azure pats my hand. "When you meet your mate, we'll explain what happened. I'm sure he'll love you no matter what." He rubs my stomach. "*Both* of you."

I stare into my brother's eyes. He has no idea what he's saying. "Azure, I don't think…"

"Listen. Luna gave us our fur partners to complete us and make us stronger together. Living without them is sentencing ourselves to a lifetime of loneliness. We are pack animals. And just because you had this little setback, it doesn't mean your search is over. You'll see. Your mate will have no choice but to understand and accept what happened. Then you'll get your happily ever after. You have my word," Azure tells me, and his words hang so heavy in the air I nearly choke on them.

Jackson

Young Love

Past

It's calling me. Begging me to touch it...

"Jackson?"

I look up and meet a pair of kind eyes watching me. "Frost asked me to bring these to you." I hand Raven the containers of paint I have nestled in my arms.

Her smile brightens. "My mate never stops thinking about me." She runs her fingertips over the bottles like they're as precious as gemstones. Then she tilts her head at me. "My husband could have brought these to me himself."

I shrug. "I'm just the messenger."

She grabs the paintbrush I was ogling a moment ago and waves it in the air. "Maybe your alpha knows more about you than you'd like to admit, Jackson."

"Like what?"

She lays the wooden handle on my palm. "Like maybe I should add another young pupil to my children's art class." She nods to the empty stool in the corner, and a sudden fire burns in my chest.

What is this feeling? Passion? Excitement? After the numbness that's taken over my existence, it's both scary and thrilling.

"I can't burden you again," I push out. "But thank you for the offer." I extend the brush to the alpha's wife.

"A burden?" Her amusement drops into a frown. "Jackson, you've never been a burden to me or this pack."

I rub the back of my neck. "You took me in when my parents..."

I swallow down the memory of the night they lost their lives. A battle for rank between shifters that turned into a bloodbath. Their blood. That same night, another pup was orphaned too. I shudder at the thought of *Spike*. Ruthless and hell-bent on seeking revenge, he ran to Carson City to lick his wounds. Our alpha tried to bring him back to the safety of our pack, but the stubborn shifter declined.

"When they left, you were forced to shelter me."

Raven lifts my chin with her finger. "You listen to me, young man. You will never be a burden. Do you hear me? Never have been. Never will be. We love you as our own," she says before pulling me into a hug.

The bell over the art studio entrance chimes and we both turn. My jaw hits the floor as my eyes meet the beauty gliding through the door.

"Sorry I'm early." She fluffs her hair. "Robert wanted to come with me to talk to Frost. Something about asking for permission for me to travel between territories for the class."

Raven smiles at the goddess. "Robert didn't have to do that. He has his own pack to run."

"I told him as much too." The girl shrugs. "But like my mom always says, *he's a man and never listens*."

Raven smirks. "Don't I know it." Their gazes land on me, the only male in the room. "Speaking of men who don't listen." Raven pats my elbow. "Ashely, this is Jackson, a very loved and wanted member of our family."

Ashely tilts her head as she assesses my jeans and rock band t-shirt. "Is he mute?"

I clear my throat and offer her a sweaty palm. "No, he isn't. I mean, *I'm* not. It's nice to meet you."

When she slides her fingertips over mine, a spark ignites in my chest. My brain malfunctions and my heart races. I know I'm only twelve years old, but I fight the urge to slam her against the wall and taste those plump lips of hers. Her pupils dilate, and I know she's having similar thoughts. But she's smart enough to drop my hold and step back.

"Yeah, nice to meet you too." She throws a thumb behind her. "I'm going to find a good canvas to work at." She scurries past us and settles in a dark corner.

Damn, she's beautiful.

"Are you staying?" Raven directs the question at me while tapping her foot on the tiled floor. It takes me a minute to realize she's talking to me. She offers me the paintbrush again. "I think our alpha's meddling was Luna's way of connecting two unlikely individuals."

"I don't know what you mean." It's not a lie. I honestly have no idea what just went on there. It was like nothing I've ever experienced before.

"Well, why don't you stay, learn a thing or two about painting, and get to know other shifters with similar interests." She bumps her hip against me. "What's it going to be, son?"

I glance at the girl texting in the back of the room. She meets my gaze and blushes before returning to her phone. I grin and take the paintbrush from Raven.

Challenge accepted.

Our flourishing relationship all started six years ago with some buckets of paint and a few brushes. I thank Luna every day for that chance encounter. We started off as friends, and now we are engaged to be married.

"Jackson! This is amazing!" Ashely squeals.

"Do you really like it? Or is this like that time I cooked for you and burned the lasagna?" I wrap an arm around her waist. I can't stand to be away from my mate. Every moment we're apart twists my heart into knots. I need to see her. Feel her. Make her smile like this.

"Hey, lasagna is very complicated. You're being too hard on yourself." She pushes up on her tiptoes and places a kiss on my cheek. "I love this."

I twirl her in a circle and her new gown fans out before it settles around her ankles again. "I can't wait to tear this off you."

"You'll do no such thing, mister!" She smacks my chest. "This dress is going to be worn for our wedding ceremony."

"*Then* I'll tear it off you," I repeat as I nip at her ear. Her floral scent is intoxicating.

She mews softly. "Yes, then you *tear it off me*... with your teeth."

My dick weeps with anticipation. The things this woman does to my body and soul. I growl before nuzzling into her neck. "I love you, Ashely."

"I love you too. Now kiss me before I melt into a puddle and ruin this beautiful gift."

"Your wish is my command." I devour her mouth, not holding back as I bite her tongue and she molds her frame into mine. "Are you sure we have to wait until we're official to have sex?" My hand glides up her thigh. "We could have a few test runs..."

"It's only a few days away." She giggles. "You can wait."

I grind my erection against her. "I'm afraid I'll explode before then."

"Well, it'll give your hands something to do," she teases. "Just don't jerk too hard. I'll need him at his best on our wedding night." Her phone dings, and she sighs. "Time to go."

We're from two different packs, and until we're united in the eyes of Luna, we have time limits on when we can see each other. But that's only for a few more days, then she's all mine. I squeeze Ashely's ass. Well, more like mine and a new member of the Tala pack. It's tradition here in Cold Creek. When a female bonds with a male, she joins his pack. That's usually why packs don't like their females to travel. They're afraid of losing them.

Oh, well. Their loss is my gain.

I knead her cheeks with the palms of my hands. "I'm going to miss you."

"I'll be back soon." She rubs my biceps. "Will I see you in class tomorrow?"

"I think I'm hopeless as an artist. Maybe I should quit while I'm ahead. I still can't create anything worth mentioning. It's a lost cause."

"Jackson. Don't quit because it's too hard. Do you hear me? Unless it doesn't bring you joy." She stomps her foot for good measure. "You're better than that."

"Am I?" I tease her. "How about you remind me how good I am?"

"Only if you show up to class."

"Fine. But I'm only going because I get to sit next to you and play footsies." I wink at her.

"You're impossible."

"Well, I am a man," I mock.

"That's right." Ashely pulls away from me. "But you are *my* man." She blows me a kiss. "Don't forget that, mate."

She peels off the white lacey fabric and hands it back to me, while I eye-fuck her delicious curves. My wolf begs for a taste. Her hips sway before she morphs into fur and gallops off towards Robert's territory. Her tail swishing wildly as she goes. It takes every ounce of my willpower to not chase after her. I can't imagine my life without her sweet smile brightening up the room.

My soul mate.

After we tie the knot, Ashely and I spend many sleepless nights under the covers. But eventually, we emerge and are forced to rejoin society. And even though we've been married for a few years, I still can't keep my paws to myself.

"Babe! Your friend is here," I holler over my shoulder.

"Jackson. I know my way around the house. You don't need to shout." Bridgett shoves her way past me.

I grind my jaw. Bridgett is Ashely's bestie from Robert's pack. She's annoying, but my wife's been going through a tough time.

The bathroom door cracks open, and Ashely's head pops out to wave her fur companion inside. I lean against the wall and listen as their conversation leaks under the door.

"I'm bleeding again. Why is this happening?" Ashely's cries are muffled, as she presumably rests her face against Bridgett's shoulder. Just like she did with me this morning when I tried to comfort her. "It's been years and still… nothing."

"Sweetie, calm down." Ruffling noises ensue and then someone blows their nose. "Luna will bless you with pups on *her* time, not yours."

"But we've tried everything. What if I'm not worthy to carry a child, in her eyes? What if I'm damaged?" my mate screeches.

"Then we'll do what we've talked about. I'll fuck Jackson and carry the baby for you."

The girls giggle together. "As long as I can be a part of it," Ashely replies.

"Sure thing. It'll be just like *The Handmaid's Tale*."

"Oh, Luna, no! That's horrible. I want everyone to have fun and enjoy themselves."

"We will."

I shake my head. Girls talk about the weirdest things. And, somehow, I got roped into this too. Considering it's my dick and sperm they're openly discussing. I pinch the bridge of my nose. I told Ashely I didn't even want kids. That I'm happy the way things are with us. I love *her*. I desire *her*. Not a snot-nosed brat. Or a high-maintenance second wife. Just my mate.

More laughter wafts from the bathroom to my ears. My frown twitches. If Bridgett can keep my woman in good spirits, she's welcome in my home anytime.

My nose tremors and I pivot to the front door to see the alpha's wife leaning on the frame. When our eyes meet, she waves me over, so I join her outside. The early morning sun warms my skin as we stroll around the yard.

Once we're out of wolf earshot, Raven sighs. "Her bleeding

started again?"

"Yes," I push out.

"It's hard. I remember those days. Just give her time, son." Raven rubs my back.

"I'm not pressuring her to do anything." I grind my jaw. "She's just dead set on having children, making it out like it's do or die."

"She wants to be a mother." Raven bites her lip. "It's hard to explain, but it's what our wolves crave. To hold and cherish a piece of our mate's life force. To have something of ourselves to carry on when we cross the rainbow bridge."

My eyes shoot to my surrogate mother. "Is your health okay?"

"Yes, of course. Frost won't let me die first anyway. He's already set that law into stone." She elbows me, and we share a laugh. Her husband leads with an iron paw. I respect him and loyally serve as his beta, but he can be a little hard-headed at times. "Ashely will be fine. You'll see. And don't worry about Bridgett. The pack likes her, so if you do decide to allow her to be your surrogate, I'm sure you'll get approval on our end. It's Robert who might complain about losing another female."

"I only deal with her because of Ashely. I'm not planning on allowing another woman into our bed or to steal my sperm."

"Bridgett has a beautiful soul," Raven tells me, as if that solves anything. "You're lucky she's willing to help out with this sensitive issue. Not many females would agree."

"Did Frost consider a surrogate?" I bark, knowing damn well he wouldn't, even when they were facing their own conception issues.

I know it's a dick move, and I instantly regret it. Frost and Raven finally gave birth to a little girl shortly after I turned twelve. But it didn't last long, because the pup ran into the woods when she was three and no one has seen her since. Of course, we searched, but we never had luck finding any clues to her whereabouts.

Raven sighs and shakes her head. "But you aren't Frost. You can see clearly without allowing jealousy to cloud your judgement. Your wife is begging you to give her a child, any way that you can. Maybe you'll be able to listen better than my husband did."

"No wolf can replace your mate," Frost booms from the pathway in front of us. "Why are you putting these ideas in the boy's mind? He's got a good head on his shoulders and knows how to make the best decision for his family." He slaps my back. "Right?"

Raven rolls her eyes and moves towards her cave. "Men."

"I'll show you what a man is capable of tonight," Frost calls after her as he drools over the sight of her backside. Once the door is closed, he guides me towards the lake in the center of our territory. "I've noticed that Bridgett is getting cozy in your home."

"Against my better judgement." I shrug. "But she makes Ashely laugh, even when I can't, so I'm okay with it."

"Has she mentioned if Robert has crossed the border lately?"

My ears prick up. *Is he asking me to spy on the other pack's shifter?*

"No, she hasn't."

Frost itches his scruff as he stares out over the water's edge. Ducks quack and paddle as far away as they can from the alpha's intense gaze, not wanting to become his next prey. "Could you try to slip it into the conversation while she's here? I've heard rumors that he's been visiting another pack, and I want to make sure he's not planning to combine territories and move towards ours next."

"Why would he do that? That would break the treaty we have with the wolves in Cold Creek."

"A good leader stays on top of these things. I'd rather be safe than sorry."

"As you wish, alpha." I owe this man my life for taking me in as his own and showing me how to lead. "Speaking of staying on top of things, have we checked up on the Fangs in Carson City?"

His eyes darken, and his fangs elongate. "They are bullying the people of the city, so the lot of them are in the Guardian's hands now. Not mine."

I know damn well he's still keeping tabs on the rogue beasts. Rumor has it… they are doing the dirty work of the local drug dealers in exchange for cash. As a result, they are also slowly climbing the hierarchy of the decaying town. But since it's not in our territory, I guess Frost isn't involving himself. Plus, he feels guilty for killing Spike's brother in battle, and I know that's clouding his judgement. So much for being safe instead of sorry. But he's our leader and knows best. I'll gather the intel that he needs, and eventually he'll trust me with more sensitive information.

"Happy anniversary, babe." I kiss Ashely's cheek as I place her favorite cake in front of her.

"Aw, you didn't have to do all this for me." Her eyes light up at the mountain of gifts.

"It's not every day that we celebrate five years of being married." I cut into the moist dessert.

She dips a finger into the creamy frosting, pops it into her mouth, and groans. I can't wait for her to do that same thing in the bedroom later. Her wink tells me that she's reading my mind. "Sit next to me and relax, mate. You've been serving me all day. Take a break."

I do as I'm told. These last few years have been the best of my life. I sink my teeth into the cake. It's sweet, the perfect way to end the night before the real fun begins in the bedroom.

After we've devoured our tasty treat, Ashely slides over a gift bag.

"Where'd that come from?" I arch a brow in question.

"Just open it."

"But, seriously, where the fuck...?"

"From my folds!" she grumbles. I blink at her thighs as I take a moment to consider her answer. "I hid it under the table," she clarifies. "Now please open it."

I tug out the layers of annoying tissue paper concealing the gift inside. Why do people even use this stuff? It's ridiculous and wasteful. My finger catches on a tiny hanger. I pull out a miniature shirt, which is clearly too small to fit me. "Uh. Thank you?"

"There's something in the bottom of the bag too," Ashely urges.

I fumble around until I reveal a white plastic stick. I wrinkle my nose at the smell of urine. "Why?" I whisper to myself.

"Jackson. You can be so dense. Turn it over."

I follow her instructions and the words "pregnancy test" scream back at me from the stick. I squint at the display window and tilt my head. Why the hell would anyone decide to pee on something like this? Don't they have bloodwork instead?

"You're not happy."

I meet Ashely's glittering eyes. Then I glance at the items in question again, and everything clicks together. *Shit. This means...*

"You're pregnant?"

She runs to the bathroom and slams the door shut. I rub my forehead. Man, did I fuck up her surprise. I walk to the locked door and knock.

"Go away!" she sobs.

"Ashely," I groan. "I'm sorry. I'm just exhausted—that's all. I spent all day putting this amazing dinner and dessert together for us."

"And my gift isn't important?" she screeches in reply.

"Of course, it is, sweetheart." I bang my head on the wall. "It's amazing. Honestly. The best present anyone has ever given me," I tell her and listen as her sniffles lessen in frequency. "And, bonus, we don't need Bridgett's assistance. Right? Honey?" Silence echoes back. "Ashely, you should be proud. Now, get out here so we can continue this celebration and practice for the next pup."

There's a click before she swings open the door. "Are you really happy?"

I lift her chin. "Ecstatic." I kiss her softly.

"And you want another pup?"

I wrap an arm around her waist and guide her back to the dinner table. "Let's have this one and see how much we like it before we try for baby number two."

She smirks as she picks up her fork. "That's true. I mean, you do have an enormous head and it'll be tough to push that melon out of my vagina."

I thump my palm against my chest to clear my airway as I choke on my beer. I forgot about childbirth. I hold back a shudder. Gross. But happy wife, happy life.

Ashely raises her glass of water as if reading my mind. "To new life."

Her smile warms the room. I've only seen her this cheery once before, and that was the day we completed the bond and officially became mates. It's contagious.

I grin and clink cups with her. "To new life."

Months later, we finally get to experience this *new* life Ashely mentioned.

"I don't understand why you don't just have the baby at the hospital?" I say as I brush the hair away from her sweaty brow.

"We've talked about this," she grunts as another contraction seizes her body. "And the midwife said that a home birth shouldn't be a problem."

"But she's still relatively new to this," I remind my wife as I push an ice cube past her lips.

"I trust her." Ashely squeezes my hand. "Please support me on this."

I kiss her temple. "I'll support you until the day I die."

She screeches as another pain rips through her frame. It's hard to watch my mate suffer. My heart is splintering bit by bit. How could a woman want this? It's madness. You get fat, endure stretch marks, then you have to pop the thing out. Luna has a sick sense of humor.

Ashely leans forward and her breast rubs against my arm. I guess there is one wonderful benefit. My wife's tits are full and two sizes larger. Plus, last week, while I was sucking on her nipples, a delectable liquid seeped into my mouth.

I shake my head and focus on the task at hand, while reminding myself that the milk is for the baby. The infant will need to suckle in order to grow strong and healthy. At least that's what my mate tells me. We even bought a little bassinet for our bedroom, so it'll be easier for my wife to nurse.

"I wish Bridgett could be here," Ashely huffs.

The other woman has grown on me too. Even though she talks too much.

"She would be here if she could," I remind my wife.

"But, *no*, she's too busy," Ashely whines.

"Honey, she's traveling in the other territories, searching for her mate."

"She couldn't have waited until after I had the baby?"

"Your due date is still two weeks away. It's not her fault our pup didn't want to follow the timetable."

"How are we doing?" The midwife strolls into the room.

I grind my teeth. She's acting like this is a walk in the park. I want to squeeze her tiny head between my paws and squish her.

"It hurts," Ashely answers.

"Do you want me to call an ambulance? The hospital can give you an epidural."

"No. I want to do this all natural, like we discussed. It's better for the baby," Ashely groans through another contraction. "My back is cramping."

"Why don't we walk off some of the pain?" The midwife flutters to the other side of my mate. "Ready to help, Dad?" She motions to me. "We'll lift her up and let her stretch her legs a bit to get the blood flowing." She rubs Ashely's arm. "Does that sound good?"

"Yes," my mate breathes out. "Anything to take my mind off *this*."

I bite my tongue to keep my comment to myself. I wish she'd just go to the hospital, where there are real doctors and proper medical equipment. I don't give a fuck if this is the way it was done a hundred years ago. There's a reason women rush to the labor and delivery department to have their children. Especially when it's their first. Frost and Raven had their little girl Maya at the local hospital, and they are the alphas of the Tala pack.

My lips tug into a frown at the thought of their lost child.

"I love you." Ashely leans her head on my arm, dragging me back to the present. "Can we name the baby Ash?"

"Why?"

"Why not? It's short for Ashely. After all this work, shouldn't I get to name our first pup?"

"But we don't even know the gender," I counter.

"So?" She pauses to power through another contraction.

I can't watch her like this. It's too much. "If you go to the hospital, you can name it whatever the fuck you want."

"No," she huffs. "I've come this far. I'm not going to the hospital now. This baby will be born amongst its pack. Surrounded by love."

"At least let me call Celeste," I beg one more time.

"She works at the *hospital*," Ashely grinds out.

"But she's a doctor."

"Stop!" my mate yells. "If you can't support my decision, you won't be welcomed at my home birth."

"But, honey…"

"No *buts*. I mean it, Jackson. I'm perfectly capable of having this pup. Trust in me."

"Yes, dear." I kiss the top of her head, send a prayer up to Luna, and wait for our child's arrival.

Hours later, the three soon-to-be four of us are crowded into our bedroom. The midwife is between Ashely's legs and I'm encouraging my mate to push. Ashely is a champ. She is stronger than I thought. No matter what comes her way, she rises above it. Pride brightens my features. She's amazing.

"I see the head. Way to go," the midwife sings out. "The shoulders are the hardest part, Ashely. I need a big push."

Suddenly the once-quiet room is filled with a wail. I rub my eyes. I can't believe that thing came out of my wife. The midwife hands the baby to Ashely first.

"My sweet child." My wife kisses the newborn's forehead. "My little Ash."

"Here, Dad. Let's cut the umbilical cord."

"No thanks." I cringe. "I'm good." I brush my fingertips down Ashely's cheek. "You're incredible, honey."

"Thanks," she whispers. "I can't wait to show Bridgett."

"Want me to take a picture and send it to her?"

"Would you?" Ashely's eyes flutter closed. After this ordeal, I'm sure she's exhausted.

I tilt my head as I give my mate a closer look. She's pale. "Are you feeling all right?" It's a dumb question to ask a woman who just gave birth, but something is off. Her hold on the newborn relaxes. "Shit!" I catch the bundle before it hits the floor, and it screams at the sudden movement. I hold it close to my chest. "It's okay, buddy. I've got you."

"I need an ambulance stat!"

My head snaps to the midwife. Blood. That's all I can see. Buckets of it. "What's going on?" I turn my attention back to my mate. "Honey?" I rub her chilled arm. She doesn't move. I shake her gently. "Ashely!"

My roar echoes against the stone walls as I frantically beg anyone in earshot to spare her. I can't lose her.

Please, Luna. Have mercy!

"Jackson?" Raven rushes inside the room, closely followed by

Frost. She stops at the threshold as the scent of blood fills her nostrils. "What happened?" She meets my eyes.

I pass my adoptive mother the newborn and clutch Ashely's cold hand.

Frost rubs his wife's arm. "I need to call Robert."

Raven nods at her husband but doesn't speak. Instead, she turns to me. "I'm sure she'll be fine." Raven strokes the baby's cheek as tears slide off her chin. "I'll call Celeste. She'll know what to do," she says while reaching into her pocket.

Before she can dial the phone, however, the paramedics rush in. Then it's a blur of activity. One minute, I'm standing with Raven amidst chaos. The next, a pain jolts through my body, followed by an eerie silence. I stare at Ashely. Our mate bond has been severed.

The medics share a glance before turning to me.

I swallow the lump in my throat. "Don't say it." I release my wife's limp arm. "No." Agony blazes where our connection once burned with a much more pleasant intensity.

Raven pales. "Has she passed?" she whispers, though I'm not sure if it's aimed at me or the others.

"I'm so sorry." The midwife swipes her cheeks. "It happened so fast."

I tug at my hair, trying to calm the rage boiling up my throat. But nothing is soothing the inferno of pain. My vision blurs. My clothes explode off my frame as fur takes over. I leap at the only person I can blame for this atrocity.

"Jackson, no!" Raven screeches.

My wolf is out of control as he tears through flesh and breaks bones. *Ashely is gone because of you!* my fur-conscious screams. *She trusted you!*

A projectile slams into me, and I slide across the cave floor until my head slams into the wall, and everything goes black.

A nightmare. That's what it was. I mentally reach for the mating bond to assure myself of its existence.

"Easy, Jackson," someone says but my head is throbbing. It's hard to recognize who's speaking.

"Is he awake?"

"Give him a minute to get his bearings."

I groan and rub my scalp. Then my eyes flutter open as I cringe at the bloodbath surrounding me. My wife's life force coats my skin. Or is it the midwife's?

Shit.

"How are you feeling, son?" Frost asks.

I push off the ground. I fucked up. I know that.

"You've suffered a concussion and a contusion." Celeste reaches for me. "You need to sit."

I shove her away with a growl. My alpha and his wife retreat a step.

They're afraid we'll lose control again, my wolf tells me.

"Jackson," Raven coos. "Do you want to hold Ash?"

That name. I backpedal. "I... I can't."

"He needs you, son," Frost adds.

My gaze locks on my surrogate parents. How disappointed they must be in me. I'm a murderer. I've lost my mate. I'm not fit to be a parent, a son, or a beta. My fur breaks through my pores, and I shoot for the exit.

"Don't go!" Raven shouts at my back.

"Let the boy clear his head," Frost tells her.

I don't deserve their devotion…

I gallop into the woods. Branches scratch into my skin as I jump over fallen trees. Anything to get as far away as I can from my deceased wife. The ache in my heart is too much. I want it to stop. I should just fail to exist. Be swallowed up by darkness so I can join my mate over the rainbow bridge. My breath comes out in heavy pants.

Is this enough to kill me? I dash through the forest until I collapse by a ravine. My chest heaves as tears coat my cheeks.

Can you take me now, Luna?

A blanket of darkness covers me once again as I slip into a different kind of oblivion this time.

I cough and sputter on liquid. What the heck? I shake my shaggy mane, and water droplets fly into the air.

"Well, I wouldn't have had to shove it down your throat if you weren't so stubborn," a woman yells.

Of course I chose to die in a place inhabited by nosey individuals. I turn away and lie in the dirt again.

Her toes poke my rib cage. "What's your story?"

I snap at her ankle. Warning her I'm not in the mood.

She smacks my hip. "Boy! I'm your elder. You will respect me."

Great, not just annoying individuals but an annoying *pack*. I curl into a ball and lay my tail over my face. She gets the hint and leaves me to rot in my own personal hell.

"Stop *pushing* me, Nana."

"I'm not. I'm *encouraging* you to walk faster. Now pick up the pace, youngin'."

"That's the definition of shoving," the new female voice grumbles in reply.

"See? This is why I asked my smarty-pants grandpup to help me."

Four human feet stop by my snout. The younger woman taps her boot on the grass. "You dragged me out here to look at a shifter who desperately needs a bath?" the girl says, and the older woman responds with a pointed glare. "What do you want *me* to do about it? It's obvious it wants nothing to do with us. So why are you pushing?"

"Because he needs a *push* in the right direction."

"And you think I'm the person to do that?"

The elder shoves a bowl into the other woman's hand. "Yes."

"Wait! Where are you going?" the young girl yells out.

"Papa's calling me."

"No, he's not!" the girl insists. Once the annoying, gray-haired lady turns the corner, the younger one growls, "I don't have time for this." Then she narrows her eyes at me. "You're seriously going to just sit there?" She scratches dried paint off her elbow. "Nana is just going to keep sending me over here until you get off your ass and move."

The girl watches a yellow butterfly flutter from flower to flower, and a smile brightens her face. I tilt my head as she chases it. She laughs as she skips through the foliage.

Luna, I want that. The carefree attitude. The pain-free existence. My mate back in my life.

The golden-winged insect drifts up into the sunbeams, and the young shifter falls into the leaves beside me.

"Do you think butterflies get to choose their wing colors?" She props herself up on her elbows. "I'd choose bright blue. Oh, or even better, a sparkling rainbow."

What's she talking about?

I pivot to make sure she isn't smoking anything funny. She meets my gaze and her smile falters. I wish she'd continue her ridiculous bug talk and ignore me again.

"Someone lost their wings. Didn't they?" she says, and I realize she's not all there in the head. Her eyes water as she plucks a strand of grass between her fingers. "My parents died in a car accident," she whispers to herself.

I turn away. I can't add her misery to mine.

The shifter spends the next hour telling me stories about her mom and dad. Then she explains how hard it was to pull herself out of her state of grief, until she found a community college that offered free art classes taught by local students.

"I'm going back to school, and when I return here, I'm going to give others what they gave to me."

I arch a wolfish brow. *What could they have given her other than paint stains?*

"I know it sounds weird, but those classes brought the light back into my life and taught me to move on." Her toes dig into my side. "What will pull you out of it, Stinky?"

69

I growl at the nickname. It's not like I want to be unclean or mourning the loss of my wife. But here I am. I should leave and find another location to slowly decompose and become one with the earth. Obviously, the spot I've chosen is too chatty and cheerful.

I ignore the other shifter and stare at the bushes. I don't want to be yanked out of these emotions. I *deserve* to feel like this. The female shuffles, before the sound of her footsteps falls into the distance. I release my breath, glad to be alone to drift into the darkness again.

Cold water splashes over my coat. I yelp and jump. But I'm too late to get out of the way as another bucket soaks through my fur. I shake it off and snarl at my attacker.

"Nana isn't here to stop me from cleaning you up." Miss Sunshine waves a scrub brush in my direction. "We can do this the easy way or the hard way, Stinky," she says, and before I can leap at her, she tackles me and viciously rubs at my matted hair. "You'd feel so much better if you just took care of yourself."

This woman is fucking crazy! Jumping a shifter like this! Especially one who doesn't want help.

I shift to two legs and wrestle the brush out of her hands. "Just leave me the fuck alone! I don't want to live! Can't you people just respect that?" I hiss at her.

I'm panting. My frame is all bone and dirt. I clench my fists. I'm a failure. A murderer. A worthless nobody…

The girl kicks me in the chest, and I tumble backwards head over feet. I stare up at the tall oak trees. Apparently, I'm also a little bitch who gets their ass kicked by tiny girls.

"My nana didn't give up on me when I wanted what you wanted." She places her hands on her hips. "That's why she asked me to help you. I'm paying it forward." Then she taps her foot and nods to the lake. "Either you jump in, or you let me continue to help you."

I shake my head. "I told you…"

"Fine. We'll do it the hard way." The girl doesn't let me finish before she dunks her brush into the water and begins to wipe off the dried blood, while I remain glued to my spot. Tired. Defeated. Accepting my fate. When I stop fighting, her strokes become gentler. "Look at that. I can see your skin color now." She pokes my foot. "You aren't from around here, are you?" She wiggles her dark-toned toes in my direction. "The packs here aren't this shade." When I don't speak, she continues to ramble on. "No matter where you're from, I bet your family misses you." She wrinkles her nose at my frail body. "Why don't we get you back to normal so you can return to them?"

"I can't," I push out the words.

"Sure you can. You just put one paw in front of the other."

"I did something unforgivable. I can't show my face there."

The girl's hand stills as all the pieces click into place. "Did you kill something you weren't supposed to?"

"Yes."

"An animal?" she whispers as though she already knows the answer.

"A person," I admit, and her eyes dart towards her pack, as if she's gauging how fast she can run to them if I turn my rage on her. "It won't happen again."

"What did your alpha say afterwards?"

What *did* Frost say?

I honestly can't remember. My memories are blurred together. I squeeze my eyes shut. I don't want to relive that day. I tug at my hair as it all floods my brain like a tidal wave of agony. Ashely screaming in pain. Ash being born…

A warm hand pulls me back to the present, and I blink up as a palm wipes away my tears.

"You can't run from the pain. Trust me. I've tried and failed. Learn from my mistakes."

"You didn't *kill* someone."

"No, but I could have stopped something bad from happening."

I meet her gaze. "How?" I find myself curious about her story.

The girl rubs at her arms. "Let's just say Luna has blessed my family with gifts. At the time, I thought my brother was the only one with special abilities. But the night before my parents' accident, I saw it happen in a dream. It was horrible. But I thought it was just a nightmare and never told them about it. If I'd said something, they'd still be here."

That's a tough situation. If I had seen Ashely's death before it happened, I would have tried everything in my power to protect her. But would it have made a difference? Would she have listened to me or just thought I was being overprotective?

Only Luna knows…

"Well, looks like you're making progress." The older woman returns with two plates in her hands. My nose twitches at the scent of grilled fish. For the first time since I found myself amongst strangers, my mouth waters at the thought of food. "Here you go." She offers us dinner. "There's more where that came from too." Then the old woman turns and leaves as quickly as she came.

I devour the meat before licking the grease off my fingertips. The girl taps her shoulder against mine. "No more running. Face your demons head-on." She nods towards the rough scrub brush at our feet. "Otherwise, I'll have to do this again."

I roll my eyes before snatching her food and scarfing it down too.

"Hey! That wasn't yours to eat, Stinky," she grumbles.

Days pass. How many? I'm not sure. The world moves differently when you're engulfed by loss. The slowly passing seconds are a reminder that you are here, and they aren't. Each painful heartbeat pushes you forward while theirs is silent.

The darkness surrounding my existence fades to a navy blue. Has Frost buried Ashely's body? Then navy blue morphs into a pale yellow. What's happened to the infant? Did he join his mother in her grave?

My lashes flutter open. The sun stings, making my eyes water. Will my pack turn me in to the authorities, or deal with my sentencing on their own? Birds flutter in the treetops, welcoming another day, while their songs generate a false sense of security.

"Will today be the day?" The old lady settles onto the fallen log beside me.

Every morning, she asks me the same question. I'm not sure what answer she's hoping for. But she asks it nonetheless when she brings me food. I don't even know her name. Yet she's taken care of me as if I were her own. The others in her pack have done the same. Especially the girl.

I don't remove my gaze from the sun's ascent. "Thank you."

"Just make sure you pay it forward when another wolf needs help one day." She pats my leg. "This world desperately needs more compassion."

I glance over and see a single tear drop from her chin. "I'm sorry to hear about your family's loss."

"Thank you." A breeze tousles her silver hair. "You know, we've all lost pack members, but it's how we allow the loss to define us that shapes who we are, what we do, and if any of it has meaning."

73

She swipes her cheek. "They wouldn't want us to live anything *but* happy lives, filled with hearty laughter and tender love." The old woman nods with finality. "And that's what I'll do. I'll live my life *for* them, because theirs was cut short. Until my dying breath." Then she pokes my chest. "Now the question is… what will you choose to do?"

This stranger has more fire inside her than I'll ever have, and without Ashely, I'm just a lonely wolf. Never to find love again.

A butterfly flutters between us, momentarily drawing my attention away from my self-pity. The golden wings remind me of the girl's question. The creature lands on my nose and I resist the urge to blow it off.

Maybe we do get to choose our own wings?

"My pack believes these creatures carry messages from over the rainbow bridge." The elder points to my face. "Messages of peace and hope."

The insect flaps its wings and disappears into the sky. And a shard of my broken heart clicks into place. Maybe she's right?

I push to my feet, and my stiff limbs scream at the movement. I lift my chin towards the north. It's time I face my pack *and* the consequences of my actions.

Jackson

Welcome Home

Amillion scenarios run through my head as I gallop through the forest towards my pack. I imagine their angry glares. I *killed* someone. A family is mourning the loss of the midwife my wolf tore apart. What if the pack fears me? I've served as their beta, protecting them from prey and invaders for most of my life.

I wince. I made a mistake. Surely my friends and family will understand that?

I shake my mane. No. It wasn't a mistake. I *chose* to rip that woman apart for taking away my mate. Ashely trusted her midwife, and it was a horrible error in judgment on her part… as well as the last one she'll ever be able to make.

My paws quiver from exhaustion. I slow to a trot as the familiar scent of my alpha tickles my nose. I'm almost home. That word feels so wrong to think or say without my mate to welcome me on the doorstep. I skid to a stop, inches from our boundary.

I can't do this.

I pivot and stride away from the Tala territory. I can't return to our cave and our way of life as if nothing has happened. I only make it a few steps before a wounded bark tugs at my heartstrings.

"Son?" I freeze. *"Jackson?"* Raven communicates through our wolf connection. Her heavy breathing indicates that she's been running to catch up to me. Her emotions are pushed through along with her words. Love for me and fear that I'll leave again. *"Come home."*

I lower my head, unable to meet her gaze. *"I don't belong here anymore. Not without Ashely."*

She whimpers. *"What about me and Frost? We've lost so much. Please do not add to that sorrow."*

I wince. In all my misery and self-loathing, I forgot about Maya. Their lost pup. Before I can answer my surrogate mother, she rubs her head under my chin and warmth spreads through my chest. I've missed her.

I return her nuzzle. *"I didn't mean to cause you pain."*

"We know you didn't. Your own suffering clouded your judgment." Frost's voice booms as he stands on two legs. Watching us. He opens his arms. "Welcome back to the pack, Jackson."

I shift and meet his gaze. I thought he'd yell at me and demand I leave. "You're going to *allow* me back? After everything that's happened?"

He pulls me into a tight embrace. Then whispers, "Nobody knows what you did to the midwife except for a few individuals. We took care of the *mess*."

"Why?" I blurt out. "I should be punished. Banish me or turn me into the authorities."

Frost pulls back and slaps his palms on my shoulders. "You were distraught when the mating bond snapped, son. Considering what happened, no one blames you for that little accident. Everything is taken care of and we're moving on." He waves me into our territory.

I backpedal. I figured they'd hate me. Not *this*. They're willing to overlook everything I did…

"You're a good person, Jackson. The pack needs your protection," Raven coos. When I don't move, she grabs my wrist and pulls me towards her cave. "At least have some chili before you go."

I enter the stone home and sit in the same chair I occupied as a lost pup. It's come full circle now. Lost pup and now a lost man.

"I brought the biscuits." Granny emerges from the other room with a basket in her arms. "Well, I'll be damned. The prodigal son has returned."

"Mom. Language," Frost grumbles as he helps her sit.

"Don't you dare lecture me on what I'm doing," Granny snaps. When Frost goes to the kitchen to help Raven, the elderly woman turns to me. "I'm sorry for your loss." She pats my hand, as she gazes at her own wedding band. "It's not easy. When I lost my Michael…" Her voice trails off as she closes her eyes. "I can still feel the bond snapping between us. It's a pain I'd never wish on anyone. Especially someone so young."

This woman has been around decades longer than I have. Even though I never met her husband, that didn't stop his memory from living on through his wife's actions and speeches about his contributions to the pack. Maybe I can do the same.

I squeeze her wrist in a silent response. I'll get through this. Somehow.

"Here we are. Venison chili with buttermilk biscuits." Raven serves us each a bowl. "Eat up, before it gets cold."

The recipe is exactly as I remember it. It's full of fresh herbs and vegetables from the garden with chunks of the pack's recent prey. The alpha's wife always makes a massive pot and feeds the entire pack during gatherings.

My spoon pauses at my lips. *How long was I gone? What event is today?*

Frost slides his chair back. "Everything was perfect, dear." He kisses his wife. "I'll bring the rest of the food to the ceremony." He walks to the door. "Mom, do you want me to help you to the tree?"

Granny grumbles and waves him off. "I'm old but not too old to walk, child."

Then it hits me. They're saying goodbye to a pack member. *Ashely.* I meet Raven's eyes, and she gives a small nod as confirmation.

"Will I see you there, son?" Frost asks me.

I open my mouth to respond, but quickly close it. Can I go? To say farewell to the love of my life?

"Give the boy some breathing room." Granny clicks her tongue. "Get going and we'll see you soon." When Frost and Raven leave, Granny shakes her head. "Everyone is walking on eggshells around you, Jackson." Her bones pop as she pushes up in her chair. "But they need to be supporting you and pushing you forward so you can get on with your life." She offers me her weathered palm. "Now walk this old lady to the ceremony, and with any luck, we'll arrive before sunrise."

"I don't think I can…"

"Stop," she demands. "I will not let you doubt your abilities."

"But…"

"Don't make me pull you over my knee and spank you, young man. You are *never* too old for a good wallop." She wags a finger at me. "Now stand tall and uphold your duty for your wife, child, and pack. Don't show any weakness in front of her family tonight. They need to know their baby girl was cherished and that her memory will carry on through you."

I swallow the lump in my throat. I forgot about the friends and family Ashely left behind too. I'll have to confront them with my tail between my legs. I couldn't protect my mate. What a disappointment...

"Are you ready?" Granny taps her foot on the floor. "I'm not going to live forever, you know."

That simple act of impatience reminds me of the pack I visited in my time of grief. I lift my chin.

I can do this. One paw step at a time.

I square my shoulders. "Yes, I'm ready."

"That's a good start." Granny smiles. "And with a little more practice, I'll actually think you believe it."

We stride into the night air. The crickets serenade us as we follow the candlelit path laid out in front of us. The territory is full of Robert's and Frost's family members. The crowd is overwhelming, and I fight the urge to gallop into the forest to mourn by myself. But when they see us approaching, everyone rushes over. They wrap me in a blanket of comforting hugs and sympathetic words. Even though they are suffering too, their main concern is my pain.

We continue to make our way towards rows of candles that lead to a large oak tree. I place my palm over the sturdy trunk. "This tree has been here longer than we have and will remain long after," Granny says from beside us as she pats the bark, staring intently at a wind-swept spot. "The Native Americans believe that its roots grow to the center of existence, which allows us to communicate with our loved ones in the beyond. When a pack member passes on, we mark its trunk and guide the wandering spirits with candlelight." She leans her forehead on its surface. "Then we dance around its lush branches, hoping that it will encourage the spirits to join us in celebrating their new life. A painless existence with our creator and the mother of all, Luna."

I've heard this speech before—it's recited whenever a shifter from our pack passes away. But this time, the words slam into my gut and cause me to bend over as all the memories crash into me, reminding me I'll never see Ashely again. The roaring inferno of pain engulfs my entire being.

No. I need her. To touch her. Love her.

When I open my eyes again, I see everyone has wandered off to the open field to drink, share stories, and dance the night away. Everyone except...

Bridgett dabs her lashes as her finger glides through the fresh tick mark in the bark. Ashely's mark. "It's a load of shit." She chugs from a plastic cup. "Do you really believe all that?" Bridgett can't even meet my gaze. I let her best friend die. She'll never get to watch chick flicks or drink a fresh cup of tea with her bestie again.

"It's just to offer hope, Bridgett." I force out the words, as if to convince myself too. "Besides, there's no proof it doesn't work."

"They're stupid stories. I can't just pick a branch..." She tugs on a twig above her head. "...and reach Ashely." Her facade splinters with her agony, and she blubbers into the leaves. "Why her?" she roars into the night air. "I hate you, Luna! Do you fucking hear me! You stupid fur dictator! Fuck you!"

Her statement slices into my soul. The threat burns deep in my heart. My wife's best friend's hatred towards our deity matches my own. But I don't have the balls to scream it to the world.

Robert rushes over and whispers in Bridgett's ear in hushed tones, reminding her of her place and that she's a guest of the Tala pack. She stalks off to refill her beverage, tears ruining her painted face.

"I'm sorry, Jackson." Robert pats my back. I'm not exactly sure what he's apologizing for until he clarifies, "When Bridgett returned from her mate search empty-pawed, I had to break the news to her about Ashely's passing, and it wasn't easy." He rubs a hand over his face. "Maybe you two should swap stories and remember the good times."

I can only nod. Sharing memories won't bring my mate back.

"Here." Bridgett shoves something that smells like toxic waste into my open hand.

I wrinkle my nose but chug the contents. I slap my chest to keep the concoction from rising. "What was that?"

Her slender shoulders lift and fall. "It numbs the ache. For a few hours anyway."

A violinist plays from somewhere in the shadows, and I close my eyes to listen. The music is calming as the soft notes lull me into a comforting silence. And in that blissful darkness, there's my mate again, living inside my sweet daydreams.

Wrapping her palm over my thick erection… Begging me to steal a taste of her sweet nectar… Telling me how much she loves me…

The sun glares down from the sky, burning my naked flesh. "Fuck," I huff as I shield my face.

Polished fingertips dance over my chest. *What the hell?*

I shoot up into a sitting position and take inventory of my surroundings.

"Quiet down," a feminine voice demands as she clutches her head. "I need some aspirin and a burrito."

I blink at the nude shifter. "Bridgett?"

"Oh, good. We weren't drunk enough to forget who we were." She smacks her lips together and stretches.

I must have blacked out. How could I have slept with my mate's best friend? The contents from last night fight their way up my throat at the thought.

Bridgett wraps me into a hug from behind. "I can still smell her on you." Her tongue flicks over my shoulder. "If we close our eyes, we can pretend *together*." Her wrist snakes through my chest hair and down to my hips. "Please. I can't forget her." She strokes me as she bites my earlobe.

My nose twitches. She's in *heat*. A shiver racks my body as my primal desires attempt to push past my wavering logic.

She's not Ashely.

I hiss as Bridgett's nails dig into my balls, dragging my attention to my traitorous erection. I should tell her to stop. A moan parts my lips. My grief-riddled mind pushes reality aside, and suddenly Ashely is the one taking my cock. Her eyes water as I thrust into the back of her throat. Spittle mixed with my fluids slides down her chin. I wrap her hair around my fist and pump into her. Her guttural moan vibrates against my rod, and I combust with a roar.

Yes, this eases the sorrow. Remembering my wife through meaningless sex. The sound of panting fills the space. This is how I'll survive without my mate.

A few hours later, we're standing outside my home.

Wipe your paws. The cutesy welcome mat mocks me. Even the wreath screams *she's gone!*

"Robert said I need to return to our territory before sunset." Bridgett bites her lip from where she's positioned beside me.

We fucked until we passed out again, but now...

I swallow the lump in my throat. The hard work begins. Frost said there was no rush. That I could stay in my old room in their cave, but I want to be back in our den. Be close to my wife's beautiful paintings. Breathe in her fading scent.

"If you want to do this without me, I'll understand," Bridgett whispers, even though she begged to join me so she could grab a few mementos before she's forced to return to her pack.

I shake my head. "She would want you to have some of her drawings." My palm rests on the door handle. "Plus, you can take back that nasty-ass tea you forced her to drink."

"Hey! Those herbs helped her conceive…" Bridgett's words fall between us.

Yes, conceive the child Ashely desperately wanted. The same one who's alive and well while his mother isn't.

"Just throw that shit away. Burn it for all I fucking care," she snarls with clenched fists.

Frost told us that a married couple is looking after Ash until I decide how I would like to proceed. The family is hoping I agree to allow them to adopt the furball since they can't have children of their own. But I'll deal with that tomorrow. Today I'm going to tackle this mess.

I push through the threshold. Although I can still make out a few stains on the stone wall, the alpha did his best to clean up the carnage from the home birth. He even had the place straightened up, the ruined furniture replaced.

A crash from the kitchen has me turning in that direction. Bridgett rips apart all the herbs Ashely consumed—the ones that inadvertently resulted in my mate's death during childbirth. She's on the verge of losing it. Her face is red, tears are brimming at the corners of her eyes, and her actions are rage-fueled. She attacks the mugs next, sending shards of ceramic all around us.

"Fuck!" Bridgett screams as she claws at the counters, cutting her hands on the remnants of her fit. "Why!" Her back hits the wall and she slides onto the cold floor. She hugs her knees and rocks back and forth.

I wish I could unleash the beast of grief boiling inside me, but I know the consequences of doing that again. Instead, I allow numbness to take over as I sweep up the shattered ceramic on the floor and begin to put my life back together.

Piece by aching piece.

Lily

Moving On

"There're my grandpups! Get over here and give your nana a hug!"

"Easy, Nana," Azure warns as she runs to me. "Lily is a little roughed up right now."

Nana skids to a stop and her frown darkens her usually sunny demeanor. "Baby girl, what happened?" She wraps an arm around my waist and helps Azure guide me towards our family cave. "Don't you worry about a thing. The Pawson pack takes care of their own. You'll be galloping through these woods soon." She strokes my hair. "How long are you staying, Azure?"

My brother sighs. "Not long, unfortunately."

Honestly, I'm surprised my brother's been by my side the whole time I was in the hospital. Not once did he mention leaving me. It was nice having him so close.

I lean my head on my twin's shoulder. "Don't worry about me.

I'm with Nana and Papa." I smile at the older woman. "You know how they love to spoil me."

Nana gives me a toothless grin and I question her age. I've only ever asked her how old she is once, because she smacked me upside the head and told me it wasn't any of my business. That you're only as old as you feel. I believed her up until my parents died. That accident aged my grandparents more than they like to admit.

"I dusted and changed the sheets and towels when you called, Azure," Nana says to my brother while rubbing my back. "It's been years since I've gotten a visit from my favorite pups. The others have been fishing all day, so I hope you're hungry."

"You didn't have to do all of that, Nana." I wince as Azure helps me get into my old twin bed.

"Sorry. Did you pull a stitch?" My brother frowns.

"Stitches?" Nana questions as she assesses my hot mess. "Is someone going to tell me what happened?"

I can't tell her and see the pity flash over her features. So I feign a yawn and snuggle under the covers. "Azure can tell you what happened, Nana. I'm really tired."

"Of course, baby." She brushes her lips over my forehead. "I'm just glad you're home."

Home? This place hasn't been my home for over four years, and it hasn't felt safe since my parents' car accident. But Nana and Papa have always taken such good care of us, and I'll need all the help I can get.

"Do you want me to bring you some food, sis?" Azure asks. "You know, Tilly can cook an amazing grilled trout."

"Actually," Nana cuts in. "Tilly joined Luna."

We're all silent as the words surround us. Tilly was younger than Nana by a decade or two. It feels like our pack members are dropping like flies. I do mental math. That means the Pawson pack only has six of us left: Azure, me, Nana, Papa, Jimmy, and Jackie. And you can't really count my brother because he travels so much.

"I'm sorry." Azure breaks the quiet atmosphere.

Nana pats his back and sighs. "You two better get busy and find your mates or the Pawson pack might cease to exist."

I cringe and meet my brother's gaze. *Welp. Guess we should rip the bandage off now.*

Azure nods and guides Nana outside. "Why don't I help make dinner and explain what happened?"

Their voices trail off as they join the others and leave me alone with my thoughts.

I stare at the stone ceiling. What a mess I've weaved. I pinch my eyes closed and allow my tears to flow over my cheeks. The doctors say I'll make a full recovery and that the baby shouldn't be affected by my injuries or the medication I'm currently taking, but they don't know what kind of genes it has.

Brock was obviously on the run from someone or something. Was he a fugitive? A felon? An experiment of some kind?

I swipe at my lashes. This child is half me, so I have to have hope that no matter what, it'll be a good kid. I lift the hem of my shirt. Most of the bruises have healed. My finger traces the scratch on my back. This one was the worst. I can still feel the pain when they sewed it closed. I shiver at the roughness of the stitches. I'll have to get them removed soon. I lean into the pillows. Not only will the memories haunt me for the rest of my life, but I'll have a physical scar too. No amount of healing oil will hide this one. It was too deep.

A knock stirs me from my inner turmoil.

"Thought I'd bring you something to snack on before it's time to take your medicine." My brother leans on the doorframe with a plate in his hand. "Are you hungry?"

"I think I've lost my appetite for the rest of my life," I grumble.

The bed lowers as he sits on the corner and passes me my dinner. "I gave them the quick version of what happened in the cabin."

"Thank you." I scoot my food around with my fork. "How did it go?"

His chuckle warms the air. "Papa grabbed his shotgun and Nana is sharpening her talons, while Jimmy and Jackie are trying to convince them to let it go, especially with you safe and back home."

I smirk. "Sounds like them. Luna, I've missed them."

"Me too."

The silence envelops us again as we are each lost in the past. One where the pack was flourishing, and everyone was happy. The good old days. Now it seems like the family is dying off, along with the cheerful moments.

Azure wipes my cheek. I didn't realize I was crying again. Our eyes meet. Pity lines his face and he looks older than he is.

"I'll be fine." I push past the lump in my throat. "One day," I whisper. "Just not today."

He squeezes my leg. "I'm only a phone call away."

I look at my hands. "You've said that before."

He tenses as he recalls the last time I tried to get in contact with him. "Lily, I promise things will be different. I already told the other Guardians about our situation and explained that you come first." He lifts my chin. "I never meant to make you feel like you weren't important." Then he hugs me gently. "I'm going to be a better brother."

"And what about an uncle?"

He pulls back and grins. "I can't wait for that. I'm going to spoil it so much!"

"Not too much," I warn him.

"No promises."

The tension around us dissolves as we each seem to consider the future of the pup.

"Are you going to name it what I think you're going to name it?" Azure lifts a brow with the question, and I laugh.

"I forgot about that. How old were we when we decided on that?"

Azure scratches his scruff. "We were six, I think. We both had the flu and were bedridden."

"Then we fought over the remote, and when I won, you broke my doll's arm."

"Sorry about that." He shrugs. "But then I promised you if you didn't rat me out to Mom that I'd let you name my firstborn."

"We were weird kids." I shake my head.

"No, you were weird! You kept calling your dolls odd things like Fluffermutt. I wanted nothing to do with that horrible name. But I was desperate to stay out of trouble."

"Then I suggested the name Maxi for your first pup."

"And I said it was only fair that I get to name your child too." He snickers.

"Yeah. Peanuts." I shake my head. "I'm not calling my pup that."

"That was for a girl!" he reminds me. "My boy name was pretty cool."

"I don't remember the boy name." I nibble my lip. "All I recall is Peanuts."

"It was Hunter." Azure elbows me. "Then you said a kid shouldn't be named after an activity."

"Oh! Yes!" I grin, and we share a chuckle. "I actually don't hate that name."

Azure blinks at me. "Really?"

"Really." I run my hand through his wild, dark hair. "You have good ideas every now and then."

He kisses my palm. "Is Hunter a unisex name?"

I shrug. "It will be for this little thing." I rub my flat stomach. "Assuming it stays inside long enough to be born healthy."

"It will." Azure nods with finality. "I'll be praying every day to Luna for that to happen." He sends a zap of electricity through me with a grin, reminding me of his closeness to our deity. "Or she'll have to find another bodyguard for her wolves."

"Best uncle of the century." I punch his heavily corded bicep.

"Best uncle of a lifetime!" he corrects me.

"My mistake." I settle into the pillows and eat my dinner. "When are you heading out?"

"Tonight."

My fork freezes an inch from my mouth. "That soon?"

"I can request more time off if that's what you need…"

"Stop babying your sister!" Nana breezes into the room. "We can take care of her." She nestles beside me. "Right, baby girl?"

I lean my head on her shoulder and nod. "Nana is right. Go save the world, Guardian."

My brother and I stare into each other's eyes. "But, Lil, you are my world."

My lip trembles and that voice in the back of my head nags at me. *Just wait until he finds out you killed your mate and the father of your child.*

94

Nana grabs my brother's arm and tugs him into a group hug. "Your mama would be so proud! I know I am."

I wish that were true...

Lily

New Life

"I've changed my mind!" I scream. "I want to go to a hospital and get an epidural."

"Too late now. The pup is coming," Nana mumbles from where she's positioned between my legs. "It's got a nice tuff of hair! That's why you've been having heartburn."

"That's an old wives' tale." Jackie pats my forehead.

"No, it's not! I had heartburn with mine and they all had hair when they were born." Nana points at us, never taking her eyes off the baby trying to make its entrance into the world.

"Can we argue about this later?" I grind out as I push through another contraction.

"You heard her. Quit your yapping and grab the child," Jackie demands. "Poor Lily has been at it for ten hours." The elderly woman worries her lip. "Maybe we should call an ambulance?"

"I've delivered all the pups in this pack! Never have I had to call in reinforcements, and I won't start now."

"Well, you were a bit younger the last time you had to catch a pup," Jackie mumbles under her breath.

"When my great grandpup is out, I'm going to smack you upside the head for that comment, Jackie," Nana growls in response.

"Nana!" I wheeze through the pain. "I'm not strong enough!" I cry out.

She meets my eyes. "None of that talk, Lilith Cassandra Pawson! I won't hear it! I will never give up on you! Do you hear me? Now shut your mouth, use that energy to your advantage, and push this baby out. Or so help me, I'll shove my hands up your vagina and tug it out myself."

I clamp my lips closed. I'm in enough pain. I don't need any more.

Jackie wipes my brow and smiles encouragingly. "You got this." Then she whispers in my ear, "Don't worry, we can take the old girl down."

"I may be old, but my wolf ears work just fine," Nana snarls. "Oh! The shoulders are the hardest part, and they are pushing through now!"

I take a breath and shove with all my might. My head falls back, and a cry rips through the room. I jolt up. Nana holds the baby in full view as tears fall from her chin. "There, there, little pup. Great Nana has you."

Jackie runs over and cuts the umbilical cord before wrapping the screeching child in a towel. I reach out, begging to hold the tiny creature who caused so much pain just a moment ago. Jackie walks over and lays the infant in my arms.

"Congratulations, Lily. It's a healthy baby boy."

I sob into his hair. "My sweet son," I whisper. "Mommy loves you."

His cries soften as he nuzzles into my chest against the beat of my heart. My finger glides over his jet-black hair. He's amazing. My phone vibrates from my bedside table. I smirk and answer the video call from Azure.

"Did I miss it?" he asks, sounding out of breath. I twist the camera to the sleeping newborn. "Aw, look at it! Good job, Lil."

"Hey, she had help, you know," Nana grumbles in the background. She's still between my legs.

"Good job, Team Pawson." Azure laughs.

"Don't mind Nana. She's been working so hard and hasn't slept in almost two days. She and Jackie have been Luna-sent." I smile at my packmates. "I wouldn't have been able to do this without them."

"Popping the baby out is the easy part." Jackie smirks. "Now we have to raise the little beast."

We share a laugh as we all watch the child sleep.

"Sweet dreams, Hunter." I kiss my son's forehead and hold him tight as I'm surrounded with love, while I pray my child's future will be bright and full of many blessings.

A few weeks later, my brother actually visits to see the new bundle of joy face-to-face.

"Lily!" Azure wraps his arms around me. "You look well."

"You were always a terrible liar," I grunt as I shift Hunter into my other arm. "I haven't slept in days. All he does is cry unless I'm walking around with him." I let out a breath. I love my pack, but they can't keep up with an infant's demands. And they shouldn't have to. He is my responsibility. My punishment for bashing his father's head in. I clear my throat. "Do you want to hold him, Az?"

I frown as I notice the distant look in my brother's eyes. His brows furrow like he's assessing the shapes of the dark clouds drifting in the sky. He's worried about something. I squint into the tree line. Nothing feels amiss. But it could be my lack of sleep that has my judgement feeling off.

Hunter squirms in my hold and I offer the pup to my brother for a second time. Azure continues to ignore his nephew. I roll my eyes. Why visit us if he's just going to drift off into his own world?

"Hello? Are you even *listening* to me?"

Azure shakes his head and his eyes meet mine. "I'm sorry."

"Were you having another vision?"

"Not exactly." He rubs his forehead. "I need to cut this visit short. There's something developing in the northern quadrant."

He's hiding something. But what? We used to be able to tell each other everything.

Because he knows how weak his little sister really is. My inner voice screams at me, but I push it down.

Should I press Azure for information on his next mission?

Hunter whimpers in his sleep, and I stroke his cheek. The movement reminds me of the rumors of a pup being abducted north of our pack.

"Oh, isn't that where that poor pup disappeared from?" I ask my twin.

"You're thinking of Cold Creek, Lily." Azure's jaw ticks. He's lost in his mind again, but this time, he clenches his fists and his blue veins shimmer with power.

"You'll get through this, big brother." I rub his arm until he smiles and nods.

"Thanks, Lil."

I wish he'd talk to me. But he'll recite his tale when the time comes. I need to be patient.

"Nana says you've denied their request to visit the other packs to narrow down your search for a husband."

I don't want to chat about *that*.

"I have enough on my plate, brother. I'm not scouring the land for a man. *He* can find me. Now, quit stalling and get over your fear of fragile newborns and hold your nephew." I shove Hunter into Azure's arms. "How about *you* tell me when you're settling down?"

He cradles the pup, embracing the warmth. "He has Dad's rosy cheeks." My brother tickles Hunter's face with his nose. "I plan on many more years of safeguarding the packs. I don't think I'll retire in the near future. But I'll settle down in Luna's time. That's when I'll find my mate, and not a moment sooner."

My son coos before tugging a fistful of Azure's dark hair.

"I do have faith." I cross my arms over my chest, feeling like an appendage is missing now that my reason for living is nestled in my brother's arms. "I guess I'm just being impatient because I don't want to be an old lady when I'm chasing after my little niece or nephew."

Poor Jackie and Nana try to keep up with Hunter but can't. I don't even want to think about how their arthritis will act up when he's running circles around them.

"I'll keep my eyes open for my mate."

Hope rises in my chest. If he finds her soon, we can raise our children together and I'll have a younger woman to talk to!

"Are you going to bring her back here? Or stay with her pack? Oh! Or travel together?" I throw out question after question.

"Can I locate her first?" Azure arches a brow at my impatience.

"You know, you could bring your pup to my mate's territory."

Anxiety builds in the pit of my stomach at the thought of traveling. The last time I left, I met Brock. I rub my arms. "Maybe I will go when the time comes," I push out, not wanting to admit that I don't want to leave the safety of our family home.

Azure's head shoots to the sky as if Luna is sending him a message. "I'm needed in Carson City." He kisses the small bundle in his arms. "I'll call you soon," he says as he passes over his nephew. "I love you, Lily, and I'm proud of you."

My lip quivers. If only he knew what I did…

"I love you too. Keep your nose up, brother. I know your mate is out there waiting for you to find her."

"And when I do, we'll figure out the rest." He embraces me. "Hopefully your mate will allow you to stay nearby so our pups can grow up together."

I cringe, knowing that won't be an option. I hold Hunter closer to my chest before rocking him. It'll just be us against the world.

As soon as my son is old enough to run, I'm finding myself in more trouble than I thought possible.

"Hunter! Get back here!" I sprint through the woods as the little boy giggles. "You better stop right there, mister, or no dessert tonight!"

"Nana burns cookies. I don't want them," the preschooler hollers back before he launches himself into the lake. "Weeee!"

Water sprays my tired face and serves as the wake-up call I didn't know I needed. I rub the droplets from my eyes.

Should I jump in and rescue him?

Hunter doggie paddles, plopping his palms into the once-calm surface of the pond. Thank Luna Jackie taught him how to swim. His laughter adds to the serenade of the early morning hours. He'll be fine for now.

I slump against the nearest oak tree, the bark biting into the skin of my shoulder. Damn, motherhood is the hardest thing I've ever done. I'd rather return to college and get four more degrees than continue on this exhausting path.

I pinch my nose. Typically, mothers have spouses to assist in the everyday adventures. Not me. Yes, I have my pack but their energy drains too fast for the preschooler.

"I thought you told him no?" Nana huffs beside me as she finally joins me by the water's edge.

"I did. But I don't want to battle him on this one because I'm not jumping into the frigid water to give him his punishment. Besides, my threat was no dessert." I elbow her. "And no one likes your cookies."

"Baking is harder than it looks," Nana grumbles, settling in beside me to watch Hunter as he dives after fish. "Why don't you head back to the den? I can wait here until he runs out of energy and gets hungry."

I smell a ploy brewing. I arch a brow. "Why?"

"No reason." She doesn't meet my inquisitive stare.

"Nana…" I push.

"There may be an eager male searching for a mate waiting to kiss you." She raises her arms at my red face. "Before you start hollering at me, remember I brought him here so you wouldn't have to travel."

"That doesn't make it any better."

"Yes, it does. You said you couldn't travel with a child." She gives me a pointed glare. "It's only a smooch. Stop being a prude. When was the last time you sought out anything romantic? Other than those books of yours," she adds. "Or that outdated vibrator you've been using since the Stone Age," she mumbles under her breath.

"Nana!" I hiss but recover quickly. "It works well for my needs. I'm *fine*."

"It runs on batteries."

Like that clarifies anything.

"They don't call them battery-operated boyfriends for nothing," I grumble.

"You know, they actually charge now and some even have remotes."

"I'm not having this conversation with my grandmother, so move on to a new topic," I beg her.

"The next topic will be anal beads if you don't march that pretty little butt to your cave right now and kiss the hunk waiting for you."

My cheeks are burning—and not the ones she's talking about either. I steal a glance at Hunter. He's now moved on to chasing a flock of ducks. I rub a hand down my face. No matter how many prospective mates come to kiss me, I'll never find the one meant for me. I should just come clean and tell her what happened.

Surely my own flesh and blood will understand, right?

"Nana, I need to tell you something." I puff out my chest, ready to let loose. To tell her to take that candidate away because I *murdered* my mate. In cold blood. The *father* of my child.

"Yes, dear?"

"I…" But the words don't form in my mouth and my throat closes up. *Fuck me.* "I'll be back in five minutes."

"For the love of Luna, just let the man give you some attention! Mate or no mate!" she yells at my retreating back.

Jet-black fur permeates my skin. I howl into the sky, eager to get this over with. My wolf gallops at full speed, putting as much space as we can between us and Nana.

Weak, weak, weak, my wolf snarls internally.

SHUT UP! I beg her to stop.

My talons dig into the leaf-littered forest floor, throwing pebbles in their wake. I miss this. The freedom, the wind whistling through my fur. It might actually be easier to track Hunter this way too. My snout twitches, alarming me of the intruder in our territory before my eyes zero in on him leaning on a cave wall. Talking to Jimmy. They laugh at something before they pivot towards me.

"There she is! Our Lily!" Jimmy opens his arms for a hug. I morph to two feet and embrace him. "I was just explaining to Sebastian that you had a degree in art." He hands me a soft cardigan. I button it up to hide the ugly scars on my back. Because we wouldn't want to scare off a prospect with *that* story.

I roll my eyes at the thought.

"I appreciate you making the trip here, Sebastian."

He offers me a boyish grin as he assesses my frame. Luna, I'd give anything to hear what he's thinking. Something along the lines of... *more cushion for the pushing*? Or... *damn, she must be a great cook to be so fluffy*? Or maybe even... *what is she hiding under that coat?*

He shoves his muscular frame off the den wall. "It's nice to meet you."

Wow. He's tall. I swallow, attempting to wet my dry throat. Those eyes of his remind me of Brock's. Sweat coats my palms.

"Well, I'm going to check on Jackie. I'll be back soon." Jimmy nods and turns to give us privacy.

Why do I feel like I'm a child again?

"Should we ease into it, or just jump right in?" Sebastian's fingertips graze my arm, causing goose bumps to rise along the surface.

When was the last time I was touched by someone with hunger plastered on their face?

He gently tugs my frame to his. "You're breathtaking," he tells me.

I nibble my lip. He's so sweet. I wonder if he knows about Hunter? Would the elders divulge that information? Or wait until later?

"Thank you," I announce with a little too much bravado.

His chuckle warms my heart. He rubs my bicep. "Can I kiss you, Lily?"

I should say no. That I know he's wasting his time. But then my gaze lands on his pillowy soft lips. "Yes," I whisper. Because why the hell not?

Sebastian dips his head and our lips brush. He smells amazing. Not at all like...

I groan and chide myself. I need to stop thinking about Brock.

Sebastian takes the sound I make as a sign to dive deeper, and he devours me. My toes curl at the attention. I can't help but wonder how his tongue would feel between my legs. I melt into him, until I'm gasping for air.

"No mate connection?" he questions as his thumb glides over my cheek.

"No." I sigh. "Sorry."

"No worries, Lily. We could always explore the *other* connection between us." He boldly rubs his erection over my stomach.

I step away from *that* beast. Maybe Nana is right. I am a prude. The old Lily Pawson would have jumped at the opportunity to ride

Mr. Well-Endowed.

"Don't be scared of him, darling. He won't bite." Sebastian winks. "Although *I* might if you're into rough play."

I most definitely am… was… But not anymore.

"Here we go!" Jimmy comes to the rescue as he hands Sebastian a mug. "Jackie's famous hot cocoa."

"Thank you." The other shifter sips the beverage. "Unfortunately, I should really head back home. My alpha will be eager to hear how this outing went."

"Yes, of course." Jimmy nods. "You're welcome back anytime."

"I appreciate that." Sebastian shakes hands with Jimmy, then turns to me. "Call me if you change your mind." Then he strides to the territory boundary before calling out, "Oh, and tell the Guardian that the Lobo pack sends our warm greetings. And that we welcome him to test our females to see if any of them are his mate."

"That's a wonderful idea," Jimmy says from beside me. "We will gladly relay the message for you, Sebastian."

The male morphs into a gorgeous red-furred beast and gallops into the darkness of the forest's canopy. I rub my arms. So that's why he decided to travel here, to take a shot at the Guardian's sister. It wasn't because of my charm or beauty.

I snort. If I even had those qualities to begin with…

You'll always remain in Azure's shadow, my inner voice reminds me.

A growl alerts us to the fact that Nana is having a hard time with Hunter. Moisture flecks against my ankle and I shield my face as she shakes the lake water off her fur. I smirk as she carries the pup by his scruff. My nana's once beautiful charcoal fur is peppered with silver and is thinning in spots.

How much longer will she be here to assist me?

I frown at the thought. I can't think about that. It's too much. The woman in question spits the troublemaker at my feet. She shifts into two legs and grumbles past us. Muttering something about a spoiled brat. I narrow my eyes at Hunter, and he cowers.

I collect him in my arms and sigh. "Come on. Let's feed you and let Nana cool off."

He looks over my shoulder at his great grandmother. His tail wags, thumping me in the face. I ruffle his mane and laugh.

"You have to be nice to her. She's our elder."

He shifts into a little boy and sighs. "When is Uncle coming?"

"Today."

"When?" Hunter pries.

I wish I could give him a definitive answer, but all I know is that Azure promised to be here for his nephew's fifth birthday.

"Soon."

"You always say that," he grumbles.

"And I always mean it. Now let's get you cleaned up and fed before he arrives."

"Can I grab the birthday hats? Do you think he'll wear one? Will he stay long? What gift will he bring me?" His questions continue to fire off as I guide us into our cave home. Hunter may not care for me on most days, but he sure does love Azure.

Shuffling feet and welcoming screams echo outside, and I smirk. "Hurry up, Hunter. Your uncle is here."

"Yes!" He jumps up and down before darting into his room. "I drew him a picture!"

I run my hands through my hair and tug it up into a mom bun. That's the most prep my brother will get from me today.

"Let's go!" Hunter dashes past me.

I follow him to where the party supplies have been laid out. And there's Azure, on the phone. I grind my jaw and try to wait for him to end his call before pouncing on him.

"Please don't tell me you're leaving already," I growl as my brother shoves his phone into his pocket.

He meets my angry mama-wolf glare. Then he snaps on a rainbow triangular *happy birthday* hat and blows a noisemaker in my ear. "I wouldn't miss Hunter's birthday." Before I can throttle my sibling, he snatches the preschooler into his arms. "We have some cake and presents to demolish!"

Hunter squeals and hugs my brother so tight I'm afraid he'll choke him out. "I missed you, Uncle Azure."

"I'm sorry, buddy. Adulting is a sick joke—trust me on this one. Don't get any older."

"Did you get me what I wanted?" My son's dark eyes sparkle with the question.

"Hunter…" I scold. "Just having him here for your party is enough, right?"

The boy side-eyes me before opening his hand, and I watch on as Azure pulls a silver trinket from his jean pocket. Hunter's eyes grow wide as my brother places the gift in my son's tiny palm. "Is this really it?" the boy whispers in disbelief.

Azure ruffles Hunter's jet-black hair. "It is, big guy. You're old enough to have it now. Just promise me you'll be careful."

"Azure…" I pinch the bridge of my nose. "You cannot give a five-year-old a pocketknife."

"His fangs and claws are sharper than that old thing. And it's not just a knife. It's a family heirloom that Dad gave to me when I was his age."

"I never got an heirloom," I grumble to myself.

"Ouch!" Blood drips from Hunter's pointer finger, and he pops the digit into his mouth.

"You see!" I rush to my son with a napkin. "Here, sweetie, let me help you."

"Mom, I'm fine!" He continues to suck on his injury. "Stop babying me." He tugs away from my embrace and runs off.

"But what about your birthday cake that Nana made you?" I yell.

"Just let him lick his wounds, sis." Azure pats my shoulder, and I fight the urge to snap at him about giving *me* parenting advice.

As I watch Hunter in the distance, my heart aches. I'm fucking him up. "Every time he lashes out like that…" I whisper. "Some days I think he hates me."

"Hey, don't say that. You're doing a damn good job!" My brother spins me around to face him. "Stop doubting yourself. You're an amazing mother."

What would he know? He's never had a child and he helps older shifters with their issues. With a heavy sigh, I feel the fight leave my body. Then the uncertainty takes over.

"Am I a good mom? I don't feel like I am." I plop down on the picnic bench, watching as Hunter sits near the pond by himself. "I'm trying so hard to do everything *right* that I'm doing everything wrong. Look at him! It's his birthday and he just wants to be alone."

"There's nothing wrong with that."

"The shifters here are all older. There're no pups for him to play with and he's learning to be okay with this solitary lifestyle."

"Do you want me to find you another location? Jimmy said you hit it off with the Lobo pack member who was here. I can even help you move your stuff."

I scoff. "You're busier than ever with your hero work." I watch my brother flinch, so I make an attempt to soothe my harsh words. "Not that I blame you, but I don't want to relocate Hunter until after you settle down with a pack."

"That might not happen."

"Then we'll live and die in these woods." I lean my head on my twin's shoulder and yawn.

"Why don't you travel to search for *your* mate?"

"Yes, let me do that, between raising and homeschooling a child. I'm so exhausted that most days I pass out while reading him his bedtime stories."

It's not the whole truth, but it's not a lie either. I'm one tired mama.

"It won't always be like this. Eventually, things will calm down and we will each have our happily ever afters," he encourages.

"You're *too* confident about that," I warn him.

"No, I'm just confident enough." Azure kisses the top of my head, and we both watch the orange and red hues touch the horizon.

I'll never have *that* ending. But I can assist my brother in finding his. I'm eager to witness his story unfold.

"I'm going to stay for a while," he asserts. "Maybe take Hunter camping and get to know him better."

"Really?"

"Don't sound so surprised. I love you both and want to spend as much time as I can with you."

"But what will happen when Luna calls?"

"I'll have to go." Azure wraps an arm around my shoulder. "But for now, your annoying big brother is home to stay." He rubs his knuckles in my hair.

"Hey!" I smear icing on his cheek.

"No, you didn't!" he huffs.

We chase each other around, laughing and throwing food. Hunter leaps onto our dog pile, and that's when our grand birthday adventure really begins.

Jackson

Life Goes On

Present

"I need you to run border patrol," my alpha commands.

Ever since his daughter returned to our pack from Carson City, he's been spending as much time with her as he can. So I don't mind taking his shift.

"Yes, sir."

The laughter of his daughter and her mate bounces off the walls, and Frost grinds his teeth. "Too bad you two didn't work out."

Frost asked me to keep watch over Maya when her mate disappeared. We searched for him but came up empty-pawed. We assumed the worst, even had a funeral for him.

But here he is. Alive and well.

"I'll get an early start on border watch," I grumble.

Hours later, my patrol is almost over, but it does little for my sour mood. I trudge through the woods on all fours, snipping at anything that gets too close.

Raven and Frost located their long-lost daughter a few years ago. On the way back to our territory, Maya even found her mate, Sable, in the process. But then Sable went missing too…

I shake off the memories. It has been an emotional day. Maya set up a stunning art gallery in our area because I couldn't attend the one in Carson City with the packs on lockdown. It was a necessary precaution after discovering that several shifters had been stolen from various territories. And, honestly, I thought it was her way of saying she had feelings for me.

Boy, was I wrong.

The second she could, Maya threw Bridgett at me and ran.

Then Maya was taken too, and the alpha chewed my ass out. I was supposed to be guarding her. But I was distracted, busy enjoying the art event. So much so I didn't even notice she was gone until it was too late. During our search of the surrounding areas, Maya came limping back… with most of the missing shifters in tow. She returned a hero *and* a married woman. Because amongst the rescued was her supposedly dead husband, Sable.

A scraggly weed tickles my nose, and I sneeze before I scratch at my face with my paw.

I was starting to really like Maya. She's kind, spunky, and easy on the eyes. But I don't *love* her like that. Not like the mate Luna took from me.

I growl at the thought.

Whenever I look into my son's eyes, I see Ashely. And it hurts.

No matter how much time has passed. Ash was adopted by Cynthia and Frank, who only live a few caves down from me. They share their parental duties with me now that I'm more stable. They have Ash every other week. We all get along so well that it feels like it's the most natural thing in the world. I owe them a lot for taking in the newborn during my time of grief. They're good people.

My ears prickle as I hear a far-off wolf snarl, warning off an intruder approaching her den.

I feel bad for whomever is nearby. That protective mama is not to be messed with. Poor unsuspecting creature. They are goners if they don't back up quickly and hightail it in the opposite direction.

I wince as a scream rips through the woods.

Shit. A *human* is in the female wolf's destructive path.

I gallop into the dense foliage. I can't get chewed out again. My ego can't handle it. I leap over a fallen log before colliding with the bitch guarding her cave. We tumble until I pin her to the ground. She snarls, saliva dripping from her fangs. But I growl right back. She's not winning this one. Once she submits, she retreats to her pups, with her tail between her legs.

I snort as she fades into the shadows of the cavern.

I turn to help the human, but they're *gone*. My ear pivots to the sounds of their heavy breathing before it suddenly stops and is followed by a thud. I cringe. Ouch. That didn't sound good. I stride in the direction of the noise. Yup, I was right. The human ran headfirst into a thick sapling. Now she's knocked out cold.

Great. What a mess. Why couldn't this have happened five minutes later? *After* my shift change...

I sniff the cool night air for other humans, but I get nothing. I yawn and stretch my aching body. It's late and I really don't want to drive her to the nearest hospital. I shift into two legs.

Who is this woman running from and why is she so far from home?

I pat her pockets, hoping to find a phone or a purse. Anything that can identify her so I can contact her next of kin to pick her up.

Bingo!

I open her wallet and freeze. Fuck me. I glare down at the blonde and contemplate leaving her to the animals, but then I think better of it and carry her back to my cave. When she wakes up, I'll have to deal with her. But for now, I can enjoy a short burst of silence. Because once this troublemaker wakes up…

Luna, help me.

"Motherfucker." The woman clutches her head. "Where is that fuzzball? I'm going to fuck it up."

I lean against the wall with a smirk. She has a fire underneath that frail skin. I'll give her that. "Easy there, scrappy. You won't be hitting anything for a little bit."

"Let me catch my breath, then I'll kick your ass." She points a polished finger my way.

"I'd love to see a tiny human like yourself kick *my* ass."

"Come closer and say that to my face."

"Why don't you stand up and come to me?" I chuckle as she struggles to do just that.

"Damn. Now I know how Little Red Riding Hood felt. That's the last time I'll go into the woods."

"You promise?" I arch a brow.

"What time is it?"

"It's almost noon." I lift my chin to the window with the sun blazing behind it.

"What! Damn it!" She stumbles and almost face-plants on the floor.

"Whoa! You need to move slower. You were attacked last night, remember?"

"Yeah, thanks for the reminder. I'll make sure to sue you as soon as I find my belongings." She glances around the room.

My brows shoot up. "Excuse me? I saved your sorry ass. If it weren't for my quick reflexes, you'd be dog food right now."

She narrows her eyes, then blinks as she greedily takes in my bare form resting on the doorframe. "Do you really think standing naked in front of me will excuse your behavior?"

"This is my home. I'm allowed to be naked."

She scans my room again, likely noticing the paintings all over the walls and how the cave is refurbished to function as a livable home with windows, running water, and electricity. "I'm sorry if you've mistaken my *compliment* for a complaint. You can stand naked wherever and whenever you want. If you've got it, flaunt it. Would you like to join me in bed?" She bats her lashes.

I smirk. She's playing with fire. My eyes lazily roam over her torn clothes and crazy-as-fuck hair with twigs and bugs adorning it. "I'm gonna take a hard pass but thank you."

"Well, at least you said *thank you*." She snorts. "Are you going to introduce yourself or should I just call you *Naked* Man?"

"My name's Jackson Tala."

"I'm Carly. Wait. Are you THE Jackson?"

This woman is full of surprises. "I have a reputation in the human world. Interesting. Is it a good one? How big is my fan count?"

"Wow, someone's cocky."

"I must be a pretty big deal if you are dubbing me *THE Jackson*," I remind her.

Her eyes instinctively trail to the package between my legs. "It's not that impressive."

"What? My fan count or my *dick*?"

Her lip twitches. "I'm sorry to be the bearer of bad news, but *both*."

A chuckle rumbles in my chest. "I knew you were trouble."

"Me? You're the one who attacked me."

"I did?"

"Yes! Or does your idiot wolf form make you lose your memory?"

Fur pokes through my skin at the insult. "My *wolf* has no memory problems. And you will do well to remember that. Especially if you want to survive the next five minutes."

She licks her lips, and her arousal stirs my beast. Is this chick unhinged? Doesn't she know I could tear her to pieces?

"If your wolf isn't the problem, then why did you attack me?"

"I told you it wasn't me."

She points to a talon mark on her chest. "Then what happened, Mr. Best-Memory-in-the-World? Because I sure as hell didn't do this to myself!"

"You got too close to a wolves' den."

"So, your kind attacks people if they get too close? Wow. Real hospitable."

She really doesn't have a clue, does she?

"A *regular* wolf assaulted you. Not a shifter."

"Wait. You're saying I came looking for your pack, then got

attacked by another one? A *real* wolf and not a shifter?"

"Why were you looking for our pack?" I rack my brain, attempting to figure out why the hell she'd trek all the way out here.

She stabs a finger into my chest. "What gives you the right to take over half my restaurant!"

Ah, so that's it.

I recently purchased Skylar Canis's steakhouse, the Wolves' Den, after the girl suffered a miscarriage, fell into a deep depression, and decided to sell off her life's work. I couldn't let her do that, so I bought it, with all intentions of giving it back to her when she's ready.

I smirk at the vixen in front of me. Apparently, Sky forgot to tell her two-legged bestie about the deal. "I'm sorry. Did you say *your* restaurant?"

"Well, not completely mine. But I do own half."

"Since when?" I don't remember the attorney mentioning Carly's name at our meeting. But then again, I wasn't really paying attention because I had to get back home to watch Ash's soccer game.

"Since forever, you jackass! And I won't have you messing up everything we've worked for."

"I purchased her restaurant because I know she's making a *mistake*. I have no intention of running it, or ruining anything. Sky is a member of my pack and, in turn, my *family*. And I know she'll regret it once she gets over the loss of her baby."

"Are you just *saying* that to get me off your back?"

I get the feeling this girl doesn't trust easily or like to work with others. "Why would I?"

She assesses me again before ignoring my question. "Where did you get that money so fast? Are you a stripper or something?"

"I have my ways and none of them involve dancing around naked."

"Too bad." She pouts.

Although she's human, my wolf is clawing at my insides, demanding to take a bite and make her howl. But this was not what I was expecting when I saw her ID in her wallet. I knew she was Sky's best friend. Hell, I even called Carly myself when I noticed that Sky was in a bad place before she miscarried. But no voice can compare to the real deal.

"I thought you were only into women?" I blurt out the first thing that comes to mind.

Her laugh warms me to my toes. So sultry and inviting. "Do you want to test out that theory, Wolf Man?"

At this rate, I'm going to be too hard to corral her out of my home. "Aren't you in a relationship with Sky?"

There. That's a much safer question.

Rumor has it the two women were romantically involved in college and for a few years after that. The pain etched on the blonde's face before she brushes past me makes me regret my words. I'm such an idiot. Of course, Carly hasn't been *with* Sky like that lately because Sky has been in a relationship with a shifter for over four years, even though Freddy used to be the beta of our rival pack, the Fangs of Carson City.

I clench my fists just thinking about them. Their alpha kidnapped a few of our females and we battled for their safe return. Once the shifters were rescued, Freddy was the only one left standing after the bloodbath. Our pack leader allowed the punk to share his side of the story and even had the Guardian Azure read Freddy's memories to make sure he was being honest. Then, when he was apparently clear of any wrongdoings, our alpha permitted him to live amongst us. But I never trusted a word that rebel spoke.

I scratch my chin. But I thought Sky broke up with Freddy after she lost their pup?

I shake my head. There's just too much pack drama for me to follow it all.

The bathroom door slams, pulling me from my thoughts. *Damn, this girl is emotional.*

I rummage through my dresser and throw on some clothes, effectively putting an end to her peep show. Hopefully Carly can see I'm only trying to help Skylar. I don't want the restaurant.

"Take me home."

I pivot and have to stop myself from collecting the girl in my arms as I take in her tear-stained cheeks. *Luna, help me.* I'm a sucker for emotionally damaged females.

"Are you hungry?" I nod towards the fridge. "You came at an odd time. I actually went grocery shopping the other day."

"I would rather not break bread with *you*." Carly raises her chin in open defiance.

A knock sounds and my front door opens, ending her standoff before I can end it for her.

"Jackson, I need a list of acceptable tattoo parlors in the area," my alpha announces. "Skylar and Maya want tattoos, and I'll be damned if it's…" Frost pauses when his eyes land on Carly. "Oh, you have company…"

Shit. We aren't supposed to allow humans onto our territory unless approved in advance. I clear my throat before stepping in front of Carly. "I can get you a list as soon as possible."

My alpha's eyes narrow in on my houseguest as he sniffs the air.

Carly pushes past my protective stance and stomps towards Frost. "I have a bone to pick with *you*, King Wolf!" We both stare down at her like she has three heads. But that doesn't stop the girl's tirade. "If you would have just let Sky move into her cave, she never would have lost the baby! You caused her so much unnecessary stress."

"Watch your tone. I never denied *her* access to the territory. I simply informed her *you* were not allowed here. And, yet, here you are anyway."

"She had a run-in with a wolf last night during my patrol. It was late, so I brought her home to bandage her wounds. Now that she's awake, I was planning on offering her a ride back where she came from."

Carly pauses her verbal assault to look at me. "I know you are strong and all, but do you really think you can keep me on your back that long?"

"I have a car."

She licks her lips. "But don't you want to test your physical abilities?"

"As tempting as that is, my car has air-conditioning."

"If you gallop half as fast as you run your mouth, the breeze it creates should be more than enough to keep us cool," she grumbles.

"Maybe." I smirk. "But you know, if you really want to ride me that bad, my front end would be a lot more comfortable." I wink at her as she zeros in on my mouth.

Frost clears his throat, reminding me we aren't alone while also instigating Carly to continue digging her grave.

"Why the hell wouldn't you allow *me* to come here? I have been keeping your secrets for years. And will continue to do so. I even have friends who are shifters. That's how I knew he was a manwhore and to keep away from him." She throws a thumb in my direction.

Who was talking shit about me? My last lady friend was Bridgett, and she knows I only sink my fangs into unclaimed wolves looking for a release during their heat cycle. I'm far from a sexaholic.

"My concern is that you do not value our beliefs," Frost declares with crossed arms.

"What beliefs are you referring to, your highness?"

He narrows his eyes at the title. "A man and woman are meant to be together in a marital relationship. That's it."

Carly bursts into a fit of laughter before she grabs her side and holds up a hand. "How old are you?" she questions. "Women have been dating women forever!"

"*Not* in our world," Frost snarls.

"Bullshit," she spits out as she straightens her spine.

"Excuse me?" Frost glares at the girl as he steps forward. His fur pokes through and his fangs elongate.

I maneuver into his path with my palms up. "She was attacked and is tired and hangry."

Frost turns that glare on me. "Get her out of my territory, *now*."

"Like hell you are, you pompous know-it-all!" Carly tries to shove me, but I stand my ground. "Let me talk to your wife! Woman to woman! I can guarantee you *she* has licked another pussy before."

Frost shreds into fur and charges.

"Shit!" I push Carly out of his path and tumble with my alpha.

It's been a while since he's been this worked up. He snaps at my leg. The last time was when another wolf was trying to steal his position. We knock over a chair and picture frame before Frost settles down and faces me. His breaths are coming out in heavy pants.

"What the hell is going on?" I dab at a small cut on my forehead.

He morphs to two legs and shoves me off him. "He was behind everything this whole fucking time! And I welcomed him into our pack with open paws!"

"Who was? You're not making any sense."

"Freddy!" he blares, and the name echoes off the walls.

Oh no. Freddy told us his leader forced him to do unspeakable things, and we forgave him. Damn! He even fooled the Guardian! Shit! I need to protect the pack before he causes any more damage. What if he gets his fangs into Ash?

Not while I'm beta and there's still a breath in my body! I leap up and run for the door.

"Jackson! Stop!" The alpha's voice rings out and my feet freeze. I turn to him with an arched brow.

Frost situates himself before walking past me and patting my shoulder. "Phoenix and I took the bastard to the police department in the trunk of my car. And the Guardian should be tearing him to pieces as we speak. The information just came as a surprise, and obviously I took it out on the wrong person."

As much as I wish those words were true, I doubt this is the last we've seen of Freddy. That douchebag seems to show up at the worst times. He's the cockroach of our world. Poor Sky. She must be feeling awful, knowing she was sleeping with the enemy. He even got her pregnant.

"Uh, Jackson?" Frost looks around the cave. "Where the hell did the human go?"

Fuck. Hurricane Carly is on the loose. And if she gets into any trouble, it'll be my ass.

The silence between us is heavy as we both glance towards the entrance, hoping to see Carly stroll back through. When that doesn't happen, we share a knowing look.

"Handle this, no matter the cost," Frost demands. "We can't have any more issues that might make our pack look weak."

I nod. We do have our plates full. "Don't worry, I'll find her."

Frost heads towards his cave, and I trail after Carly's floral scent. *Where did she go?*

"Hey, Dad!"

I turn to see Ash jogging over with Cynthia at his heels. I wave to her and open my mouth to greet them, but my son squeezes my stomach, knocking the air out of my lungs. I smirk at his excitement. He must have good news to report, no doubt something that is likely to get him a sugary reward.

I ruffle Ash's hair. "Hey, buddy. How was your spelling test?"

"Good! I only got one word wrong."

I fist-bump his little knuckles. "That's great. We should celebrate with ice cream. What do you say?" Cynthia gives me an arched brow, and I add, "After you eat your dinner."

His eyes light up. "With hot fudge and sprinkles?"

"Is there any other way to eat dessert?"

"Sounds good to me." Drool slips past Ash's lips but his tongue catches it before it falls off his chin.

"Hey, Ash, have you seen a blonde-haired woman?"

"Yeah." He picks his nose. Either this kid hasn't quite learned all his manners yet, or Frank needs to keep his finger out of his own nose and lead by example. "She was over by the large oak tree."

I scan the horizon and smirk. *There she is.*

"Sorry, bud, I need to talk to her, but I'll see you tonight," I remind my son before jogging off.

Carly pivots and glares at my approach. "Leave me alone."

"Considering you're on my territory, that'll be hard to do."

"Did Frost tell you to throw me over your shoulders and toss me out?"

I grin at the image. "I'll let you sit on my shoulders anytime."

Carly crosses her arms over her chest. "He wants me to leave, doesn't he?"

"Carly, listen." I step in front of her and place my hands on her shoulders. "You're a human. It's not safe for you to be here."

"Are you saying I'm weak?" *Whoops. Guess that was the wrong way to explain things.* "I didn't know I was amongst *gods* in the Tala pack," she hisses. "You shifters have really big fucking egos if you think..." She opens her mouth to continue, but then focuses on something behind me.

"Carly!" Maya hollers over my shoulder.

Carly waves at the alpha's daughter before running towards her. I tilt my head at the other shifter standing with Maya. Sky lost her child recently and has been quiet. It's been a while since she's visited the pack. When Carly sees Sky, they embrace and tears fall from each of their cheeks. The Hallmark moment ends with Carly pressing her hands against Sky's shoulders, putting distance between them.

"Bitch!" The word echoes around the pack. The other shifters pivot to keep a close watch over the group. "How could you? You *ignore* my calls and texts. Then you don't even *mention* you are selling our restaurant!" Carly screeches.

I keep close, just in case fur flies and the human is attacked.

"I just *lost* my child! What do you expect from me?" Sky counters.

"I expect you to at least call back your best friend! You promised you wouldn't leave me again!" Carly chokes on a sob. "I love *you*! But you couldn't give two shits about me! Just like everyone else in my life!"

"Carly, that's not true. I love you enough to stay the hell *away* from you before I fuck something else up and end up killing you too."

"What? Is that really how you feel? Sky Bear, that's so far from the truth." Carly rubs her best friend's back, then gently kisses Sky's tears away. "This was *not* your fault. Do you hear me?"

What you can hear is a pin drop. *Luna, why is Sky so hard on herself?* She miscarried a child. She shouldn't blame herself for that. Poor thing. Her tale is filled with so much anguish.

I watch as Carly grabs her friend's hands and forces their eyes to meet. I'm glad they have each other.

"I don't know how to do this," Sky whispers.

"Do what, baby?" Carly coos.

"How to do *life*."

Carly's laughter rings out, then she leans her forehead on Sky's. "No one knows what the fuck they're doing. We are just as confused as you are. The only difference is some of us hide it better than others."

The human has a point. Life is a fucking mess.

I clap and the rest of the pack joins in. Carly gives me an appreciative wink before she bows and waves at her audience. I can't stop the chuckle that rises up in my chest at her antics. Frost is right. She's hardheaded, but she's also one in a million.

The girls kiss, and Sky relaxes into her friend's embrace. She needs this crazy blonde in her life. Maybe the pack can find a way to utilize the human for our needs so the two can stay together?

If only we can convince our alpha to allow it...

Carly runs her fingers through Sky's hair and they share a laugh before walking hand in hand into the woods. If anyone can get through to Frost, it's them.

"I thought you were keeping an eye on her," the man in question snarls from where he's positioned behind me.

"I am." I can't help the twitch of my lip. Our alpha really needs a vacation.

"Having her parade around the territory with another female is not handling things."

"But it *is* entertaining."

"Jackson…" he warns.

"After losing her baby, Sky needs Carly to raise her spirits." I give him a minute to soak in the truth before I drop the real bomb on him. "We should just leave them be."

"What?"

"Let this relationship run its course. Sky will find her mate eventually, right?" I say. He remains silent but I notice the gears turning in his head. "When that happens, we can let her husband deal with the human's involvement. Which means we aren't the bad guys. Win-win."

Frost's jaw ticks. "No. This absurd companionship is against the law."

"Is it? Hey, I'm on the same team here, Frost. Team Tala, remember?" Once the vein in his neck begins to recede, I continue, "As beta of this family, I've looked through the law books, and I've never come across any specifics when it comes to female-on-female relationships."

"Then why does Luna only bless us with opposite sex mates?"

"To create offspring."

He shakes his head. "You're only doing this because Maya is back and you've been bumped down in rank."

Ouch. Yes, Maya has returned to her mate, and now I'm not next in line to be alpha, but I never wanted the job anyway. I only agreed to be second-in-command because I felt like I owed it to Frost and Raven for raising me as their own.

"You know that's not true. I'm glad your daughter is back, so I can give her and her husband a hard time." I smirk, knowing it was my alpha's ploy to get me and Maya together when Sable was presumed dead.

"What are we going to do about Carly?" Frost quickly changes the topic.

"Make her an honorary pack member," I tell him.

"Have you lost your Luna-loving mind!"

"Maybe." I shrug. "But if you make her feel included and important, she might be too busy to chase her girl toy around."

Frost scratches his stubble, then pivots to face me head-on. "Maybe someone else can distract the human." He gives me *the look*. "A shifter who doesn't mind sinking their fangs into a desirable female, no matter the variety."

"Me?" I push out.

"Why not? You are unclaimed and already servicing Bridgett monthly. What's one more?"

"Do I have 'fuck me' written on my chest? No. You're not my pimp. You're my alpha," I remind him.

"It's your choice," Frost declares. "But *distracting* Carly will also keep her out of harm's way."

"Don't play the damsel-in-distress card."

"I'll do whatever it takes to keep my pack on the right path. And this thing between Sky and Carly is not a part of that path."

Why is he like this? Old and set in his ways. I can't wait for Maya to ascend to the leadership position so more compassion can seep through to the ranks. I doubt Luna gives a shit about who sleeps with whom. She wants her people happy.

"How about a compromise?"

"I'm listening." Frost lifts a questioning brow.

"We make Carly our human representative and train her to speak on our behalf to the government. Show them that we have the two-legs' support. And I'll also make her feel at home and distract her from Sky."

The silence grows between us. I'm not going to promise to sleep with her. That's fucked up. I mean, Carly is gorgeous, and if things happen naturally, fine. But she deserves honesty in her relationships. Every female does.

"I'll think about it," Frost grumbles as he walks towards his den.

Well, that's a start.

A few days later, it seems like we're making progress.

"Are you sure that's what she said?" Maya questions as we sit at the round table.

"Yes," Frost answers. "This is what Skylar wants."

"To find her mate?" Maya arches a brow. "Even though she and Carly are..." She trails off as the alpha narrows his eyes at her. "Best friends."

The door slams open, and the wild blonde herself walks in. Her eyes bounce from person to person, until they land on Frost. "You!" She stomps over to him. "How could you deny Sky happiness?"

I intercept the female. "Carly, calm down. Maybe we should talk outside?" I'd hate for her to say something out of anger that she'll regret later or that may even get her banished from the territory.

"Fuck you!" she snarls at me. "Sky is demanding to find this elusive mate. Says it's the law that she marries him. That it's the only way for her to be truly happy." Her lip quivers. "But I make her happy."

I help lower Carly onto a chair. "Here's some water." I pass her a glass.

She sips it and leans back. Her eyes meet mine. "We love each other. Why can't she choose me?" she whispers.

"Because you are human!" Frost blares, adding fuel to the fire.

Carly narrows her eyes at him and leaps up. "So what? Just because I can't shift, it doesn't make me any less valuable!" She strides to the alpha, poking him in the chest. "You aren't any better than I am. We bleed the same, don't we?"

"We aren't saying we are better, Carly," Maya clarifies. "But Luna gifts us mates. They are our destined partners. They complete us."

"Luna can kiss my ass!" Carly barks. "Where is she anyway?" The blonde waves her arms in the air. "Not here, is she? So why are you forcing her rules on your family if you don't even know that she's real?"

"Not being able to see her tangible form doesn't mean anything," Frost declares.

Carly slams her palm on the table. "I will defend Sky with my dying breath." She points at each of us. "And you all... Human or not, you all have become my family."

"Then you can become our liaison," Frost suggests. "Be our voice to the human government and protect our rights."

"But I want to marry Sky, not become a politician." Carly crosses her arms over her chest.

Frost gives me a pointed stare, reminding me that I promised to deal with her. I clear my throat to soothe the ruffled fur but am interrupted by the sound of the door opening again.

"I'm so sorry. I didn't mean to keep you all waiting."

My mouth clamps shut as Sky enters the room. *Oh no. Could this get any worse?*

She appears to take inventory of the occupants in the room. Frost is sitting at the front of the table with me by his side. But when Sky's gaze stops on Carly, her search ends. I peek at the alpha, wondering what his plan of action will be. This meeting can go one of two ways. If he plays his cards right, it could go well. If not, it could burst into flames.

Frost slides his chair back, the scrape of metal against wood permeating the silence. "*Your* friend was just explaining how wrong Luna's mate law is."

And it looks like we'll have an inferno nipping at our heels...

Carly sends the alpha another glare. "That's what you got, out of my entire speech? This is a new millennium! Men and women should decide who they want to be with!"

To my surprise, Maya's mate stands and rubs Carly's arm, trying his best to apply his new alpha-in-training techniques. "The pack laws are what drives our wolf instincts." Frost smirks at Carly, but it soon melts into a frown when Sable continues, "*But* I have scoured the documents and I've found nowhere that states that same gender unions are prohibited." He aims his own glare at Frost. "I know it has been a tradition to ban such things, but I vote to *allow* it from here on out."

Well, well, well. Sable's returned home stronger and wiser. Maybe he and Maya will do some good for the pack. Sable sits but the rest of the room erupts into a mixture of shouts and praises. The chaos is deafening as older generations talk down to the more carefree youths.

I steal a glance at Frost, and he's staring daggers at his next-in-line. Raven grabs his wrist and squeezes. Their eyes meet and he calms. Then she stands with the sort of poise and grace that commands silence. It's rare for the alpha's wife to assert herself. She's normally maternal, soft-spoken, and allows others to lead.

So, when she does speak, everyone respects what she has to say.

"Family, please take a moment to reflect on this situation *without* judgement."

Everyone lowers themselves into their chairs. When the room quiets, Raven raises her palms skyward and closes her eyes.

"Luna, as your humble children, we beg for your guidance. We respect your laws, but we would also like to venture out to find our true loves, our predestined mates, even if they are of the same sex. If this decision does not please you, let us know through your Guardians. Or smite me down right here and now."

A few giggles stir the crowd, but other than that, the room remains silent.

Seeing as no lightning falls from the sky, Raven drops her hands. "Well, I'm still alive, so I guess that is a good sign."

Frost leaps up from his chair. "You aren't taking this *seriously*."

Oh boy, he's not happy. Maybe I should step in and cool him off...

Ignoring her husband's outrage, Raven turns to the other pack members. "Without punishment, who here has ever had sexual relations with the same gender?"

Over half of the room raises their hands, though some seem reluctant. Frost sputters as he pivots and his eyes land on his wife's telling palm. His face goes scarlet. "You too?"

Raven pats him on the arm. "I'll give you all the details later, dear. But, for now, do you see? If Luna really disapproved, don't you think she would have made her will known by now?"

The alpha plops down in his chair, not meeting anyone's gaze. "Fine. But when this blows up, let the record show *I* was against it."

Carly collects Sky in an embrace. "Now you don't have to leave your home. *We* can be mates!" she squeals.

Everyone glances at each other knowingly.

"Car," Sky pushes out. "That's *not* how it works."

"What do you mean?" Carly asks.

Maya smirks at her husband. "Apparently, when you meet your mate, you kiss and *come* in your pants."

Sable's mouth falls open. "Hey! Don't share personal shit like that with everyone."

"Like how when you…" Maya's mouth is clamped shut, her husband's hand firmly in place as he carries her outside.

Well, that was awkward. I smirk at the closed door.

"It's hard to explain." Sky rubs her neck and continues. "Your mate is someone who you can't be without, and it feels like a piece of your soul is missing when they aren't near." She holds up a palm to stop Carly before she can insert a guilt trip. "And to test that bond, you must kiss them. When your lips touch, a spark ignites inside you and it illuminates the rest of your life."

Tears pool in Carly's eyes. "But I did all of *this*, for you, and you're telling me you…" The girl chokes on a sob and runs from the room.

Sky's mouth hangs open in shock.

"Handle this," Frost grumbles so only I can hear him. "Sky came here to search for her mate. Encourage her to stay, and you go to Carly."

Raven hears the tail end of her husband's request and glares at him. "Frost!" she hisses before turning to me. "Jackson, this is *your* choice."

The wild look in Sky's eyes tells me she's about to bolt. *Fuck me.* I detest what Frost is doing, but in the end, Carly should have someone sympathetic to her situation and Sky's made her choice to locate her mate.

What a mess. Jackson to the rescue, I guess.

"Sky, you talk to Frost about traveling. I'll try to explain things to Carly." I pull her into a hug. "Don't worry, I'll make sure she's okay."

"Please don't hurt her feelings. I know she seems like a hard-ass, but she puts up a good front. She's fragile."

"I'll be patient with her. I promise."

"What happened between you two?" Sky arches a brow in my direction. "Did you sleep together?"

The whole room goes silent all over again as they appear to lean into our conversation. I bristle at her question. She's allowed to have sex with a two-legged creature, and I'm not? How is that fair?

But I also know how it looks. Male shifters rarely seek human affection because nothing can come of it. Well, not *nothing*. They can produce a child with a human, but fur and fangs won't pass down to their offspring. Only two shifters can create a pup. And that's what our animal instincts demand of us.

"Carly has proven that she cares for our well-being. Frost asked that I keep watch over her, to guide her as she becomes our pack's human liaison," I reply.

"I didn't know that was a position?" Sky pivots to the alpha.

"The Guardian is still investigating Sable and Maya's abduction, but we have a sneaking suspicion that war is brewing. And now, more than ever, we need to strengthen our connections with our two-legged counterparts," I add, before darting for the door.

I've wasted enough time. Carly could be anywhere. My fur rips through my skin as I follow her scent. I can't imagine the pain she's going through. The sting of rejection will bring down a full-grown man. My claws dig into the soil as I slide to a stop. She's not as far as I thought she'd be. I nuzzle her arm.

"Go away!"

I rub my forehead on her belly. *Come on. Take the bait. I'm a cute wolf. Pet me.*

"Stop," she huffs, but her tone is softer. "You're a shifter. You wouldn't understand what I'm going through. Jackson, the hero beta, has the perfect life. Girls throw their underwear at his feet day and night."

I hack out a laugh. Who's telling her this shit? Yes, I sleep with unclaimed females but I'm not bragging to the world about it. But maybe they are?

Carly's fingertips glide through my mane and I can't help but purr as I lean into her touch. "She's not coming, is she?" Carly sniffles. "And when she finds her stupid mate, she'll toss me aside like everyone else does."

I whimper and tilt my head, comforting her the best I can in wolf form.

"I want her happy. I do. But I also want her happy with me. I know it's selfish, but that's how it is."

I rise on my hind legs, resting my front paws on her chest, and lick her cheeks. Carly rewards me with a belly rub.

"I think you're better as a dog than a shifter." She brushes her lips over my ear. "Can I put a collar on you and lead you around?" she asks. I narrow my wolf eyes at her, and she giggles. "Can you please change back so I don't get dog hair all over me?"

I do as she says and wrap her in a hug. "Sky loves you. That's not going to change. Although your relationship may be a little different when she finds her mate, you'll always be by her side."

"Thank you." Carly's nails glide over my bare back. *Oh, Luna, it feels amazing.* She digs into the tender flesh, sending a jolt of pain and pleasure to my groin.

"Carly…" I moan my warning. "You're playing with fire."

She nips my collarbone. "Maybe I like being scorched. Especially by panty-stealing wolves." She trails kisses down my naked frame. Then she kneels at my feet, her hungry gaze meeting mine. "What do you say, beta? Are you ready to make me howl?"

My brain is melting into a puddle of desire. I massage her scalp and grin. "Do you think you can handle a *hero* fucking that human pussy?"

Carly trails her finger over my thickness. "There's only one way to find out."

Her warm mouth sucks in my length. I hiss and stumble back into the nearest tree. "Fuck, Carly."

She groans and squeezes my balls. *Luna, help me.* I fist her hair and tug her off.

"You don't have to do this," I pant.

Her tongue slowly glides over my weeping tip. "Don't tell me that the second-in-command of the Tala pack is afraid to fall for a human?"

I release my hold on her golden locks and gently push her to the ground. She squeals when I pounce on her. My nose glides over her neck, taking in her scent. She arches her back, giving me full access.

If the girl wants to tumble with my wolf to ease her pain, who am I to deny her?

Jackson

Trouble in the Pack

A week later, we continue our tumblings, but on cleaner surfaces.

"What do you mean she's in the hospital?" Carly leaps from my bed and gathers her discarded clothes. "I'll be right there." She shoves her phone into her pocket. "Shit. Fuck."

I rub the sleep from my eyes. "What's wrong?"

We've been falling under the sheets for a while now. And tonight was no different. The pack gathered to welcome back the taken shifters and celebrate the successful mission with the Guardian himself. Azure had been surprisingly chill.

I yawn and stretch. A pair of jeans smacks me in the nose. "Get up!" Carly hisses.

"I am up. Now tell me what's going on?"

"The fucker is around her for a few hours and this happens."

"Who?"

"I'm never trusting anyone around her again. That's it."

I shove my feet into my pants and tug the material up my thighs. I'm glad Ash is at Cynthia's house this week, or the crazy human would have woken him up with her screeching.

"Carly, what the fuck are you talking about? Slow down." I watch as she darts out the front door without a backwards glance. "Shit." I throw on the rest of my clothes and follow after her. "Carly!"

Where is she going at this hour?

I rub my throbbing temple. Plus, we drank a gallon of spiked punch. We shouldn't be driving. A car horn blares, and I cringe as the she-devil waves me over.

"Are you coming?"

I jog over and shake my head. She's crazy. I buckle my seat belt and sigh. And I must be a lunatic for going along with her. She spins the tires and I grab the "oh shit" handle. "Please tell me why you're speeding like this?"

"The Guardian."

I furrow my brows. "Is he in trouble?"

"Oh, he is now," she grinds out.

"Did he do something to upset you?"

"He took Skylar to the police department and now she's in the hospital."

"What? Why didn't anyone tell me?"

Carly ignores me and slams a palm on the steering wheel. "He's dead."

"You do realize he has literal superpowers, right? It'll be hard to kill him."

She taps a finger on the gear knob. "What powers does he have?"

"He can electrocute people and read their memories."

"*Electrocute!* Why the hell is Sky hanging out with a guy like that?"

I consider Carly's question for a moment. Azure is dark-skinned with blue lines over his frame. He's not a bad-looking shifter. Plus, as one of Luna's guardians, he radiates power. But I don't have time to recite these facts, because Carly squeals into the hospital parking lot before leaping out of the car.

"This is a handicapped parking spot!" I yell at her back.

"Trust me, this spot will come in handy soon because when I'm done with that dickhead protector, he'll need a wheelchair."

Five minutes later, we're turning the corner in search of Sky. Even though the women at the nurses' station told us she's fine and only here for observation, that doesn't stop Carly from tearing through the hallways until we reach the assigned room. As we near the door, we can hear the tail end of an interesting conversation between two Guardians.

"You have no right to take away the gift that *Luna* gave me!" Azure's roar bounces off the hospital walls.

"Do not raise your voice at me. I'm only reiterating what the others and I have decided." The female Guardian places a hand on his shoulder. "You know us and we do not take this lightly."

He shakes her off. "Why are you doing this?"

"The shifters are questioning your abilities as their protector because of all these... *incidents.* Azure, don't look at me like that. You know it is odd too."

"What do they think I've been doing? I've been traveling the quadrant in search of answers!"

"And yet, you have *none*. Maybe your service to Luna has come to an end."

Azure growls at the female but then snaps his attention to Carly as she brushes past him to get to her friend.

Carly doesn't even knock on the door as she pushes her way inside. "Sky Bear?" she calls out.

When I reach Azure at the entrance, I stop short. "Sorry about her," I say in greeting and nod towards the hysterical blonde.

"Who is she?" the Guardian asks me.

The woman in question straightens her spine before stomping towards us. She presses her hands flat on Azure's chest and shoves. "*Who* am *I*? Who am I! I'm her best friend! Her sister in arms!" she snarls. "That's who the fuck I am!"

I've never seen her so beautifully dangerous. But she has no idea who she's screaming at. Azure could destroy her with a single zap of his fingers. His job is to protect the shifters, not the humans.

"Calm down," I warn her gently.

"Fuck you!" Carly hollers at me. Then she returns her scowl to Azure. "You're in her life for mere hours and then she ends up in the hospital! She has enough shit to deal with! She doesn't need your drama added to the mix!" She holds up a hand to stop his protests. "Shut up. I should have protected Sky from that asshat Freddy, but I didn't. So now I'm stepping up and telling you that if you hurt her, I'll castrate you and shove your balls down your throat as I watch you choke."

Sky stirs under the covers, and Carly rushes over to kneel at her friend's bedside. Sky whispers softly before wiping her friend's tears away. Carly presses her lips to Sky's. Then the unthinkable happens. Electricity sizzles out of Azure's fingertips and he stalks over to break up the embrace.

Shit! I clasp a hand over his elbow. "Easy there, big boy. Those two have a long and complicated history."

His neck snaps in my direction. His brow arches in question. Then he shifts towards the girls. They're joyful as they laugh and touch foreheads. I let a breath out as Azure's posture relaxes.

"Are same-gender relationships allowed in your pack?" the Guardian inquires.

"Stop talking shit," Carly growls.

Her attitude is not helping the situation. I'm trying to keep the Guardian from electrocuting her. I rub her back in an attempt to soothe her nerves. "You two just took Azure by surprise—that's all. I was merely explaining what's been going on."

"Sky, my dear. I'm so glad you are up."

We all turn towards the voice and notice another Guardian is in the room. *What the hell is going on?*

Azure blocks the female's path. "Not now. She just woke up."

We watch on as the two have a stare-down. Aren't they supposed to be on the same team?

"What do you need?" Sky asks.

"I wish to see your memories in hopes of bringing light to a few mysteries," the newcomer explains.

Sky bites her lip, her gaze bouncing between each of the members of the small crowd at her bedside until her eyes fall on Azure. "Why are you against this?"

"I would rather you be fully rested." He sits on the edge of her bed. "Memory extracting is exhausting—mentally and physically."

Carly narrows her glare at her rival. "It can't be any worse than what *you* and Freddy have put her through!"

"Car," Sky soothes, as if trying to use her voice to lull the girl into complacency.

"No! Don't *Carly* me! I'm taking you *home* and locking you away in a fucking tower. No more of this fur-family bullshit."

Frost would lose his shit if that were to happen. Carly can't take Sky away from the pack.

"What do you mean?" I blurt out. "I thought you wanted to move onto our territory to be closer to Sky?"

The tension sizzles the atmosphere, but Carly waves me off. "Where have you been? Haven't you noticed that there's been nothing but blood and tears in your pack? I want nothing to do with it."

"Sky is a part of that *pack*!" I remind her.

"You know what? There is too much testosterone in this room. Why don't you and Blue leave?" Carly glares at Azure, her gaze fierce and challenging.

Does she have a death wish?

"I agree with the human," the female Guardian announces as she steps between us. "We'll be able to focus better with you in the hallway," she commands, while guiding us to the door.

"What!" we answer in unison.

"Just go. We'll be fine," Sky coaxes, and the door closes in our faces.

I shove my hands through my hair while I pace. *Should I warn Frost about Carly wanting to take Sky?*

No. She can't follow through with that threat. But he should know that we now have two powerful protectors in the area.

"What is Carly to you, exactly?" Azure asks, pulling me out of my mental pep talk.

"I'm not sure. All I know is that she drives me *crazy*."

"She definitely has that effect on others."

"What is Sky to you?" I throw back at him.

"She's my mate."

Shit! I didn't even realize that Guardians could have mates. I mean, they are shifters, so it makes sense but it's still mind-blowing. What does that mean? Will Sky have to leave the pack and join his? Will their children have special abilities?

Oh, Luna. Poor Carly. If he takes Sky, it will break her human heart. Fuck. She doesn't need that.

I plop into a chair positioned across from Sky's door. "What happens now?" I question him.

"Once Sky is released, I'll bring her back to her cave and keep an eye on her."

That sounds promising. Maybe he'll remain in Cold Creek with the Tala pack. But I steer the conversation to what we overheard a few minutes ago.

"What happens if you lose your Guardianship powers?"

"I'm not sure. I'm hoping they will see reason and change their minds."

"Would *you* change your mind, if you were in their shoes and another protector was in your place?"

"If I were in their shoes, I'd examine *all* the specifics before drawing such a hasty conclusion."

I chew on his words and try to speak as honestly but delicately as possible. "Frost told me that Freddy escaped police custody and we aren't any closer to finding the man behind the main operation of stealing shifters." I rub my chin. "As the Talas' beta, it does make me question your abilities. Sorry, man." I pat his back to ease the sting of my words. "Hey, don't worry about that now. You've found your mate, and her crazy ex will be caught soon." I snort as Carly strolls out. "Or at least one of them will be."

The human doesn't even look our way as she stomps off. *Damn, she's still pissed.*

"That being said, I'm not the only one questioning Luna's plans." I stride towards Carly before she can get too far. Then I glance at Azure from over my shoulder. "I know I speak for the entire Tala pack when I say: you are always welcome among us. No matter what happens. We are all thankful for your protection and guidance."

I jog to reach the she-devil. I catch her at the tail end of a phone conversation.

"Yes, that's right, two tickets. I want to fly out as soon as possible. Not next week! Call me back when you find an earlier date." Carly shoves her phone into her pocket before pouring black sludge into a couple of to-go cups.

"Where are you going to go?" I question her.

"Anywhere but here." Carly sprinkles sugar inside the liquid.

"You can't just leave. Do you know what's going on right now? Shifters are disappearing. If you take Skylar, they will hunt you down. You're safer if you stay within the pack, especially with the Guardians protecting us."

"Protecting? That freak landed Sky in the hospital. And your pack can't even take care of their own." She splashes creamer into the coffee and applies the lids. "No. She'll be safer away from this mess."

I'm stunned. Why can't she understand? Does she really think she can guard Sky? She's just a human.

"Where are you going? We aren't done talking about this," I shout as she scurries off towards Sky's room.

My phone vibrates in my pocket and I snarl, "Hello?"

"We just got a message from the Guardian. They're calling a

meeting to give us more information. I need you here, son," my alpha demands.

"But..."

"Sable and Maya are already on their way. I tried getting in touch with Phoenix, but he didn't answer his phone. I bet he's visiting his daughter. Can you grab him while you're there?"

"But Carly is trying to take Skylar and travel out of town," I press.

"Well, try to talk some sense into her! Raven is waving me over. See you soon." He ends the call.

This shit is always getting put on my shoulders. I growl. I don't mind helping out, but Frost is getting on my last nerve. I push through the hospital room and glare at Carly.

"We aren't done talking about this," I yell as I enter.

Sky's lips hover over her cup, pausing midsip. She looks between me and her best friend. Her lip twitches into a smirk. "What's going on?"

Phoenix, Sky's dad, clears his throat from behind me. I assess the room and know this argument will have to continue at another time. Sky is in the hospital and her family is here to offer her their love and support. Her mom and brother arch their brows at my red face. I clear my throat. I'll deal with Carly later.

"It's great to see everyone. If you'll excuse me, I need to return to the alpha." I glaze over Sky's questioning glance.

Her dad kisses her forehead. "I'm glad you are on the mend. I'm going to go with Jackson, to see if I can offer any assistance. I'll see you soon."

On my way out, I look back one more time and give Carly a warning glare, begging her to reconsider her threat to remove Skylar from the safety of Cold Creek.

Soon we are settled inside the conference room in pack territory, listening to the Guardians explain the situation.

"Thank you all for seeing us on such short notice. My name is Dahlia. This is Christian, Franklin, and most of you already know Azure. We are here to assist in capturing the man responsible for stealing and experimenting on shifters. We've been able to narrow our search down to a possible suspect. He's a pawn in a military organization, attempting to create new soldiers. At first, they were using our blood to try to gain our abilities. When that failed, they switched to capturing adults with the intent of breeding them and stealing the *pups* after a certain age, so they can be leashed for battle. We know you must have many questions, but we are limited when it comes to time and need to move quickly."

This is a nightmare. The government's involvement is shocking. Why would they do this? We've always lived side by side without incident. This changes everything.

Is war on the horizon for shifters and humans?

"Dahlia, why do you need our assistance with collecting Captain Douchebag? You are basically gods." Maya snorts.

Laughter carries in waves around the room at her colorful description. I roll my eyes, though I can't help but admire the fire the girl emits.

"Although we are familiar with these territories, your packs have been living here for generations. We are asking for your assistance in exploring those areas where we think he may be in hiding."

"How confident are you that he is this close?" Frost asks as he taps a map.

I lean towards the paper and scrunch up my nose. Those woods are abandoned. I doubt the enemy would be hiding there.

"We have read the minds of all those involved and have combined their experiences to pinpoint these coordinates."

What did she just say?

I lean in to whisper to my alpha, "Didn't your text say that pups were among the rescued wolves?"

He nods and his gaze smolders with anger.

"Surely you don't mean *everyone*?" I glare at the woman speaking. "There were children in that group." A collective gasp bounces off the conference room walls. "The laws are extremely clear." I ball my fists. "Because kids cannot understand the process or agree to it knowingly, the Guardians are *not* allowed to infiltrate their minds and extract their memories."

"Under the circumstances…" Dahlia insists.

I attempt to leap across the table, but Frost tugs me back. This is uncalled for! To subjugate the little ones to this is unethical! It could be a traumatic experience for any shifter, but for a child, it could be devastating.

"Bullshit!" Maya slams her palms on the table. "You had *no* right to make that call!" She speaks the words playing on my own lips.

Azure clears his throat, demanding our attention. "Everybody is weary from their travels as well as the magnitude of more recent events. Can we please stop the man who calls himself the General before anybody else is abducted?" Maya opens her mouth to object but he holds up a hand. "I promise we will reconvene once we have him in custody and discuss the severity of what's transpired."

"We had no choice. They have seen the faces of their transgressors," Dahlia answers. "But I agree. We will never do this again. Now can we please move on and discuss the objectives?"

Like hell am I going to allow her to escape punishment. But for now, I'll settle for justice for the fur babies. "Where are the children?"

"They are safe."

This bitch. If she thinks I'm going to let that answer slide, she's an idiot.

"Where?" I demand.

"We need to observe them for possible side effects, so their location is not to be disclosed for the time being."

She's still not answering me. *What is her problem?*

I snarl, but Maya pats my hand and verbally attacks the Guardian again. "Let me get this straight... You say you rescued these innocent children, just to shove them in another cage, and call it *observation?*" Her head snaps to Azure. "Did you know about this?"

"I was never told *any* of this. Because if I had been, I would have *demanded* that any orphans be distributed to the packs for safekeeping. They need to know they are loved and a part of a lifelong family."

Maya nods. "All those in favor of fostering the pups?"

Dahlia straightens her spine. "We have no idea what these kids are capable of. Most of them have been experimented on—*they were born in captivity.* Their parents were forced to reproduce, the offspring stolen to be molded into trained assassins."

"Correct me if I'm wrong. But you work for *us,* right? You are supposed to only interfere as *needed.* Well, we don't need you to interfere with the youngsters. We will take care of them. So, hand them over. Then we can discuss taking down the bad guy." Maya crosses her arms over her chest.

"I agree with Maya. The children will have a better life if they are surrounded by loving pack members. We can retrain them to use those skills for hunting. And we have plenty of doctors to monitor any possible physical or mental side effects," Azure adds.

"Release them into our care so we can be on our way to whoop some ass." Maya throws a fist in the air.

Frost coughs on his water before standing. "Although my daughter is still training, as the *current* leader, I fully support what she is demanding—just maybe not entirely the way she verbalized it." He gives her a look. "The children should be released to the packs for foster care immediately."

The other pack leaders nod in agreement, and Maya's eyes shine as she embraces her dad. He holds her tight and kisses her head. The interaction reminds me of how much time she spent away from her family and how she ended up in the Fang's pack in Carson City, forced to have sex with the alpha just to have a warm bed and the occasional hot meal. But now, she is with her true family and thriving. Just like the orphaned furballs in question.

"The children will be released into the packs' care," Dahlia announces. "The alphas may follow me, and I'll escort them to the orphans' location. Then we can get back on track."

Everyone gathers their belongings as we meet outside in the crisp air.

"Please feel free to roam the territory until we are ready to leave," Frost announces. "My mate is preparing a feast, and from the smell of it, it should be ready any minute. So if you are hungry, keep your ears open for her signal."

Everyone nods their understanding.

"May Luna be with you on your journey," the alpha sings before we separate into our various mission groups.

"As with you," we recite back.

I follow Frost to his cave. The aroma of earthy herbs and savory meat assaults my senses, and I lick my lips. The alpha was right. Raven is cooking up a feast.

"Jackson, I need you to stay back and look after the pack." Frost pats my shoulder. "With everyone scattering to rescue the children or capture the General, I don't want to leave the family unprotected."

"I'm perfectly capable of fighting off predators." Raven waves a wooden spoon at her husband.

He kisses the top of her head. "I know you are, but allow me this peace of mind, please."

"Wow. Did you hear that, Jackson? The alpha actually said *please*," Raven grumbles as she stirs her pot of soup.

I look between the two and realize I must have missed an argument. Or maybe she's still mad at her husband for attempting to banish Carly from the territory before her speech.

"I don't have time to argue with you right now," Frost mutters. "Can't we at least pretend to be civil while everyone is here?"

She splashes some food into a bowl and shoves it into his chest. "Eat and leave to get the children."

"Raven," he groans. But she turns to the next hungry shifter. The pain etched in his weathered face catches me off guard.

"Do you want to talk about it?" I ask my surrogate father.

He slams his dinner down on the table, shooting his wife a parting glance. "No. I need to head out."

I walk the group to the edge of the territory and wish them well on their travels, as they leave to collect the kids before facing off with the General. Their shadows are swallowed by the foliage, and I question if this is the best plan of action. Only time will tell. Depending on how far up this operation goes, the government could retaliate and crush our very existence.

But what other choice do we have? We must protect ourselves and our way of life.

I snatch a ladle and serve the remaining hungry wolves. After the shifters are fed, I double-check the perimeter and find no sign of intruders. Then I glance at my phone. Carly has been ignoring my texts, but I saw Azure slip into Sky's cave, so I know the human didn't escape with her friend like she threatened.

What is she up to?

"It's a beautiful night." Raven strides in my direction, wrapping a cardigan over her shoulders. The cool breeze tussles her silver hair. My gaze shifts to the crescent moon. The stars sparkle and dance around it. I wonder if Ashely is watching over our family from above. "What's troubling you, Jackson?"

I lift my chin, almost spewing out the word *nothing*, but one look at my surrogate mother tells me she'll keep pushing until I explain what's hanging heavy on my heart.

"I miss my mate." I rub the wedding band dangling from my neck.

"No one can compare to Ashely." Raven bumps a shoulder against my arm. "But maybe someone can fill the void in your heart and help you live a happier life."

"Like who?"

"Certainly not the women you have been bedding." Raven snorts. "Carly will always feel like she belongs to Skylar, and Bridgett hasn't found her mate yet."

I rub the back of my neck. I'm not sure I feel comfortable talking about this with her. But I know she's not dumb. She knows what goes on within her pack.

"I know," I answer honestly. "But they are the safe choices. I can't get attached if they belong to someone else," I whisper to the clouds.

Raven wraps an arm around my waist. "Son, you deserve a chance at a lasting relationship."

"No. I don't," I push out. "What I did was unforgivable and now Luna is punishing me."

"You don't really believe that, do you?"

I meet her searching gaze.

"Jackson," she whispers before sliding her palms over my cheeks. "You listen to me. I know there is someone out there for you."

"I had her. Ashely was it for me."

"Stubborn boy," Raven grumbles and releases me. "Just like your father," she adds before returning to her den.

"Good night." I chuckle at her departing form.

Once again, silence surrounds me. I stare into the sky, begging for answers. But nothing appears.

Is Raven right? Do I have a second chance at love?

If I do, she'll have to be as broken as I am. Then we'd be the perfect match.

Once everyone returns from their missions, we decide to call it a night. The orphaned children have been split between Cold Creek's various packs, and the General is behind bars until the Guardians can get their claws in him. By the time I drag my feet to my den, it's well past the early morning hours, and I'm ready to pass out. I slump onto my bed, not even bothering to shower.

"Where've you been?"

"Carly?" I pat the blob under the covers. "Why are you in my bed?"

"Because I went to Sky's, and she was… busy."

I smirk. Azure finished the mating bond with Sky. They'll be fucking for hours before they come up for air. At least that's how it was with me and…

I shake my head. "That doesn't explain why you're here," I grind out.

A pillow flies towards my nose but I dodge it. "Because I wanted a fucking friend to talk to!"

"So you snuck into *my* house?" I tease.

"There was no sneaking, jackass!" Carly throws back the blankets. "I'll just leave."

I grab her wrist. "You can stay."

"No. I wouldn't want to inconvenience you," she snarls. But I know her bark is worse than her bite. I tug her to my chest, then lie on the bed. She wiggles into my neck. "I don't know where I belong now," she whimpers. "Now that Blueberry man is here, I'll be out of the picture."

"Blueberry man?"

She yawns. "Because of his blue veins, Sky and I think his cum probably tastes fruity."

I laugh so hard tears kiss my cheek. "That's the most ridiculous thing I've ever heard."

Carly punches my arm. "Hey, it could be true."

"Why don't you ask her tomorrow and let me know?" I bury my nose in my pillow. "Now go to sleep."

"Jackson?"

"Hmm?"

"What will I do if she chooses him?"

"She won't."

"But what if she does?"

I just want to sleep. I'm so exhausted. "Then you can live here with me. Now please, let me get some rest."

Carly's lips brush over mine. "Good night."

The next morning, I slide a warm donut over to Carly as she texts on her phone. "Are you and Sky good?"

She looks up and shrugs. "We're talking with Maya today about baby shower stuff."

"That sounds boring."

"Isn't Maya like your sister?"

"No, it's more complicated than that." I don't elaborate. "Do you think you girls will talk about how handsome I am?" I ruffle her hair.

"Absolutely not."

"Well, at least communicate about what your relationship will be like going forward."

Carly shoves the sweet pastry in her mouth and chews on my words. Once she's finished, she pushes to her feet. "I'm hoping she'll dump him and just stay with me." At my arched brow, she sighs. "I know what you're going to say, but a girl can dream, can't she?"

"Give him a fighting chance. Please."

"Why?"

I don't tell her it's because it's what Frost wants, or that it'll be in the best interests of the entire pack. "Because I said so." I wink.

"You shifter males think way too highly of yourselves." Carly lifts her chin and leaves the cave without a backwards glance.

I follow her out into the warm morning air, stretching my sore limbs, and yawn. Sky has her paws full. I don't envy her.

"Dad!" Ash tackles my leg. "Are you coming on the hunt too?"

Shit. That's today?

I hardly got four hours of sleep last night. But one look at my boy's sparkling, eager gaze and I'm a goner. "I wouldn't miss an opportunity to hang out with you, little man." I snatch him up in my arms. "Are you excited?"

"Yes! I'm hoping to spot a deer!"

"They are pretty big. Are you sure you don't want to chase after a rabbit instead?"

"No, they're too fast and jump in hidden holes."

As we round the bend, I spot Frost chatting with Azure. I walk slower so I can catch what they're saying.

"Our mates change us, for the better. Which reminds me, when do you and Sky want to have your ceremony?" the alpha asks.

"Whenever possible," Azure answers.

Carly isn't going to like the sound of that…

"Well, Maya and Carly will keep Sky busy for a while." Frost nods to the laughter booming from inside Sky's den. The alpha pats Azure's shoulder. "While the girls play, why don't we go on a hunt? I have a batch of shifters ready for their first time. You'll make a great addition to the team. I can't wait to see what skills you have to share."

Frost is laying his ass-kissing on thick. He must really want the Guardian to move into the territory.

"That's high praise coming from *him*." I make my presence known while juggling my fur-child in my arms.

"Do I not give enough encouragement, Jackson?" Frost asks. "Should I also rub your bellies and give you bottles?"

"Yes, please." We turn to the giggling pup and Ash shrugs. "Hey, I'm allowed to be sarcastic too."

I ruffle my son's mane and drop him to the floor. "Are you actually going to catch something this time?"

"Nope." The kid shifts and tackles the other wolves, creating a dog pile.

"A wolf who doesn't like to kill prey." Frost smacks me on the back. "Good luck with him." Then he strides to the front of the group.

"Ash must get that from his adoptive parents!" I shout at the alpha.

"Dad! I found an arrowhead!" My son jogs over, placing his prize in my palm.

I kneel to get a closer look. "This will fit right into your collection, Ash. Great eye," I tell him and then watch as he skips back to his friends to show them what he found. I rise to my feet and stretch out. "I'm hoping the deer are grazing in the north field. Raven makes one hell of a venison chili."

"I also hear that Skylar knows how to cook an amazing venison steak," Azure adds.

"That's true. But if the deer won't play, we can always catch some fish." The pups moan in response. "It's better than nothing," I remind them.

"But they're slimy and hard to grab," one grumbles.

"Plus, they smell funny," another gripes.

"Well then, you better stay sharp so you can attack the deer," Frost commands. "And quit yapping, or you'll alert them of our presence."

The group collectively sticks their tongues out behind the disgruntled alpha's back, then they each hold a hand over their mouths to stifle their laughter.

"Well, this will be an interesting morning." Azure smirks at the kids.

"Have you spent much time with children?" I prod.

"My nephew and I recently went on a hunting trip." His eyes glaze over with the memories. "His spunk reminds me of your son."

"Luna help us." I chuckle as Ash picks his nose and wipes the aftermath on a screaming girl. "Kids are the best, aren't they?"

Jackson

Haunting Memories

Her giggles send goose bumps over my arm. "Stop, Jackson! We need to meet with Frost and Raven."

I nip at her neck. "They can wait a little longer for us."

"Jackson. They are our alphas."

"And we are their seconds-in-command. Doesn't that grant us some extra privileges?"

Ashely purrs as I run my palm up her thigh.

"Just give me five minutes and I'll make it up to you tonight."

She laughs and pushes me. "You have never finished in five minutes. Now let's go." She kisses my cheek. "Remember… absence makes the heart grow fonder." She escapes my grasp and dashes *out the door.*

I grumble at my erection. "The guys are going to give me hell for this."

"Mate!" she sings from our cave entrance. I can't bring myself to tell her no, so I follow at her heels like a loyal pooch. My wife clutches my arm and kisses my bicep. "Stop pouting and give me that smile that won my heart and paw." She tickles my side until a laugh escapes. "There it is. Oh, honey. Even in my darkest days, that smile always brightens my world." Her beautiful face blurs into oblivion as she whispers, "I'll always love you."

"Ashely!" I scramble around the covers. "Come back!"

My bed is cold. Her scent is gone. I rub my hands over my face. Then it hits me for the millionth time…

My wife only lives in my dreams.

"Fuck." I kick off the offending blankets.

"Dad?" Ash rubs the sleep from his eyes. "Is it time to get up?" he asks. I pat my pillow and he leaps on top of it. "Were you dreaming about Mommy again?"

I don't lie to my kid. He knows what happened and who Ashely is. The mattress creaks as I collect him into a hug. "Yes, I was."

"Today was her birthday." He nuzzles into my chest.

"It was." My gaze shifts to the wedding photo that sits on my dresser as I stroke my son's hair. "How would you like some pancakes?"

"With chocolate chips and sprinkles?"

"Isn't that too much sugar for a growing pup?"

"Maybe." He shrugs. "But it tastes good."

"Well, you'll be with your other dad in a few hours." I smirk. "So let's load you up."

"Yes! I'll grab the pan."

We fist-bump, then make our way to the kitchen. I glance one last time at the empty bed and sigh. I miss having a partner to confide in and just be myself with.

After the sugar rush wears down, I meet up with Frost.

"Rough night, son?" My alpha slaps a hand on my shoulder.

I rub a kink out of my neck. "Nothing I can't handle."

His amber eyes take in my disheveled hair. "It'll get easier with time," he tells me. I bite my cheek until the acidic taste of blood calms me. "Would a mission take the edge off the pain?"

My wolf's tail wags. "What kind of *mission*?"

"One that will take you away for a few days. I need you to escort the Guardian's sister to the territory."

"What? Why?"

"Don't give me that look."

"It's babysitting duty. Again," I grind out. "First Maya. Then Carly."

"I made a mistake when I asked you to keep watch over my daughter. Especially when I assumed she would fall for you so easily after losing her mate." He scratches his chin. "But I don't regret assigning you to Carly. She will always need a nanny. Trouble follows closely at her human heels. But soon, she'll be the Guardian's problem. Hopefully he can tame her before she ruins our pack."

I snort at the thought. She's a hellion for sure. But I'm glad that it sounds like Azure is claiming her as his. Let the beast take her under his paw. Even with all of his superpowers, he'll get a run for his money with her *I don't give a shit* attitude. Plus, she's been hurt so many times by males that she has to constantly thwart them by pushing their buttons. Including mine.

Frost asked me to train her to be our liaison with the humans, but she challenges me at *every* turn. And it doesn't help that the alpha doesn't trust her, so he asks me to constantly keep my eyes on the she-devil.

This morning, she found out that I was snooping on her per his request and all hell broke loose. Now Frost and I are on her *shit* list. For someone without claws, the girl's fierce. If Skylar weren't so smitten with the two-legged woman, we wouldn't even be having this discussion. But that's their tale to tell. I've got enough on my plate.

"I can't leave right now. I want to be close to protect Ash and the rest of the pack. We need all the manpower we can get," I say, and Frost quirks a brow. "I don't have a choice, do I?" I cross my arms over my chest.

The wind catches the alpha's graying hair and I question how much longer he'll be able to reign as our leader. Maybe challenging him wouldn't be a bad idea, considering everything that's been going down under his watch.

I quickly shake that thought away. It's both of our negligence that's caused all the chaos.

"You always have a choice. But I'd appreciate it if *you* handle this one."

"Why?" I press him.

"Azure wants his sister to live here and that means he plans on settling in with our pack. Can you imagine it? The Tala pack would be unstoppable with a Guardian at our beck and call. And after the mishap with Freddy, we *need* this win."

He's right. We fostered Freddy after his pack was destroyed in

Carson City. Then the little shit was working with the General, stealing shifters under our muzzles. Including one of our own, Sable. Now the neighboring territories are questioning our leadership. All because of *one* rogue renegade who slipped under our paws.

"How does the all-powerful Azure feel about me looking after his sister?"

"I told him I was sending my second-in-command to help her find her way here." His grin tells me he has a plan formulating. "And that's you, son."

"What do you have up your sleeve?"

"Nothing," he fibs. "I just think that if we make her feel *extra* special and protected, she'll want to join her brother here too." He elbows me. "And I know how special you make the ladies feel."

I roll my eyes. I'm not having this discussion with him again.

"You'll make sure Ash is looked after while I'm gone?"

"Yes. His adoptive parents are staying nearby until you return, and I promise no harm will come to him."

Maybe getting away will do me some good. "When do I leave?"

Frost claps his hands and rubs them together. "How soon can you pack?"

Lily

Journey

"I'm fine. Honestly," I remind my twin over the phone for the hundredth time. "Don't you have someone else to bug, all-powerful Guardian?"

"I know you are fine, Lil. But please give my request some serious thought."

"Stop. I don't need a bodyguard. I can travel on my own." I rub my chilled arms as I silently question my words. "Plus, Hunter has that knife you brought him for his birthday." I pat my son on the head as he shoves clothes into a backpack.

"It'll be safer to travel in a small group," my brother insists.

"Then why don't *you* come here?" I can hear Azure squirm over the phone.

He just met his mate and is eager to finish the bond with her. I gag at the thought. I don't want to think about my sibling having sex. But if he really cared, he'd be here and not pawning me off to some other shifter.

"It's not that far if you travel in wolf form, and I'll be there to greet you the moment you step paw onto the territory," he says before babbling on and on about how amazing his mate and her best friend Carly are. My throat tightens as he indicates I should find my furever partner next.

Will I ever have the heart to explain that that's impossible because I murdered him?

I stare at my hand; the gleam of blood still weighs heavy in my memory. I shake out my palms to remove the haunting image.

"Mom, it's *my* turn to talk to Uncle Azure," Hunter demands.

"Hey, Hunter wants to talk to you. I love you and I'll *consider* your offer of an escort. If anything, I'll grab Nana and she'll guide us there."

Hunter mutters something about it taking us a year to get to the Tala pack if I go along with that plan.

I pass the phone to my whining child. "Once you get off, I'll tuck you in and read to you before bed."

"Mom," he groans, then ignores me completely to talk to his favorite shifter.

Azure wants us to move into a cave near his new family. I grind my jaw as I snatch handfuls of clothing and tuck them into my bag. But I can't be under his watchful gaze. There'll be too many questions. I tighten my fists. He'll hate me forever. Disown me. I side-glance Hunter. They both will.

No. It'll be easier to stay hidden in this territory. I nod with finality. I'll go to his wedding and *return*.

I wrap my charger cord around itself but pause when an object under the dresser catches my attention. My fingertip grazes on the old paint brush covered in a thick layer of dust. The same one I used to create that mountain landscape in college. The memento shakes in my trembling hands.

How long has it been since I decorated a canvas?

My son's laughter in the other room answers my question. I shiver. That horrible shifter ruined everything I held dear in my life. He tamped down all the peace and beauty that once encompassed my soul. No more dancing, creative planning... Heck, when was the last time I laughed? Or visited an art gallery? I used to go every other weekend and eye the masterpieces while my brain soaked up the next big project.

"Uncle Azure said to tell you goodnight." Hunter flops onto the bed with his favorite chicken plushie clutched in his hands. He strokes the red comb and stares at the ceiling while his dark eyes reflect the beast that couldn't keep his paws to himself. "He told me to tell you that his friend will be here in the morning."

I bite back my string of expletives. Hunter doesn't need to add another naughty word to his expansive vocabulary. Of course Azure would have my kid tell me this, instead of telling me himself. Probably because he knows I would argue against it again. When I get my claws on my twin, I'm going to give him a piece of my mind.

I rub my temples. Who am I kidding? Azure knows how weak I truly am and that I'd never be able to protect my son on my own. I'm worthless.

I clear my throat of all emotion. "Well, then, we should rest up." I cover Hunter with the sheet and kiss his forehead. "Are you sure you don't want me to read to you?" He turns away, pulling the blanket over his head and effectively ending our conversation. "I love you, Hunter. Have sweet dreams."

Silence. It's been my worst enemy lately, and it only reminds me that I need to keep my secrets buried, or they'll destroy everything.

"Mine. Mine." His claws rip through my flesh. Blood coats my shirt until it clings onto my chest. "You can't leave me!"

I whimper and cower away from his paws. "Stop! Please!"

His hands wrap around my neck. "Mine."

I wheeze for oxygen. My neck snaps left and right. Instead of the beast of my nightmares, I see my den. The soft snores from Hunter tell me it's still early. I wrap a cardigan over my shoulders and walk into the cool night air. A breeze tickles my sweat-riddled frame.

How many times have I had that nightmare? When will it end?

"Here's some coffee." Nana trails outside behind me and hands me a mug. "I'll keep an eye on the pup if you need to take a moment for yourself."

I meet her withering gaze. She knows something is off with me. Ever since I returned from those haunting hills, I'm jumpy. I can't sleep well. But she never pushes me for answers.

I sip the hot liquid. "Thank you."

She nods before disappearing into my cave to keep an eye on my son. I trudge through the weeds until a familiar log comes into view. The same one Dad sat on while Azure and I swam in the lake. And where Mom would laugh when we attempted to catch fish.

Luna. It's been so long.

I miss them. I take another swig of caffeine. And I miss *me*. The old me. Where the canvas was my bitch and I'd conquer her with every brush stroke.

"Well, if it isn't the butterfly. Have you chosen your wing colors yet?"

My gaze pans to the masculine voice. The sun is just rising over the horizon. The orange and red hues shimmer behind the shifter standing beside the water's edge. My eyes assess the corded muscles of his arms and hard abs, then land on his pack marking.

Well, I'll be damned.

Jackson

Stinky Returns

The dark goddess doesn't even stir at my approach. The years haven't been good to her. She looks exhausted as she sips from a chipped mug. The sun sparkles all around her, giving her an ethereal appearance. That's when it clicks. She's Azure's *sister*. I'd recognize that skin tone and eye color anywhere.

Does she have powers like her brother? Because she's stealing my breath.

I shake my head. No, when we first met, she mentioned having the occasional vision but that was it. Like the one she had just before her parents' car crash. I shudder at the memory. Is that why she's so frail? I tilt my head. But that doesn't make sense. She seemed to be in a much better spot back then...

Maybe you should announce yourself and stop being a pervert.

I take my wolf's advice and shift to two legs. I lean on an oak. "Well, if it isn't the butterfly. Have you chosen your wing colors yet?"

I hold back my gasp. Her gaze has lost its light. It's the oddest thing. What the fuck is going on? I grind my molars. Is someone from her pack harming her?

"I'm sorry to say the caterpillar never broke free from her cocoon."

Even her voice sounds exhausted. I step closer and point out her rainbow butterfly tattoo. "I don't think that's entirely true. She's here. She just needs to spread her wings and fly." I sit next to her and fight the urge to hold her. Or shake her until she tells me who hurt her.

"What about you, *Stinky*? Have you spread your wings?"

Guess there's some spunk left in her after all.

"I forgot about that damn name." I can't help but laugh, until more memories rise to the surface and remind me that she knows I killed someone with my bare hands. She knows my darkest secret. And yet, here she is. Inches from those same limbs that took a life, and she's not flinching.

"What are you doing back here?" she asks me.

She must not recognize the pack brand on my neck. Or maybe Azure never told her I was on my way to pick her up?

"I'm on an errand." I cross my arms over my chest. "Azure sent me to babysit his baby sister."

She narrows her eyes, kindling that fire I know is burning inside her. "Excuse me? I am not a child," she snarls. "I'm older than you, *brat*!"

Age was never a thing to me. She'll learn that soon enough. I shrug at her attitude. "Well, that's better than the first nickname you gave me."

"Young man, come give me a hug!" Nana holds out her arms. "Look at you! You've grown since we last saw you."

The older woman walks at a snail's pace, so I get up and close the distance. I wrap her in a tight embrace. I guess everyone has had hard times in this pack. "I'm sorry it took me so long to return. I'll make sure to visit sooner next time. Or maybe you're the plus-one I'm taking back to the pack for Azure's wedding?"

"I wish." Nana lowers herself onto the log, her knees creaking with the movement. "I'm afraid this old body won't get very far."

She's older than most of the shifters I know. I'm sure Luna will call her home sooner rather than later. Poor thing. I'd hate to be that fragile and still stuck in the land of the living.

"Don't say that," Azure's sister yells, her eyes shimmering at the thought.

"I should be worm food by now. It's okay. I'm fine staying here and keeping an eye on things." Nana sighs.

"I'll be back as quickly as I can," the younger woman promises her elder.

"No, you won't. Don't baby me, child." Nana turns to me. "You make sure she stays with her brother."

"Nana!" The woman's mouth falls open.

"Don't *Nana* me! You can visit us, but you will not rot away here. Branch out, find your mate, and let your son play with pups his age," the feisty elder demands. Then she returns her attention to me. "Do I have your word that you'll keep her out of trouble and make sure she finds her partner?" She's pleading with her eyes. Telling me she's scared that her family can't protect the girl. That they've already failed once and she won't let it happen again.

My heart aches. She shouldn't have to bear that burden. Not at her age. I kneel at her withered feet and take her hands. Pushing back my own prayer that she finally rests and finds peace. "You were here for me in my darkest hours and didn't let me give up. I'll do my best to watch over her." I smirk at the girl. "Although, if she's anything like her stubborn brother, they'll both be a pain in my ass to keep in line."

Nana laughs and hugs me as she whispers in my ear, "Thank you."

"You do realize I'm sitting right here. Oh, and I was the one who made you eat and bathe, Stinky."

That fucking name!

I leap to my feet and collect the woman in my arms. "You're right. I owe you one."

"Put me down!"

"Not until I return the favor." I grin at the shimmering lake. I saunter over to the edge and throw her in. The splash echoes over the dense foliage, causing birds to scatter from their treetops.

"What the fuck was that for?" she screams when she resurfaces.

There's that fire again! Fight your demons, butterfly!

"Stop calling me *Stinky*."

She paddles to the muddy edge and shakes off the droplets from her skin. She stomps past me with a snarl. "Fine. I'll just call you *jackass* from here on out."

Jackass and Jackson are pretty similar. She's getting closer to knowing who I am.

"How about you just call me by my real name?" I shout at her back.

She flings a naughty finger in the air without sparing me a backwards glance. Once she's out of earshot, Nana sighs, her eyes glued to the sunrise. "It's been a long time since I've seen her like that."

"What? Pissed off?"

"No, feeling and reacting. She's so closed off all the time."

"Don't worry. I'll make sure she's taken care of. The Tala pack is very welcoming, and Azure has mated with one of my favorite family members."

"Lily has hit a few rough patches in her life, but I'm confident once she feels safe again, she'll open back up and paint the world like she used to."

Lily. That's a beautiful name. Wait... did she say...

"She gave up art?" I blurt out, remembering how Lily told me it helped her grieve after the loss of her parents.

Before Nana can confirm, a pup rushes over to me. "Me next!" he shouts at our feet.

I arch a brow. "Who do you belong to?"

He raises his arms and reaches up to me. "Mom said you threw her into the lake! Can I have a turn?"

I ruffle the young man's hair. "Your mother is Lily, huh? So that makes Azure your uncle?"

The kid nods and jumps up and down. I pivot to the older lady for permission. She rolls her eyes but waves me forward with her blessing. I swoop the little guy up and stomp to the water. He claps and squeals in anticipation. I toss him forward and then hear the satisfying splash. I tense until I see him reemerge in a fit of laughter.

"Again!" he sputters as he doggie paddles to shore. His dark eyes glimmer with mischief and I know that he and Ash will become quick friends.

I look over my shoulder to where Lily has disappeared inside the cave and wonder if, under the Tala pack's watchful eyes, the butterfly will finally spread her wings and soar.

"I'll be back soon." Lily pulls her family into her embrace. "I love you."

"Come on, Mom!" Hunter tugs her wrist. "We're losing the light."

Lily looks at each of her pack members, then over towards the canopy of trees. Her lip quivers, and her hands shake. I rub her back and she meets my gaze. She's scared shitless. Why?

"Do you want to stay another night and leave tomorrow?" I ask.

"What? No!" Hunter grumbles.

"Hey. Take a chill pill," I snarl at the youngster, and he snaps his mouth shut. Then I squeeze Lily's elbow. "We can take all the time you need. I'm here to escort you to the territory at your pace."

She nods, takes a step towards the woods, and freezes.

"I won't let anything happen to you. I promise."

Hunter is literally holding his breath to keep his protests under control. I make a note to remind him how pack laws work. He shouldn't speak to his mother with such disrespect.

Lily pivots to her Nana before she runs into the older woman's arms again. "I'm not strong enough."

My heart splinters at her words. *Luna, what's happened to her?*

"Yes, you are. Remember this is for your brother. He wants you by his side for his wedding." Nana kisses Lily's forehead. "You got this, baby girl."

Lily wipes her cheeks and walks back to me and Hunter. She lifts her trembling chin. "Let's go."

"Yes!" Hunter screams. He shifts into a shaggy black wolf and prances a few feet in front of us.

"Are you sure, Lily?" I question.

"Who told you my name?"

"Well, I couldn't very well call you *Butterfly* in front of the other pack members." I wink at her. "That's just between us."

Her cheeks gain a pink streak across the sides. "I'll just continue to call you *Stinky*," she declares.

I reach for her as I threaten, "Then I guess you're going for another swim."

"Stop!" she half shrieks, half laughs. "What should I call you then?"

I offer her my palm. "My name's Jackson."

Her eyes gain more light as she shakes my hand. "I'm still going to call you *Stinky* when we're alone."

My fingertips brush her wrist. "I'm looking forward to it. Just be warned that when you do, I'll be forced to get you soaking wet," I whisper.

She swallows and licks her lips. A bark reverberates off the trees and we both turn to see Hunter running in circles while chasing his tail.

"We should go." Lily clears her throat.

"After you." I wave her forward.

She morphs into her fur suit and chases after her son. I salute the Pawson pack elders, turn tail, and gallop after the two wolves. My tongue hangs out as the wind whips through my hair.

Let the adventure begin.

Lily

Tala Pack

I'm so out of shape. It's embarrassing. This mom bod must go.

"There's a ravine up ahead," Jackson sends down the wolf telepathy.

"We're stopping, again?" Hunter whines in reply.

Jackson gives my son a pointed stare, and the pup sighs but doesn't say anything more when we slide to a stop at the water's edge.

I greedily lap up the cold liquid. Then collapse onto the dirt. This is why I chose an art major and not a labor-intensive degree. I hate exercise.

There's a loud splash before droplets spray my heated frame. I peek over and see Jackson and Hunter racing back to land. Jackson splashes water at the pup, which causes Hunter to leap at the older shifter. They wrestle under the surface, until they decide to plop back down beside me. Both are heaving in heavy breaths with their eyes closed.

My heart warms. This is what Hunter's been missing. A father figure. Maybe going to the Tala pack isn't such a bad idea.

Soft snores have me smirking at my son. I guess I'm not the only one out of shape. He's out cold. Something glides over my arm, and I turn to see Jackson tracing one of my scars. His brows furrow. Anger smolders behind his lashes. I tug away from him, as if his touch somehow burned me. He meets my gaze, but instead of the rage that was there a moment ago, I see sorrow.

I'm not sure which one is worse.

Just when I think he's going to ask questions that I'll refuse to answer, Jackson gently pulls me to his chest. His heartbeat is strong and steady. So unlike the one racing inside me. He wraps his arms around my back. It's as if he wants to shield me from more pain.

As if that's possible...

"Whatever did this to you," he whispers. "If it's not dead already, I'll hunt it down myself."

"You would do that?" I question him. "Kill another shifter?"

He tenses. "A shifter did this to you?" The silence grows between us. "You don't have to say anything more. But just know, when you're ready to talk, I'll be here to listen. No judgement."

I'll never be ready. Ever.

"Get some rest. I'll keep watch." Jackson releases me and I snuggle closer to my son. Wishing for the very first time that I could tell someone all of my dirty secrets. If anyone could understand, it'd be another shifter who acted out in rage like I did.

Or would his love for his lost mate have him questioning why I destroyed the bond Luna gave me and cause him to resent me instead?

"How much longer?" Hunter drags his paws through the fallen foliage. *"My feet are sore."*

If I weren't decades older than my son, I'd also vocalize how exhausted I am.

Jackson's furry beast sniffs the air and his tail sways side to side. *"We're almost home."* His big eyes assess our hunched forms. His wolf morphs to two legs before he grabs Hunter and carries him. My son burrows into the strong hold and purrs.

How does Jackson make it look so easy? Hunter never lets me carry him. I glance at my paws. Would I even be able to baby him like that? I need to work on building up my muscles.

"I can wrap you around my shoulders," Jackson shouts back to me. "I've been looking for a fur-skinned scarf anyway."

I roll my eyes and keep pace with his long strides.

"Don't worry, it's only two more miles." His fingertips massage my ears to ease the shock.

Two more *miles*! I lean into his touch. *Luna save me.*

"You can rest when we arrive." He smirks. "That is, once everyone smothers you with affection. Oh, and Raven will shove all kinds of food down your throat. You'll be fat and barely able to walk."

I wince. I definitely don't need that. Nana is an amazing cook. Not the greatest baker, but she makes the best stew. My mouth waters at the thought of the thick chunks of meat, sliced vegetables, and earthy seasonings.

"They adopted me when my parents died," he whispers to the foliage. I'm not sure if he's talking to himself or us. "I owe Frost and Raven everything."

He's an orphan too. That sucks. My paws bark in pain as I stumble over another jagged rock. Fuck this. I shift to human form and join his slow pace. "That's Nana for me and Azure."

"Speaking of, I'm sure your brother will be excited to see you guys again." Jackson bumps my shoulder. "And just you wait, his mate owns the Wolves' Den steakhouse, and she and her business partner know all the ins and outs of making a mouth-watering feast."

"They sound amazing. I can't wait to meet them."

"Do you see that ridge over there?" He nods into the distance. "That's where we're going and we're almost there."

"You said that already," Hunter mumbles.

Jackson chuckles. "Complain one more time, mister, and you'll be walking. Then your mother can be the one I carry."

Hunter grumbles under his breath again but doesn't argue. Jackson winks at me and picks up the pace. It's endearing how excited he is to see his fur family. I smirk and attempt to stand by his side, even though my muscles continue to scream their objections.

When we finally crest the hill, I'm drenched in sweat and ready to collapse. But we made it safe without any issues. Hunter wiggles out of Jackson's hold and his eyes go wide.

"This is huge! It's so much bigger than our old place."

Jackson clasps the boy's shoulder and puffs his chest in pride. "You're going to love it here." He nudges me with his elbow. "Both of you."

"I never agreed to stay here," I grunt out. "Nana may want me to live with Azure, but..."

"Lily!" Speaking of my pain-in-my-ass brother, he smashes me to his chest. I hold back a gag. He smells like sex. Lots of it. But I know I have no room to complain. My scent resembles old gym socks. He tugs me towards a woman leaning against an oak tree. "This is Skylar."

The joy in his breathless introduction surprises me. The last time I heard him this ecstatic was when he uncovered that he had powers from Luna. I guess it makes sense. Tonight is a big night for him. He's tying the knot with his mate and living with the Tala pack. They are achieving their happily ever after.

I clear my dry throat. "Hi, I've heard so much about you." I embrace my soon-to-be sister-in-law. "It's nice to meet you."

"Azure has been talking nonstop about you too." Sky beams at the man in question. Love laces each syllable. The hearts are almost fluttering in her eyes.

Why couldn't that have been me and Brock?

"Hopefully my brother has only told you about the good moments." I jab my elbow into his stomach.

He bends and grunts. "Hey! That hurt."

"He was always a big baby." I smirk.

"I was not!" He straightens his spine and shoots me a glare. "Why do you have to be so mean to me?" He turns to Sky, hoping to gain sympathy from her. But his mate is grinning from ear to ear.

She appears to love this sibling rivalry we have going on. I bet she has a big family that she messes with too. Maybe we can share prank ideas? I wink at her, knowing we'll get along just fine.

Sky kneels and offers a palm to my son. "You must be Hunter." He shrugs, ignoring her attempt at friendship. "Do you like to whittle?" She nods at his small knife, and he clutches it tighter.

I bite back a laugh. This child hasn't even heard of that word before. No one from our pack would have the attention span or the hand strength to scrape wood into inanimate objects.

"Incoming," Jackson alerts. And that's the only warning we get before Hunter screams as a group of pups bullet towards him with their tongues hanging out and tails wagging. I yelp as they tackle their new friend and bark their enthusiasm.

"Hunter?" I lift him to his feet and brush the dirt from his red knees. "Are you okay?"

The shock plastered on his face melts into a grin. "Can I play with them?"

Well, shit. It didn't take long for him to warm up to other kids. Why can't he be like that with female adults too? Have I ruined him that much?

"Of course," I push out. "Just don't go too far."

He shifts and growls before chasing his pals. I can't believe it. Maybe Nana was right. But does that mean I really have to leave the Pawson pack and join this one?

I catch a stray tear with my fingertip. I hope not.

Azure wraps an arm around my neck. "See? I told you. There's nothing to worry about."

Before I have a chance to respond, more women flock in my direction. I give Jackson a pained stare and he nods as if to say: *See? I told you so.*

"Oh my! There she is! My name is Celeste. I'm the mother of the bride. It's a pleasure to meet you. Welcome to the family!" All of her excitement has her talking a mile a minute. "Where's your little one?"

"He's getting into trouble." I point to the pond where the youngsters have shifted to skin so they can grab a rope and swing into the water. I rub my arms. "I feel like I'm missing something without having him close by."

"All mothers do." Celeste smirks at her daughter, likely reliving some childhood memories. "Even when they grow up, they're still our babies."

"There you two are! I've been looking everywhere." Another shifter saunters over, adding to the growing crowd. "We're ready to begin."

"Raven, this is my sister—Lily." My brother smiles.

"Oh! Where are my manners?" Raven shakes my hand. "Pleasure to meet you, dear. Your brother is pretty adamant that we prepare to welcome you to our pack as an official member soon. He even staked claim on a cave by Skylar's."

Great. Now I'll really be held under Azure's microscope.

"I wouldn't make arrangements yet. It's a long way from where we grew up and I'd have a lot to move," I fib, hoping to get everyone off my back.

"We'd have your things shipped here in a pinch!" Celeste interjects. "Plus, free pupsitters."

"What's taking so long?" A male pops into our conversation. The vibes rolling off him tell me he's the alpha of the pack, Frost. "I asked you to find them, not talk their ears off."

"Stop it." Raven smacks her husband.

"Let's get this over with." He trudges past us, muttering to himself.

Raven smirks. "Ignore him." She laughs. "This ceremony is a little different from what my husband is used to."

Well, this is news to me. Azure is usually a very strict, follow-the-rules type of shifter.

"Oh?" I sneak a peek at him.

He's blushing! Wow. What is going on?

"You'll see." He winks. "I'm not spoiling the surprise."

Now I'm really curious.

"You must want to clean up," Celeste suggests.

I stare at my travel-worn body. "Yes, please."

"You can join the girls in my cave. We're all primping together." Sky wraps an arm around my neck.

They are strangers. I bite my lip. Can I trust them? I glance over at Hunter. Will he be okay without my supervision? All these questions are giving me a headache.

"Why don't you girls get a head start, while I show Lily to her cave?" Azure comes to my rescue.

"Don't take too long." Sky kisses him softly, and then Azure picks up the heat.

Yuck. I step away from the horny mates and let them get it out of their systems.

"They'll be at it forever if we don't split them up." Jackson smirks.

I urge my eyes to stay on the beta and *not* my brother's growing bulge. "This is awkward."

"You've never seen your brother date before?"

"There's dating, then there's *this*," I groan as my twin kneads his mate's ass.

"It's pretty intense when you first meet your mate. Ashely and I were hot and heavy for weeks."

I swallow the lump in my throat. I did feel that with Brock. But it quickly morphed into pain and regret.

Jackson must have misunderstood my facial expression, because he wraps an arm over my neck and grins. "Don't worry, you'll have it too. But while you wait, we can always set the covers on fire *together*." I go to shove him aside, but he holds tight and whispers, "Three, two…"

Azure's head snaps in our direction, and he narrows his eyes at

Jackson's hold. A Cheshire cat grin spreads over the beta's face. This man has problems. But he did end the make-out marathon.

Praise Luna.

"Don't worry, I'll grab Hunter," Jackson offers before he separates from me.

"He is *my* nephew." Azure puffs out his chest. "I'll go get him."

Jackson waves my brother in front of him. "As you wish, *Guardian*. I guess that leaves me to take your sister to her den. Isn't it the one between my cave and yours?" He taps a finger on his chin.

"What?" my twin growls.

I love this. I've never seen anyone get under my brother's skin as quickly as Jackson has. Normally everyone bends over backwards to keep Azure happy. But not Jackson. He seems to revel in pushing the other shifter's buttons.

"I'll take her, babe." Sky clutches my arm. "While you grab Hunter."

Azure pecks his mate on the cheek, then stomps towards the pups.

Jackson sighs. "I think he likes me."

"Why are you antagonizing him?" Sky smacks Jackson's arm.

"Because I can."

"You are a child," she hisses. "Isn't it enough that you get Sable all wound up when you mess with Maya?"

"Nope." He pops the P as he ruffles her hair. "Now go get ready for your wedding."

She claws at him in response. "Jerk! Now I'll have to curl it again!"

"Don't back talk the beta," he taunts. "There're punishments."

"I'll give you a punishment," she snarls.

"I got Hunter," Azure announces. He smacks his nephew's butt as my son hangs over one shoulder. Hunter squeals and kicks out with laughter. "Come on, Lily. Let's go check out your new home."

Sky gives Jackson a parting gesture, then follows at Azure's side.

I mouth *thank you* to the beta, and he play bows before twisting to address the alpha.

"What do you think?" My brother encourages me inside the den. "It has three bedrooms. I figured one for you, Hunter, and a spare to use as an art room."

"I'm not sure I need all this space," I say, observing the furnished home skeptically.

"If Mom doesn't want the spare room, can I turn it into a gaming space?" my son begs. "Please."

Azure shakes his head. "You have a whole pack of friends now. You can spend your time outside with them and not on video games."

"That's not fair," Hunter grumbles.

"Life rarely is, buddy. Now let's get you in the bath so we can get ready for the main event."

They turn the corner, leaving me and Sky in the kitchen. She fidgets with the coffeemaker. "I'm really glad you could make it. Azure is too," she adds hastily.

I lean on the stone counter. "It's okay. You don't have to force small talk with me."

She relaxes as she lets out a breath. "I just want to make a good impression."

"You already have." I pat her hand. "Welcome to the family. Let me apologize for all of our baggage now."

She laughs and nods. "Ditto. My family has their dirty secrets too."

"Don't we all." I snort.

"Well, I have to meet the other girls at my place. When you're done showering, come over. Carly and Mom would love to have the chance to fawn over you. They'll insist on helping you with your makeup and hair."

"Sure."

She embraces me. "See you soon, sis."

My heart aches. She's going to be my sister-in-law soon. I'll have another sibling to worry about.

"Bye, Lily!" She waves as she slips through the front door.

I eagerly stand under the scalding water as it soothes my sore muscles. Why couldn't we have driven here instead of shifting and prancing through the woods?

I suppose it was probably safer that way.

I glide the loofah over my arms. The floral soap smells amazing and leaves my skin soft. My fingertips drag over the scars over my shoulder. I shudder at the phantom pain of claws slashing through me. I yelp as the puddle at my feet is tinted red. My eyes flick around.

Am I back at the resort?

"Lily? Is everything okay?" Azure pops his head into the bathroom. "I heard you scream."

I zero in on the clear water and rub my temples. I just need sleep. That's it. "Sorry. I saw a spider."

"Do you need me to kill it?"

If only you could.

"No, I took care of it."

"Okay. Do you want me to stay until you get out, or can I bring Hunter to meet the rest of the pack?"

The excitement in his voice makes me laugh. "Go ahead. I'll see you guys soon."

"Hey, Lil?"

"Yeah?"

"Thanks for being here for me."

I lean my forehead on the cold bathroom tile. How many times have I wanted to say those exact words to him? During my graduation… When I called from the resort and needed him to rescue me from my mate… When Hunter was born…

"You're welcome," I push out.

"Could you do me a favor?"

I pop my head out of the shower. He places a simple ring on the counter. "Could you hold on to this for me tonight?" I arch a brow. I thought he said Hunter was the ring bearer for their ceremony? "It'll make sense later. I promise."

"No problem."

"See you soon."

His retreating steps have tears springing free from my eyes. I'm the world's worst sister. *Why can't I be happy for him?*

I towel dry and dress quickly. I don't even bother looking around the new den. It's too much right now. And for him to suggest I create another masterpiece again, what was that about? He knows I haven't touched paint since…

"Hey, Lily!" Sky's singsong voice calls from the house next door. Then she waves me inside.

I force a smile and step into the perfume-fueled home.

"I think your hair would be beautiful with a few curls," Sky coos. "Oh, and some red lipstick!"

I shrug as she guides me over to a vanity. "I'm pretty low-maintenance. Do what you think is best."

"Really? I get free rein?"

The eagerness dripping from her voice has me rethinking my response.

"Sure." I do my best to make it sound like an answer and not a question.

A blonde saunters in and passes out wine glasses. "Sky Bear, remember she's a mom and not a hooker."

Sky smacks the girl. "Don't say that."

"Hi, I'm Carly." The blonde extends a polished palm in my direction. "And before you ask, no, I'm not a shifter. Just an ordinary human who fell for a fur beast." She winks at Sky.

My head is spinning. They're together too? Or am I misreading the signals?

Carly nods to my untouched drink. "You'll need a few sips to understand our tale."

"I'm not a big drinker."

"Trust me, girl. You *will* be with this family in the mix." She clinks her glass against mine. Everyone giggles and I sip the white wine. It's cool and crisp. "You don't have to skimp." Carly smirks. "We have barrels full."

I like her sense of humor. I chug my alcohol.

"Atta girl!" she sings. "Now the party really begins! Let's paint our faces on, ladies!"

"Tonight, we gather to bring the Guardian Azure Pawson and Skylar Canis together as mates," Frost announces and aims to move forward, but Raven elbows him. "Along with Carly Smith," he mumbles. "Luna, in all her mighty wisdom, has brought them together. Thank you, Luna. We praise you." Frost sips from the ceremonial wine before he passes it to Sky.

She swallows the red liquid, mimicking the alpha's actions and handing the goblet to my brother. His eyes never leave hers as he repeats the process, then presents the wine to Carly. The blonde hesitates as she sniffs the substance. The alpha clears his throat, and she guzzles a swig before passing it to Sky's parents.

After the pack has all partaken from the goblet, and it makes its way full circle to Frost, he holds it in the air. "Luna, may you bless them in holy matrimony and help us support them through their amazing journey." He meets the eyes of each of the pack members before he continues, "The grass withers and the flowers fade…"

"But the love of the pack lasts furever," everyone finishes in unison.

Then he takes the final sip and steps aside. "Azure."

My brother stands in Frost's spot, his eyes scanning the crowd. He pauses on my face and his smile widens. It's the same one he wears whenever he's done something sneaky, like hide a frog in my shoe and watched me put them on without saying a word. Then he meets Sky's gaze and collects her hand. "Skylar. I feel like I've waited an eternity for you. I'm sorry for not fighting for you in the beginning of our tale. But with Luna as my witness, I vow to never make that mistake again. I love you, and from now on, you are my world—my everything." He glances at Hunter's wolf form, and my pup prances to his side and leans in. Azure unties the ring that's around the kid's neck and slides it over the woman's finger. "Skylar, will you make me the happiest shifter and be my wife?"

It's a bittersweet moment. I wish my parents were here to witness it too.

"On *one* condition," Sky answers. The group chatters around us. She pivots to grab Carly's wrist. "Will you, Azure, also love, protect, and fight for the woman I love? And welcome her into our lives as an *equal* in our relationship?" Carly blubbers as she embraces my sister-in-law, her makeup smearing down her face. "That's also *if* she still wants me as her wife."

Celeste sneaks over with a few tissues and she helps Carly collect herself. "I never thought this day would come." Carly pats her lashes. "Sky Bear, of course I'll be your wife. And I guess I'll *deal* with him too, if I have to." She smirks at my brother.

The field is silent as we all collectively hold our breaths. This has never been done before. When you join with your mate, that's it. And for one of Luna's Guardians to be the first one to marry two women...

I peek at my brother. His smirk answers all my questions before he speaks. He nods to my pocket, where I placed the simple ring he asked me to hold for him, and everything clicks into place.

"I was going to talk to you *privately* about this, but you've given me no choice but to address the elephant in the room." Azure holds out his hand. I tiptoe closer and place the wedding band in his palm. He meets Carly's gaze. "You have been here for Sky when I couldn't. You even went toe to toe with a rogue shifter so you could remain by her side. Your love for her has *no* limits. Will you do us the honor and become an equal partner in our marriage? Through sickness and health *and* dirty diapers? In return, I'll love, protect, and fight for you too." He extends his hand.

Carly stares between us, her eyes watering as if she might start crying again. She swallows her sob. "You better make sure you change *your* share of diapers too, blue boy." After the laughter dies down, she adds, "I accept. And I'm honored to be a part of an incredible family." He slips on her ring. She pivots and smiles at the crowd. "Now you all are stuck with me forever." She makes a point to wink at Frost.

We all laugh as we clap.

"Now let's get the party started!" Sky calls out.

Music blares and everyone shouts their enthusiasm into the night air. I slide into a dark corner and enjoy the quiet as I people watch. I nurse my third drink while I keep an eye on Hunter as he piles more food onto his plate. That boy can eat. But I don't blame him. The girls said the dinner was catered by their restaurant and that it's the best in town. The bonfire sparks into the night sky, its soft crackles creating a shiver that runs up my spine as it resembles bones snapping. The face of the delivery boy haunts my memories.

"Lily?" I jolt and fall back onto my butt. "Whoa. It's me."

My gaze focuses on the figure in front of me. "Jackson. Sorry. You startled me." I brush the alcohol off my arm.

"Is everything okay?" He scans the area.

"Yes, fine," I snap. "Did you want something?"

"Hunter wanted to know if he could stay the night with Ash at my place."

"I don't know." I rub my neck.

"My door is always open. You can come and check in on him at any time." He nods to my drink. "Plus, it'll give you more freedom to have fun with the girls." At their mention, a few female giggles can be heard, and I know I'm on the radar to get drunk next. "What do you say?"

"If that's what he wants, that's fine with me."

"If you change your mind, just let me know."

"Stop hogging Lily!" Carly slurs as she pushes Jackson away. "Come on, sister, sit with us and tell us some secrets about Azure."

"Yes, please!" Sky adds. "We know he can't be as perfect as he pretends to be."

They hand me another cup and guide me to a picnic bench. I lower myself onto the seat and grin as I seize the opportunity to move away from my haunting memories and create happier ones. Even if it's at the cost of embarrassing Azure.

"How much time do you have?" I lift a questioning brow. They cackle and lean in, eager to soak up the gossip. "My brother thought crayons were flavored."

"No, he didn't!" Sky laughs.

"He did! And after he tried what he thought was a sour-apple flavored one, his teeth turned this moldy green color."

"We've married a good one." Carly smirks over the rim of her wineglass. "Maybe that's how his veins turned blue!"

"There he is! The *crayon* eater!" Sky giggles.

Azure trudges over and narrows his eyes at me. "Really? You told them *that* story."

I shrug before bringing my cup to my lips. "It was either that one or the one when I found you jerking off…"

He slaps a hand over my mouth. "I think you've had enough to drink. Why don't I show you to your cave?" He stalks off as I drunk-wave behind him. Then he leads me into the dark home. "You shouldn't have told them that story. What will they think of me now?"

"That you're just as fucked up as the rest of us." I hiccup.

He blinks at me. "That's a given. No one expects perfection. That's an impossible goal to obtain."

"So why do you care about what I told them?"

"Because it's embarrassing. You don't see me telling Hunter that you used to eat your boogers."

"You could. I wouldn't care."

"But I respect you enough to not speak ill of you to someone you care about."

"Just go back to your family." I wave my brother towards the door.

"You are my family."

"No." I shake my head. "Your *new* family. The ones you promised to always be there for."

"Lil…"

"No, I understand. But just so you know, being a Guardian *and* a husband won't work out. You're gonna fuck up at least one of those duties."

"How can you *say* that?"

If I were more drunk, I'd take the chance to really rip into him. Tell him how I feel about his broken promises to me as a brother. Instead, I plop onto the couch. "Your wives are waiting for you."

"We'll talk tomorrow when you sober up." He kisses the top of my head. "Get some sleep." He pauses on the doorstep. "You're going to move here, right? Hunter loves it and I want you closer."

What he doesn't mention is how he won't have time to visit two packs on his rare days off. So if I don't join the Tala pack, he'll never see his nephew or his sister. Because he'll always choose his mate over us. So, now it's on me. *A very intoxicated me.*

Should I be a bitch and make it harder on my brother?

I sigh. I can't do that to my son. He should be closer to his cousins and aunts-in-law.

"Fine," I draw out.

Azure rushes back over and hugs me tight. "That's great! I'll tell the girls!" Then he dashes outside, leaving me alone with my thoughts.

I strip out of my clothes as I yawn and stretch my sore limbs. It's been a long, emotional day—as well as physically exhausting. I curl up into a ball in my new bed, begging sleep to take me. But nothing is familiar. Darkness is pressing in on me.

"Mine. Mine," the shadows whisper.

My eyes snap open. Is that a pair of golden eyes in the corner? "Stop." I squeeze them closed again.

"You can't hide. I'll find you and my son."

Hunter! I leap out of the house and stumble next door. I peek into a bedroom and see my son snoring softly. I rub a hand over my face.

Fuck. I'm losing it.

A creak in the distance has me jumping and clutching at my chest.

"Lily?" Jackson rubs the sleep from his eyes. "Did you need something?"

What a loaded question…

All the strength I've built up seeps out in a single sob as I fall to my knees.

"Oh shit." Jackson scoops me up and rocks me into his arms. "Hey. It's okay."

"No. it's not." The tears won't stop. My drunken mind is sick of bottling everything up. "Don't make me go back."

"Where?" Jackson asks.

"To that house."

He looks over my shoulder towards the open doorway. "Are you talking about your new cave?"

"Yes."

"Why don't I bring you to your bed so you can sleep this off?" He strides towards the one place I asked him not to bring me. I thrash in his hold but he tightens his grip. "Okay. How about I let you stay here?" He lays me on his bed instead. He tugs the covers over my bare chest. "You're safe." His fingertip dances over my arm. "Get some rest. I'll sleep on the couch." He pivots but I clasp his wrist.

"Don't leave. Please." The waterworks start up again. "I need protection," I beg.

He tenses. "From whom?"

I rest my head in my hands and sob. "From myself," I blurt out.

The bed creaks as he sits next to me and rubs my back. I lean into him for support, and he strokes my hair. "You're safe," he repeats the mantra. "I won't let anything happen to you. But you need to tell me what you're so afraid of? Who hurt you?"

I shake my head. "I can't. You'll hate me."

"I don't necessarily *like* you now," he teases. "Come on. You ran to my house for a reason, right? I know you're a little tipsy, but somewhere deep down, you trust me to watch over you *and* your pup." He holds me tight. "So tell me. *Who* do you need protection from?"

His heartbeat is steady. His touch is soothing. *Luna, help me.* I feel safe with him. He's so different from Brock.

"My mate," I whisper so low I think he may not hear me.

"Is he close by?"

I nuzzle into Jackson, not wanting to remember what happened in those snowy mountains. "No. I *killed* him." I release the burden that's been weighing me down for years.

Then I take a deep breath and feel reborn. Like magic, darkness takes over my vision and I drift off to sleep. Surrounded by the beta's promise of safety.

Jackson

Protection

*H*er words replay over and over again in my head as I try to digest them.

"Who do you need protection from?" I ask gently.

Lily remains silent. If her heart weren't racing so fast, I'd think she was finally sleeping off the booze. But I don't relent. I continue to stroke her arm, trying to remind her that I've never given her a reason to doubt my loyalty. Hell, I owe her for saving my life when I lost Ashely.

"My mate."

My brain just can't comprehend her words. Lily's *mate* hurt her? No. Surely not.

I stare at the many scars littering her frame. *Fuck*. There's no way a mate would do this kind of damage. The bond wouldn't allow it. Would it?

I scan my brain for my known history of our kind. But nothing compares to Lily's tale. Then her statement from earlier clicks into place. She said it was a shifter who hurt her. Plus, she's jumpy as fuck around new males. My mind reels all the wonderful memories of Ashely. That's what Lily deserved. Laughter. Sweet, love-fueled actions. Not whatever it was she endured.

Not only is this rogue brute a danger to her, but he's a threat to her pack as well, which now includes the Talas. The same pack I'm sworn to protect with my life...

Shit. Does this mean Hunter is... the spawn of that creature? Will her mate try to take the pup back? This complicates everything.

"Is he close by?" I demand.

Lily relaxes in my arms. Like a weight has been lifted. Did she think I wouldn't believe her? She nuzzles into my chest.

"No. I *killed* him."

Well, so much for needing to get my hands dirty.

Wait... I blink into the darkness. Did she just admit to murdering a shifter? And not just any shifter, but her Luna-blessed mate?

Her breathing is even as she drifts into dreamland. I hold her closer and stroke her hair. "Oh, Lily." I sigh. "What are we going to do now?"

As the sun crests over the lake, I slip out of the bed and tuck a blanket over my surprise houseguest. She's going to have one hell of a hangover when she wakes up.

Then I set the coffee machine to brew twelve cups. I nod. That should be enough. I check in on the sleeping pups and smirk. They must have woken up in the middle of the night and played with Ash's toys. There're army men littering the floor and Legos on their chests as they snore.

Hunter is a good kid. I lean on the doorframe and continue to watch the pair. What will Lily tell the child about his father? Will he even care to know? I scratch my scruff. Of course he'll care. When he's older. I know I did.

I hear a knock coming from next door and I poke my head out to see who it is. There's Carly, looking radiant as ever. I smirk. I bet Azure fucked her crazy last night.

I clear my throat. "You're knocking on the wrong door, sweetheart," I taunt.

She yelps and clutches her chest. "Jackson!" she hisses. "I'm looking for Lily."

"Why?"

"What do you mean *why*?" She crosses her arms.

"Why don't you step into my den and I'll show you?" I wiggle my brows up and down.

"You're an asshole." She snorts before shoving her ring finger in my face. "Plus, I'm in a committed relationship now."

"I'll be sure to mail out the sympathy card for you."

She narrows her eyes at me. "Are you going to tell me where she is or not?"

"Once you tell me why you want to know, I will."

Her lip twitches. "Oh, I see. So, since I'm not an option anymore and Bridgett isn't in heat, the Guardian's sister is keeping you company." Before I can answer her, Carly storms past me and peeks into my room. "Well…"

I clamp a hand over her mouth and slam her against a wall in the kitchen. Out of Lily's earshot. "Shh. We didn't do anything. She came over drunk and is sleeping it off. That's it. Now drop it," I explain. "She'll be mortified if you start a rumor like that." Carly taps her foot and I remove my palm. "Please, Carly. If you don't do it for me, then do it for her."

She takes a minute to evaluate the truth of my statement. Then she shrugs. "She's a grown-ass woman. Who she sleeps with is no one's business but hers."

I let out a breath I didn't know I was holding. "Thank you. Do you want a cup of coffee?" I fill two mugs and set them on the table.

"Jackson…" My eyes flit to my bedroom door. Damn. Hearing Lily speak my name while sleep still coats her every word does amazing things to my libido. She halts the moment she notices Carly sitting with me. "I…"

Carly waves at her sister-in-law. "Hey, sexy mama! Why don't you join us for some java?"

Lily glances at her bare chest and her cheeks flare.

"I have some t-shirts in the third drawer." I point to my dresser. "Help yourself."

She scurries back into the darkness. Carly shoots me a look and whispers, "What the fuck happened to her? She has so many scars." Her voice is a mix of sadness and anger.

I shrug and nod towards the newcomer. "There's a whole pot of coffee on the counter."

"Thank you," Lily mumbles as she reaches on her tiptoes to grab a cup. My shirt rises along the waistline, giving us a peek at her ass.

Damn. I resist the urge to tilt my head to get a better look.

Once she takes a few swigs of her coffee, Lily meets our inquiring eyes. Fear fills her vision.

Does she think I told Carly something?

"So why are you here?" I direct the question to the blonde sitting in front of me. "You said you were looking for Lily. Why?"

"I'm taking her shopping."

"Oh, no. I don't think that's a good idea," Lily blurts out.

Carly waves a hand at her. "Don't worry about money. I have a shit ton. Let me spoil my sister."

"That's not it." Lily chews on her bottom lip. "I have Hunter."

"Jackson has Ash this weekend, so he can keep an eye on him too." Carly's phone vibrates and she leaps to her feet. "Sky is up. I'll see you in a few hours." Then she winks at Lily and struts back out the door.

"You don't have to go if you don't want," I remind Lily as soon as Carly is out of sight.

She hides behind her mug. "You didn't *tell* anyone did you?"

"No."

She meets my gaze. "Thank you."

"Lily. Please tell me what happened."

She rises from her chair and ignores my request as she walks around my modest home. The various artworks adorning the walls appear to catch her attention. She runs a fingertip over the last one Ashely painted before she died. It's a stunning canvas with two wolves as its focal point. They stare into the sunset as they overlook Willow Creek.

"Are all these yours?"

I stand beside Lily, my shoulder brushing hers. "Most of them are, but a few are Ashely's."

Talking about my mate eases some of the ache in my heart. I miss her, but as the days pass, it does get easier. Stupid Frost was right.

"They're beautiful. Your technique is exquisite." Lily taps the masterpiece directly in front of her now. "I'd love to watch you perform."

I smirk, watching the pink creep up her cheeks as soon as she realizes her poor choice of wording.

"I mean, to witness your strokes firsthand," she attempts to clarify, then face-palms. "You know what I mean."

I grab her wrists and gently pull them down to her sides. My eyes meet hers and I grin. "Well, I'd love to observe *your* unique techniques. Have you ever painted a subject *nude*?"

She nibbles her lip while she scans my body.

Luna, she's adorable. What I wouldn't give to listen to her internal monologue right now.

The tips of her fingers graze my abs. I hiss at the cold they bring with her touch. She tugs them away as if I burned her.

I kiss her palms and rub them together with mine. "Sorry. Your hands are freezing."

She tugs her arms to her sides and clears her throat. Fuck. I shattered the moment. She was coming out of her protective shell and opening up.

"I don't paint anymore," she tells me.

"But I thought you said it helped you heal after your parents' death? Don't you think it could help now too, considering the circumstances...?"

"No," she answers too quickly. "I can't."

Her eyes lose their light as she gets lost in her trauma again. I wrap an arm around her waist and guide her back to the kitchen. We don't say a word as we sit together. I know she needs space right now. I've said too much. I can't ruin what we have.

What do *we have?*

A friendship for sure. I peek through my lashes. Maybe it's more than that though. We've both lost our mates to tragedy. We're unclaimed. Have sons. It's as if the stars are aligning, reminding us that even through grief there is hope. There's the chance for a new beginning as well as the possibility of an unconventional happily ever after.

I shake my head, dislodging the hope. That can't be us. Our fairy-tale ending has long past. Buried six feet in the ground.

"Mom! Can I go to school with Ash!" Hunter tugs on Lily's hand. "Please! I'll be good. I promise!"

"I'm sorry, sweetie, but you're homeschooled, remember? Uncle Azure said your schoolbooks should be here by the end of the week."

"But that's not how everyone here does it." The pup stomps his foot. "I hate you."

Lily flinches as her son's words appear to slam into her chest. My eyes narrow, and I grab Hunter's shoulders. "That is not acceptable behavior, young man. Apologize to your mother."

He looks between us. "You're *not* my dad. You can't tell me what to do."

A tiny gasp leaves Lily's throat, and I fear she's on the verge of a panic attack. I puff out my chest and use my beta tone on the unruly pup. "You listen to me right now." My snarl vibrates off the stone walls. Even Ash cowers. "If you ever want to hang out with *my* son again, you'll watch how you speak to your mom. She has done everything for you, and she deserves more respect than what you're giving her."

He swallows and I know I've made my point, but I'm far from done.

"We can walk Ash to the bus stop, and you can play a little more with him. But after that, you and I are going to talk with the alpha about your recent behavior while your mother spends some time with your Aunt Carly." I pivot to Lily's pale face. "Is that okay with you?"

She only nods before excusing herself, walking into the bathroom, and locking the door behind her. I hear tissues being pulled out of the box, followed by silent sobbing. My heart clenches. I want to hold her and remind her that everything will be all right. But right now, I have more pressing matters to deal with.

I return my attention to the sharp-tongued child in front of me. "Are you ready to take Ash to the bus stop and play with the other pups for a bit? Or do you want to stay here and go shopping with your mom?"

"I'll go with you." He swallows before he adds, "Sir."

I nod and allow him to scurry back to Ash. "We leave in five minutes."

I rub my hand over my face. *What a mess.*

"She better be ready to go." Carly rushes in a few minutes later with an attitude in tow.

"She's in the bathroom." I nod to the closed door. "What's up with you, Miss Sunshine?"

"My new husband is crashing my family outing." She pouts. "I wanted one-on-one time with Lily and he's ruining it."

"But he's your life partner and he wants to spend time with you too."

She snorts and mumbles, "I only married him for Sky."

"Carly…" I push out. "Give the man a fighting chance." I remind her.

"Yeah, that's what his mate said too." She rolls her eyes.

I peek over at the bathroom door again. "Keep an eye on her, okay?"

"Why?" Carly draws out the word.

I give her a pointed stare. "She's new to the area."

"She's also a shifter with a great sense of direction," Carly tells me what I already know.

"Please. Just promise me. Don't leave her alone."

My words are cut off as Lily makes her way to the kitchen. She stops short as soon as she spots Carly, who takes in the other woman's tear-stained cheeks and glares at me. "What did *you* do to her?"

"Me?" I shout. "Why are you blaming me first?"

Carly raises her hands and looks around the vacant kitchen. "Who else can I blame, other than the only idiot in the room?"

"Excuse me?" I snarl.

"I'm going to get dressed. I'll meet you out front in a few minutes." Lily shuffles past our bickering.

Carly scowls at me. But stops when Hunter approaches with a frown. "Don't blame him. I made Mommy cry."

Her scowl melts into a smile and she ruffles his hair. "I can excuse your manners, little man, because you have many years of learning ahead of you." Then she narrows her eyes at me again. "But he's old enough to know better."

"Dad! I'm ready!" Ash passes us with his backpack bouncing as he goes. "Bye, Carly."

"Bye, buddy! I'll see you after school."

"As much as I love our heated arguments, I should see him off to school."

I brush past Carly, but she grabs my elbow. "Were you serious about keeping her close?"

There's the woman I adore and call my friend. She'll protect those in need, just like me. I've even heard the stories about how she's set up cheating husbands and boyfriends just to show their partners their true colors. She's a force to be reckoned with and I know she'll make Lily feel safe.

I let my gaze answer for me. Once Carly nods her understanding, she releases her hold on my arm. I walk into the early morning air, eager to get these outings over with so I can catch up with my butterfly.

Lily

Red Thong

"You don't have to go with us," Carly snips at my brother.

"Yeah, I know how much you hate shopping." I arch a brow at him.

"I want to spend time with you. Is that so wrong?" Azure lays it on thick with his wife. "Plus, Sky is helping Maya with the baby shower again and Hunter is chilling with Ash. So I'm all yours." He wraps an arm around us. "Let's go shopping."

Carly ducks out of his embrace. "I'm driving."

The tension between them is so thick it could be cut with a knife. What the heck happened last night? They were all hot and heavy when I left.

As we approach the vehicle, I quickly shout, "And I call shotgun!"

My brother looks hilarious as he tries to squeeze into the back seat. His knees crush into his chest and his chin is tucked in. I shake my head at his large frame. He could just shift and meet us at the shopping center.

Why is he acting like this?

Carly changes the radio station to some rock music and thumps her fingers on the steering wheel. Oh! That's right. I forgot she was a human and not a wolf. Maybe that's why Azure is riding in the back? To help his new wife feel included in their everyday activities.

Or he's watching over his weak sister.

Carly slams on the brakes at a red light and we lurch forward. Azure releases a few curse words and she cackles.

"Is everything okay, Carly?" I whisper to her.

"Peachy," she replies.

"Are you sure?"

"Yes, and I would like to change the subject."

"Oh? To what?"

Her sinister smile spells out trouble. "How about we chat about your sleepover last night?"

Not this topic! Abort, abort!

"It wasn't like that," I attempt to clarify.

"Sure it wasn't," Carly drags out.

She wants to play, huh? Okay then, here come the claws.

"I thought *you* and him were a thing," I counter with a teasing wink. "That's what the other shifters are saying anyway."

"Jackson is just a pain in my ass," Carly grinds out. "His *alpha* forced him to keep tabs on my every move, like I'm some kind of criminal."

"I'm sorry he did that to you."

"I'm not. I'm finally living my happily ever after. With *Sky*. I know she loves me wholeheartedly." Carly scowls at my brother in the rearview mirror.

Great. There's that tension again.

"Well, you and Sky do look happy together."

"We do, don't we," Carly sings.

Okay, we need a serious change in conversation. One that doesn't place me or my brother in the hot seat. Just simple things.

"Not that I'm complaining, but why did you want to take *me* shopping?"

"Because you are the new girl in town and I want to get to know you better. Plus, you can give me all the dirt on your brother."

Oh, Luna. It's going to be a long trip. These two are going to be at each other's throats all day.

"I'd love to get to know you better too, Carly. Especially now that we are sisters-in-law," I admit, attempting to rein in her attitude and remind her that we are all family and should try to get along.

My twin winks his approval.

Carly's knuckles whiten around the steering wheel. "In the spirit of getting to know each other, Ash said he found you naked in Jackson's bed this morning. What's up with that?"

Fuck! She's like a volcano! Willing to turn anyone and anything in her path into rubble.

"I was drunk!" I sputter.

"I put you in *your* bed!" My brother turns his temper on me. "How the hell did you get to the beta's house?"

"I probably had a nightmare and was searching for help. It is a new place. I got turned around," I rush to explain.

Carly's grin is all we need to confirm that she's pinning us against each other to take the heat off her. *Damn. She's smart.*

Once she pulls into the parking lot, Azure leaps out of the car and rips open Carly's door. "And why are *you* so damn concerned about Jackson? If nothing happened between you two, why is his name constantly on your lips?" His fur pokes through at the thought of his spouse with another wolf.

Carly stands to meet his gaze, the best she can with the height difference. "Why do you think I have to explain myself to you?" She sizes him up. "You only want to be with your mate. I'm just scraps. A side-lay for you." She lifts her chin. "However, as long as I get to be with Sky, I don't give a fuck. But don't you dare think you have a say in what I do."

Electricity sparks from my brother's fingertips.

"Shit," I sputter as I unbuckle and make my way over to them.

Azure's chest crushes Carly against the car. "You will *not* have sex with another man or woman while you are married to us."

"Azure! Let her go." I've never seen him this distraught. Not even when I was in the hospital. I pull on his arm. "Enough of this."

But his wolf won't hear me. He snatches her wrist. "This is a symbol of our promise to be loyal and devoted." He wiggles his ring in her face. "We need to hold each other accountable if we want to have a successful marriage."

"She gets it. Now why don't we go inside the mall? You're probably just hangry."

He continues to ignore me and dips his lips to hers. Carly stiffens and clenches her fists, while doing whatever she can to not return the kiss. He steps back to give her space. Hurt etched over his features.

Carly slides past him and grabs my hand. "What store do you want to check out first?"

I guess we're not talking about their fight.

"Uh…" Her mood swings give me whiplash. "Any of them is fine."

Carly tugs open the door and waves me through. "Is it true that the Pawson pack doesn't have a shopping center?"

I nod. "I had to travel to go to a university too."

"I wouldn't be able to survive like that." She sighs.

"We make do with what we have."

"Well, thank goodness you are among civilization now. We have lots of options!"

Azure scans the crowded mall for any signs of danger. Most of the shoppers gawk and move out of our way in a hurry, while others lick their lips as they take in my brother's muscled frame. Of course they ignore me. I'm not a threat *or* a treat.

"I need to drop into the lingerie store." Carly loops her arm with mine.

"Oh no. You're going in there solo." I tug on the excess skin on my abdomen. "No one wants to see this in lace."

My brother looks absolutely relieved to hear my quick refusal.

"Stop, you are beautiful." Carly frowns.

"No, I'm not." I hug myself.

"I'd have sex with you," she offers.

How do I answer that?

"Thank you…?"

"Azure, you can wait at the car. We don't need you." Carly shoos my brother off at the store's entrance.

"I'm *not* leaving," he insists.

"Well, we don't want you following us into a clothing store.

Especially one like this."

"Why? I'm going to see it anyway." He crosses his arms over his chest.

She arches a brow and throws her chin at me. "Really? You're going to see them on your sister."

"Well, not on *her*."

"And not on *me* either. I'll wear it while you're off doing whatever Guardians do," Carly huffs before pulling me into the shop. Azure's snarl vibrates against my back as the door closes him out. "Is he always this bossy?"

"He's usually pretty even-tempered." I smirk.

"Why are you grinning?"

"Carly. Come on," I groan before turning to face her. "As much as I love watching my brother squirm, you're not being very nice to him. Or to me, for that matter. Especially bringing up Jackson like that." I cross my arms over my chest. "Would it kill you to be nicer to your husband? Because if you can't, I would like to go back to the pack right now."

She appears to assess me for a moment. "I'm glad to see you aren't a complete pushover," she says, then saunters towards the lacey thongs.

"Who said I was a pushover?"

Carly holds a red string of fabric against my hips. "With your skin tone, these would look hot!"

"Carly..." I warn.

"No one has said it, but that's been the vibes you've been sending out. At least until you spent the night with Jackson." She winks at me. "Did he perform that amazing tongue flick on your clit?" She swoons. "God, his tongue should be molded and made into vibrators." She hands me a white pair of underwear next.

I stretch the material in front of me. "So, you and Jackson had sex?" Not that I should care, but my chest is tight and bile rises in my throat.

"Didn't he tell you?" Carly meets my gaze. "We've never hid it from anyone. It was a way to blow off steam, nothing more." She clasps my hands together. "Hey. He's with you now. No more of his bed-hopping. I see the way he looks at you. That shifter cares about you. Not me or Bridgett."

I gawk. *Jackson has been seeing multiple women at the same time? Wow...*

I shake my head. No. I don't care who or what he does. "You've got it all wrong. We are not together."

"Are you sure?" she teases.

"Uh, yes."

"Well, when he does fuck you, make sure to request some tongue action," Carly suggests before throwing more lingerie into the shopping basket. Then she drags me all over the store, making me watch as she tries on more flimsy material.

I love the sisterly bonding, but I've had three cups of coffee and I need to go pee.

"Am I boring you?" Carly elbows me in the rib. "Because you keep looking at the door."

"I just have to use the bathroom."

"No problem. We'll check out and ask them where the closest one is located."

We unload Carly's goodies onto the counter and the clerk starts scanning everything at the register.

"Excuse me, miss. Where's your bathroom?"

"It's right around the corner as soon as you exit the shop." The young woman gestures to the left.

At this point, I'm bouncing on my tiptoes. I turn to Carly. "Can you meet me there when you're done?"

"Do you want my pepper spray?" She dangles her keys in my face.

"I'll be fine." I wave my phone. "I'll call if I have a problem."

I jog out of the store and around the corner so fast I swear I leave one of those comical puffs of air behind me as I go. When I finally relieve myself, I sigh with contentment. Stupid bladder. It's never been the same since I had Hunter. It's like pregnancy somehow managed to shrink it.

I wash my hands, screeching when I pivot to grab a paper towel and notice two men in suits blocking the exit. My heart races.

What do I do? I reach for my phone.

"I wouldn't do that if I were you." One of them tugs his jacket open to reveal a gun. "We just want to talk, Ms. Pawson."

I swallow my fear. "If you only wanted to chat, then why did you stalk me in here?"

"Do you remember this man?" The stranger ignores my question as he shoves a picture into my palm.

I don't even bother looking down before handing it back over to him. "No. You got the wrong woman."

"Take a closer look."

My knees grow weak as I stare into the eyes of my dead mate. "Sorry. I can't help you," I tell the stranger again. Then I push past them, leaving the bathroom as fast as my legs can move.

Should I shift and hightail it out of here?

Just when I think they're going to let me leave, one grabs my wrist and slams my back into a dark corner of the hallway.

"We aren't idiots, Lilith. When you were admitted to the hospital, you had his blood under your fingernails."

I press my hands over my ears, images of the carnage reflecting behind my eyes as pain slices through my healed-over skin.

No. This isn't real.

I'm having a panic attack or something.

"Then nine months later, you had a son."

My blood turns to ice. My eyes shoot open at the implication. They somehow found out about Hunter.

"That child belongs to us."

"Lily!" Carly slams into the men and stands in front of me. "Get the fuck away from her! Can't you see you've upset her? She's shaking like a leaf." She pulls out her pepper spray. "Did you put your hands on her?"

One of the men knocks the weapon from her grasp. "We were only asking her a few questions." He aims to meet my gaze. "Just tell us where he is, and we will let you leave."

"You better let us go right now!" Carly demands, but I see the way she's trembling.

We're in trouble.

"Get your hands off them," Azure snarls. "Now."

They stiffen and pivot. Their arms return to their sides. Then the taller man clears his throat. "We mean no harm. We were only asking them some questions."

Carly kicks the closest one in the nuts. When he falls to the floor, she claws at his chest like a rabid dog. "Fuck you! How dare you scare the shit out of my sister!"

I cower to the floor, wishing I could disappear. It's all my fault. I murdered Brock and now they're coming after me.

The other male reaches for Carly and Azure's eyes go wide as fur shreds his clothes. He slams the lackey to the ground and snaps at the guy's ear.

"Whoa! Easy!" He waves a government badge. Drool drips from my brother's canines onto the man's suit. "We are investigating the murder of Brock Robinson and it's led us to his mate."

Azure's gaze snaps to me. The wheels are turning in his head, likely recalling that Brock was the shifter who abused me.

Carly strokes his dark fur. "We don't care who you are. This is no way to conduct an investigation."

"We are just following orders."

"Who's your boss?" Carly demands. "We need to meet with them and settle this misunderstanding." She pats the wolf's shoulder.

My brother's jaw ticks before it closes around the man's neck. He squeals and fidgets as his colleague offers a business card.

"We'll be by his office *tomorrow*," Carly says, and Azure releases his would-be prey. "Make sure he's available for questioning." She narrows her eyes to emphasize her point.

They dash into the crowd, leaving us alone in the hallway. My big brother shifts, collects me in his arms, and strokes my hair as I cry into his shoulder. "Let's go home," he tells me. "We need to talk to Frost about this."

Carly cringes at my twin's naked body. "You demolished your outfit." Her gaze trails his frame as she shoves her lingerie bag into his hands. "I hope you look good in a thong."

Numbness. That's all I can feel. Mind-numbing iciness. Because I can't begin to think about the other stuff and what it means for me and my son.

As soon as we return to the Tala territory, we trek over to Frost's cave to discuss a plan of action. If government officials are after me, we need to find out *why* while also ensuring the pack's safety.

"Why are they after you?" Azure asks as if reading my mind. When I don't immediately respond, he begins to lecture me. "Lily, you have to tell us. This is serious."

I start at his condescending tone. "Don't you think I know this? I was the one cornered and interrogated like some sort of criminal!"

"Lil…"

I stomp out of the house. He's acting like I'm a child. He has no idea what's going on, and until he can talk to me with some respect, treat me like the grown woman I am, he can just fuck off.

I drag my tired limbs to my new home, but pause on Jackson's doorstep when I hear Ash and Hunter's shared laughter. I lift my chin as my own plan formulates. If the government has tracked us to Cold Creek, it's only a matter of time before they realize we're staying with the Tala pack. I need to protect my son at all costs.

Jackson

Beta Duties

I battle my urge to chase after Lily as she leaves the alpha's house in a foul mood. Poor thing has been through a lot and her brother is treating her like a shifter he intends on interrogating and not his own flesh and blood.

"Jackson." Frost pulls me out of my thoughts. He nods to the exit, giving me the thumbs-up to check on the woman while he deals with the hothead. But I pause a moment to hear what the others know about the situation.

"They were after the kid," Carly mumbles. "They kept asking where the *offspring* was and informing us that *it* was government property," she spits out the words. "I need to meet with their boss."

"No, you don't. They were just talking out of their asses," Azure growls. "There's no way a child can be property."

"Unless they believe he's one of the kids we rescued from the General's compound," Frost interjects.

"But they knew who Hunter's father was," Azure reminds him. "And they thought the sperm donor was my sister's *mate*."

Shit. Now they know the one secret Lily has been desperately trying to keep.

"They know nothing about shifters and their way of life. They probably assume *baby daddy* and mate are interchangeable." Carly snorts.

I let out a breath. Leave it to the fiery blonde to save the day.

I stride to my den and pause when I see Lily standing at the threshold. Her shoulders are slumped as if the weight of the world is upon her. She meets my gaze and her lip trembles. I crush her to my chest.

"It's going to be okay," I say as I guide her to her house. "We'll figure it out together."

"Can I stay with you?" she pushes out, and my heart aches at her tone. Those government asshats broke her spirit.

I stroke her back. "Of course, you can." I wipe away her tears and lift her chin. "As long as you tell your brother it was your idea."

She smirks and leans her head on my chest. "Deal."

I guide Lily towards my room, but she backpedals, staring wide-eyed at the bed. Haunted memories appear to swim in her vision. "I can put some blankets on the couch. It's really comfortable."

"That sounds great," she whispers while appearing dazed.

I help her snuggle into the plush cushions, then I drape a blanket over her huddled form.

"Mom! Look what I made!" Hunter comes barreling into the room and shoves a clay planter in Lily's face. "I'm going to grow you some flowers when it's finished."

"That's wonderful, honey." She kisses his forehead and hugs him.

"You're squeezing me," the kid grumbles.

"Sorry."

He skips towards the open front door. "I'm going to show Uncle Azure!"

Bad idea. Especially with the pack in a heated discussion about the boy and his mother.

"Hey, buddy, why don't you hang out in the house and I'll go grab him for you?" I offer instead.

Hunter shrugs and returns to Ash's room.

I run my fingers over Lil's arm. "Do you want to talk about what happened?"

She shakes her head.

"You do realize that your brother suspects the thing you don't want him knowing, right?" I say carefully so the kids can't overhear me. Lily squeezes her eyes shut and hides under the sheet. I pat her leg. "I'm going to let Frost know where you're staying, okay?" When I'm met by silence, I add, "I'll be back soon."

As I exit my cave and approach the alpha's house, I can overhear the conversation again.

"We need answers," Frost demands.

"What do you have in mind, boss?" Carly coos.

"Don't call me that."

"How about fur-king?"

"I'll have Jackson escort you to the location and you two can poke around."

"They're after *my* sister. I'll go with Carly," Azure insists.

"Great idea. They'll be scared shitless of you and more compelled

231

to give us answers," Carly agrees.

I step into the room and wait until everyone acknowledges my presence. "Lily is resting."

"What did she say?" Frost asks.

"I'm still attempting to get her to open up to me."

"Guard her and her child with your life." He pats my back. "We're counting on you."

"Of course." I nod to my alpha, then pivot to Azure. "Hunter is asking for you." The Guardian is quick to turn on his heel and head to the door, before I call out, "They are staying in my cave and Hunter's sleeping in Ash's room."

"What?" he snarls.

"Just for the time being, until we can figure out who's after them," I attempt to reason.

Azure bumps chests with me. "She's my sister! She'll be staying with me for protection."

"Sweets. Lily is an adult." Carly pets his arm. "You have to let her choose her own path."

He tugs away from her. "I couldn't protect her from that monster. But I can now."

He gives me a parting look, then stomps into the night air while I rub a hand over my face. This is a mess. I don't want to start a war with the Guardian but I also want to respect Lily's wishes and not impart her tale to the world.

"Don't worry, he'll calm down, eventually," Frost says from beside me.

Carly brushes past us. "Jackson, we have an appointment tomorrow. Don't be late. I texted you the details. We're going to give those suited brutes a piece of our minds.

"Who's going to keep watch over Lily?" I blurt out.

The alpha raises a brow. "We won't let anything happen to her, son. But we need to get to the bottom of who attacked her."

"Of course."

"Why don't you go home and get some rest?" he offers.

"Good night," I agree with a nod.

I stride towards my house, but lean by the front door, not wanting to interrupt the Guardian's visit with his family. My ears twitch towards the conversation going on inside.

"Wouldn't you rather stay with Carly and Sky?" Azure asks.

"Their house isn't exactly *child* friendly. I love you guys, but I'm not ready to have *that* conversation with Hunter yet."

I chuckle. Yeah, I can only imagine all the questions the kid will have about his uncle's relationship with two females.

"I understand." Azure sighs. "I'm here for you, whenever you are ready to talk."

"I know. Just not right now."

An hour later, Azure strides outside again, appearing exhausted. He leans against the stone exterior, appearing lost in thought. Either he doesn't notice me, or he doesn't care that I'm here.

"I never meant to step on your toes," I tell him. "But it's my job to protect the pack, even the newest members."

"And it's my job to guard all the shifters, including my baby sister."

What is his problem?

I grind my jaw and attempt to be the bigger wolf as I reach out a hand to squeeze his shoulder. "Then the pack is truly blessed to have two mighty warriors fighting for them."

Azure's gaze darkens. "If I find out you were anything but a *gentleman* to Lily..." Electricity shimmers, lighting up his blue veins before slipping out to zap me. I tug my arm back and shake it. "*You'll* need protection, beta."

This little shit! I'm going to rip him apart. Guardian or not!

"There you are!" Sky embraces the soon-to-be dead man. "Are you okay?"

I got electrocuted and she's asking *him* how he is doing?

His lips graze hers. "I'm fine. Where's Carly?"

"She said she needed to shower and wash the grime of the day away." Sky frowns at my scowl. "What happened to you?"

I ignore her and stomp into my cave, slamming the door behind me. I did initially feel bad about keeping Lily's past a secret from her brother, but after that incident on the porch, I'm going to sleep like a puppy tonight. A grin spreads over my face. Snuggled up next to his sister.

"Jackson?" Lily whimpers from the couch.

"Go back to sleep." I kneel by her side.

"I can't." She clutches my wrist. "What am I going to do now that they're coming for us?"

I scoop her into my arms and hold her tight. "We're going to stand our ground and fight for a better tomorrow."

The next day, I find it difficult to leave Lily's side.

"Are you sure you're feeling up to this?"

"I kind of have to go." Lily rubs her arm. "Maya is the next alpha and my sister-in-law planned the event."

"It's just a baby shower. It's not like it's some mandatory pack meeting."

I can feel the ripples of fear radiating off Lily. The whole incident at the mall really shook her. I tried to talk to her about what happened but she keeps saying she isn't ready yet. I respect her choice, but I really wish she would open up to someone. Especially since she's not able to sleep and her appetite is less than what a mouse nibbles.

"It feels like it *is* a mandatory pack thing," she scoffs.

"Want me to talk to Frost about it? I'm sure he'll excuse you if that will make you feel better."

"No, I'll survive." She peeks over at Hunter as he plays soccer with Ash and Sky's younger brother Aspen. "And you're going to keep an eye on them?"

"Yes. I'm running an errand in a little bit, but Frost said he'll take the boys fishing if the shower isn't over by then." I can't add more stress to Lily's plate, but I hate *not* telling her the whole truth.

Carly and I are going to shake down the man responsible for the attack at the mall. My jaw ticks. Because that shitshow will not be tolerated on my watch. No matter what the asshat said about *just asking questions*. You don't corner two females in a dark hallway to do that.

Lily side-glances the alpha as he speaks to Raven, who's carrying a massive stack of gifts in her hands. Lily appears to assess the man in question for a minute and nods. "I guess if they stay on the territory, they'll be safe."

I gently grab her chin. "Hey. We will figure this out."

She shakes me off and pivots to enter the cave without another word or a backwards glance.

Does she blame me for not protecting her?

235

I'm doing everything in my power. I pinch the bridge of my nose. She's going through something right now. I need to give her space to process what's going on. With time, I know she'll be back to her normal, happy, paint-loving self.

A few hours later, I pull up to my rendezvous point and look for my blonde partner in crime.

"Why aren't you answering your phone?" I shout into the receiver. "Carly. Our appointment is in fifteen minutes. Where are you?" I yell at her voicemail. "Fine. I'm going inside without you."

I tuck my phone into my pocket and glare at the towering building. The pillars are bright white and blind me as the sun's glare bounces off its facade.

"Fuck me," I hiss under my breath, causing a few women in suits to sidestep me. I attempt to offer them an apologetic nod, but they still give me a wide berth as I climb the steps leading to the main entrance.

I scan the catacomb of office doors and spiral staircases. This place is massive. I walk towards the reception desk but no one is there. So I peek over the top and curse.

Of course, everyone's at lunch.

I double-check my watch and tap my foot as I glance at the grand entryway. There's no one here. A janitor wheels a cart in front of him and exits through a back door. Well, everyone's on lunch except for the low men on the totem pole I guess. My nose twitches.

Wait a minute...

I maneuver around the space until I hear Azure's baritone voice call out, "Who sent you?"

What's the Guardian doing here?

"The General," someone answers.

My blood runs cold. Does he mean the man who's been stealing shifters and breeding them? Is he still out in Cold Creek?

I shake my head. No, Frost told us that the monster is locked up in Carson City.

"Impossible. We have him in custody," Azure repeats what I'm thinking.

"Obviously you've never been in the military. When one falls, *another* takes his place."

I've heard enough. I push open the door with a growl, claws extending and ready for a fight.

"What the fuck?" I skid to a halt. The Guardian already has the guy knocked out. *Dick ruined my fun!* "What happened in here?"

"What are *you* doing here?" Carly demands.

"We had an *appointment* for this afternoon to speak to the douchebag. Why are you here this early?" I cross my arms over my chest.

"I came during their lunch break so I could snoop in their office."

Why is she so damn difficult? She ruined the mission. It was supposed to be peaceful.

"Well, great job, genius!" I wave at the limp body. "How are we going to explain *this*?"

The Guardian leans into the she-devil and sways. "Azure? Oh, no." Carly lifts her now bloody palm. "He's been stabbed."

"Shit." I rush to her side. "We need to get out of here. Can you walk?"

"Maybe he should shift? Don't you heal faster that way?"

"If he turns to fur with the weapon inside him, it'll cause more damage. Guardian, can you use your powers to help us get out of here?"

He shakes his head. "No."

Carly inspects the gash. "Ew. There's green slime coating the blade."

We're in deep trouble. Our contact at the clinic mentioned something similar happening to her son.

"Bastards," I snarl. "That sounds like the same serum they used on Sable. They knew we'd be here. It was a trap."

"Well, if we don't leave soon, we'll be in handcuffs." Carly rubs her neck.

"There's a back exit. I saw a janitor walk out to a dumpster—this way." I let Azure lean on me before I tug him forward. "I can't believe I'm saving your ass after you fucking shocked me. You better remember this moment the next time you want to use your talents on me."

As far as I'm concerned, the blue bastard owes me one.

"What about him?" Carly points to the man passed out on the floor. "We can't just leave him out in the open."

Shit… I forgot about him. Azure staggers, adding more of his weight onto me. We are running short on time. He's going to pass out soon, and it'll be really hard to get him to the car once that happens.

"Are *you* going to drag the body out?" I toe the man at our feet. "It'll cause too much of a spectacle. Just leave him. Now let's get out of here."

But the stubborn brat never listens. Instead, Carly snatches the assailant's ankles and tugs him into the closet. "Don't look at me like that. Putting him here will buy us some time. Now you can sneak out the back."

Carly and I weave through the hallways leading to the rear of the building. The passageway is clear, except for a few receptionists, but they're too busy chatting to notice our attempt at a quick getaway. Sweat drips down my back. My legs quiver. Once we're close enough, I kick open the door so we can move right through.

"We're almost there," Carly grinds out to her husband.

"How much do you weigh, Azure?" I huff. "You need to go on a diet."

We ease him into the back of the vehicle. I slam the driver's side door closed and start the engine. I look back and see the Guardian's head fall against the seat.

"Hey, stay with us!" Carly taps his cheeks.

I slam the vehicle into gear and the tires squeal as I crush my foot onto the gas pedal. There's no way he's dying on my watch. My mind whirls. Lily has had enough mental trauma to last her a lifetime. I will not add more to it. I turn the corner, going twenty over the speed limit. Carly hisses as she grabs the "oh shit" handle but doesn't complain. Once I'm on a straightway, she gives me a weak smile in appreciation.

"If I don't make it..." Azure whispers, "tell Sky I love her."

"Shut up." Carly sniffles. "You'll be fine." Then her neck snaps to me, as she silently begs me to pick up the pace.

I nod and press the pedal to the floor while praying to Luna we make it in time.

"I love you too, Carly," the Guardian pushes out.

"I know you do, you big blue idiot," Carly murmurs into his neck. "We're almost home." She's lying. Even with me breaking every traffic law, we still have a little way to go, then we have to get him to the hospital. "Azure?" Carly panics when he doesn't respond. "Jackson! Wha... what do I do?" She's hyperventilating. If I can't calm her, she'll go into shock.

"Carly?" When she doesn't answer, I glance into the rearview mirror. She's pale. "Carly!"

She jerks to attention. "I can't lose him," she whimpers.

"You won't."

"How do you know?"

"Because we won't *let* him cross the rainbow bridge. Not today." I grind my molars. "Grab my phone and call Sable. Explain what happened and have him meet us at the lake with his mother. Celeste will know what to do. But they need to be there when we arrive. Can you do that? For your husband?"

Her hands are shaking but she manages to dial. "Sable? It's Carly." She bursts into tears but is able to force out the words between sobs.

I clench the steering wheel until my knuckles are white. Hunter will get his uncle back in one piece and Lily will have her annoying brother at her side soon. I attempt to shout my thoughts into existence. Only a little farther.

The car bumps over stumps and twigs as we create a shortcut through the pack's territory. I screech to a halt and leap out to help Sable with Azure's limp frame. Celeste trails behind us, shouting instructions as we push through her front door. We lay him down on the bed in her guest room, then she shoves us out of the way to work on him.

I run my blood-soaked hands through my hair and lean on the wall. That was intense. Screams erupt from outside and I cringe. Sounds like the rest of the family knows what happened to the Guardian. I glance towards the makeshift operating room. As much as I don't care for the blue-veined jerk, I really hope he can pull through.

240

No Turning Back

"I'm so glad you could make it. Come on in, dear." Raven leads me to the couch and hands me a glass of punch. "How are you feeling?"

"Tired." I sigh before sipping the tart drink.

The alpha's wife frowns and pats my leg. "Do you want a sleep aid?" She nods to another woman. "I've known Celeste most of my life and she's an amazing physician. She could provide you with something to help you."

"Thank you, but I'm going to try to get through this on my own."

"I respect that. But just know you're never alone in your struggles. We are your pack now and we got your back."

"And front!" Sky sings as she stabs my shirt with a diaper pin. "Don't say the word *pup* or you lose this. The goal is to get as many as you can before the baby shower is over."

I adjust the bright blue pin and nod. "Thanks for the warning."

Sky moves on to her next victim and Maya joins me on the couch. "She's energetic, isn't she?"

I smirk at the bubbly woman running around the room. "Yes, she is."

Poor Azure has his paws full with Sky. Her headstrong temperament is nothing like my brother's chill demeanor.

"I don't think we've officially met yet." The alpha-in-training holds out a hand. "My name's Maya and Sky is my sister-in-law too. I married her older brother, Sable."

I miss my tiny pack. My head spins with all of these names I'm expected to remember.

I shake her palm. "It's nice to meet you. And congratulations." I nod to her belly. "It's a boy, right?"

Her eyes appear to sparkle with joy as she rubs her stomach. "Yes, it is. Wasn't your first pup a boy? Do you have any advice?"

That's a loaded question. Motherhood is exhausting yet rewarding at the same time. There's a lot I could say to her like: sleep when the baby sleeps, enjoy the special first-time moments, and buy earplugs for the various tantrums that are sure to ensue. Instead, I give her a word of warning. Something I wish someone would have told me.

"Cover their junk before you change them, or they'll pee on you."

"Hey! Give me your pin, little sister!" Sky skips over and adds Maya's pin to her ever-growing pile. "Remember not to say the P-word, guys!"

"You mean *penis*?" Maya shouts, and everyone giggles.

"You're just jealous that I took yours." Sky sticks out her tongue.

"Well, it is *my* party. Shouldn't I get a freebie?" Maya grumbles under her breath.

These two are competitive. Or maybe it's just the pregnancy hormones? But what's Sky's excuse?

I pat Maya's hand. "I wish you and your new *pup* many blessings," I say, then immediately hand over my pin, so she has one again.

"Aw, thank you." Maya squeezes me.

"That's cheating!" Sky objects.

"Skylar," her mother warns from a distance. "How about we eat some of that delicious cake that Raven baked, so we aren't hangry?" She gives the girl a pointed stare before adding, "Please."

The other woman rolls her eyes but obeys her elder. "Everyone can help themselves. The food is in the kitchen."

The group shuffles over to the stone countertops. I pause as my phone rings and an unknown number blinks across the screen. I send it to voicemail and pick up a plate.

"These cupcakes are heavenly," Maya gushes. "I know Mom made the cake, but didn't you make the cupcakes, Sky?"

"They are red velvet with a cream cheese frosting." Sky beams. "The secret is adding sour cream to the batter." She winks at her other sister-in-law. "The more white stuff, the better."

They share a giggle as I grab one of the baked goods in question. I settle back into the living room as a text message comes through, and the blood drains from my face.

We have your pack surrounded. Bring the boy tonight. Or your loved ones are dead.

The ominous warning includes a few pictures of Nana and Jackie cooking in the kitchen back home. *What the fuck?* I bite my lip as I zoom into the image. Could this be a prank?

Bile rises in my throat. Why would someone do this?

I set my cake on the table. My appetite is gone. I scan the room as my heart races.

Can I ask the Tala family to help rescue my grandparents?

Their laughter warms the air as they coo over the towering gift pile. I could sneak out and no one would notice. I tap my finger on my arm. I should at least tell Azure what's going on when he returns. He could zap the idiots threatening our family. I rock back and forth. But there's no way I'm bringing Hunter into this mess.

No. He stays here. No questions asked.

Sky throws a roll of plastic at me. "It's your turn, Lily! Come and guess Maya's belly's circumference."

"Oh, I don't know…" I push out, trying my best to appear normal.

"Don't be a party pooper." She pouts. "Join the fun!"

Even with my head throbbing with all the *what ifs*, I swallow down my fear and plaster on a fake smile. "Sure, I'll take a guess."

An hour later, my foot is bouncing with anxious energy. I have to do something about that message.

"Thank you again for coming," Sky says as she walks a guest to the door, before collapsing onto the couch.

"You did an incredible job." Maya squeezes her hand. "The baby shower was absolutely perfect. Especially the *pin the tail on the pup* game."

Sky smirks and holds out a palm. "Give me your pins."

"What? The game is over." Maya covers her chest, protecting her goods. "No way. I won fair and square."

Before the girls can continue, Celeste wraps an arm around Sky and says, "I can't wait for your first child."

"Then I can steal your pins and keep the title of reigning queen." Maya grins.

Raven sends her daughter a pointed stare before quickly changing the subject. "Did you have fun too, Lily?"

All eyes are on me. I force a nod. "It was my first baby shower," I admit, knowing it'll probably be my last one as well. "My former pack members were a bit older," I whisper, thinking about Nana and how my time is trickling down. But Azure still hasn't returned…

"I'm glad you could join us. It was fun spending more time with my fur-in-laws," Sky adds with a yawn.

"Thank you for having me. It's nice to have the opportunity to meet all the ladies of the family," I answer honestly. They make it easy to feel welcome.

We all jump as Sable bursts through the door. He scans the cave before tugging his mom away from our group. The rest of us blink his way before meeting each other's concerned stares.

"That jerk didn't even say hi to me!" Maya dashes out after her mate.

We leap to our feet to follow the chaos outside. Carly slams into Sky's chest. The girl is covered in blood! We all gasp at her appearance. What the hell is going on? I scan the horizon. Was Jackson with her? Is he wounded?

Carly's frame is racked by sobs. Sky strokes her wife's hair. "Sweetheart? What happened?"

"He saved my life," she blurts out.

I hold my breath as Sky asks the question on everyone's lips. "Who?"

"He threw me out of harm's way and got knifed. It should have been me! I killed him." Carly crumbles at our feet. "I gave him such a hard time, and now I'll never have the chance to tell him how much he means to me."

I cover my lips. It *is* Jackson. They are always bickering. No... My heart clenches in my chest and I waver on my feet. *Anyone but him*, I beg Luna.

Movement in the darkness catches my attention. Sable and Jackson are carrying in my unconscious brother, who's drenched in blood and unmoving. I can't breathe. Luna actually heard me this time... and somehow made it worse...?

"Azure?" I push out, my voice trembling. "What happened?"

"He'll be all right," Sky whispers to us before she huddles with her wife.

"Skylar?" Sable helps the girls over to their parents' cave. "Don't worry. Mom's working on patching him up."

When Jackson walks out into the night air, I throw my arms around his waist. My mouth opens to spew the list of questions building up in the back of my throat, but then I notice that he's covered in blood.

"Are you hurt?" My hands rove across his chest.

"No. This isn't my blood. I had to move Azure to the car."

"What happened?" I fist his shirt as tears well in my eyes.

"He was attacked inside the government building."

I stumble back a step. "Why?"

"We don't know yet, but Frost is contacting the mayor and hopefully we'll have answers soon."

"They found him. They found us," I whisper. My neck snaps up as my eyes scan the grassy terrain. When my gaze lands on Hunter, I run towards him.

"Mom, what's the matter?" Hunter frowns at my tear-stained face.

I take a steadying breath. My son is safe. I need to *mom up* and force my fears down so I don't freak him out.

I kneel in front of him. "Uncle Azure's been hurt."

"Is he going to be okay?"

"They are helping him right now."

"Can I see him?"

"Not now. But I was thinking maybe you could draw him a get-well card for when he wakes up."

Hunter's lip quivers, as his friend steps up next to him. "I'll get the others to make some too," Ash adds before looking over my shoulder. "Is that okay, Dad?"

"I think he'll love some cards from everyone. Why don't you go to your parents' cave and get started while I take Lily to talk to the doctor?"

The pups take off towards another den without answering. Once the boys disappear inside, Jackson tugs on my elbow. "Please talk to me. I know, with everything going on, you must be freaking out."

He's not wrong. I'm running out of time. And now I can't count on Azure's help. I'm on my own as usual. I clear my throat. "I'm worried about my brother. That's all."

He wraps an arm around my waist and guides me to where Sky and Carly are waiting on the couch in Celeste's home.

"Any word on his condition?" Jackson asks the group.

Sable rubs his face as he glances at the guest room door. "Not yet."

My leg bounces and I fight the urge to keep checking the time. It isn't long before the doctor emerges with crimson-soaked clothes and sweat-drenched hair. "The good news is there wasn't any internal damage. I was able to disinfect the area and stitch him up. Now he's resting peacefully, and he'll make a full recovery." Everyone collectively releases a breath. "The bad news is the dagger was doused in that anti-shifting serum and he can't use his Guardian powers to assist in the healing process."

Oh no. That means he can't protect the Tala or Pawson packs. They're on their own against the government's forces.

"I thought you developed a cure that counteracts the effects?" Sable interjects, and hope leaps in my chest.

"I did, but I'm still in the testing phase, and until Azure's conscious and aware of the possible risks of the vaccine, I don't want to inject him without his consent."

I deflate in my seat. I'm glad he'll be fine, but I can't let him know what's going on for his own safety.

"Can we see him?" Sky pleads.

"Just don't wake him. He needs to sleep so his body can mend itself."

My sisters-in-law and I scurry through the hallway and peek into the room. We halt in our tracks as we take in his pale frame. Sky runs her fingertips over his forehead. Azure looks older, lying in the bed like this.

"I can't believe you took a knife for me," Carly whispers as tears kiss her cheeks. "You put my life before your own." Her lips graze his. "Thank you for teaching me that not all men are the same."

This moment steals the air from my lungs. He was there for Carly and saved her. My brother can have his happily ever after. He's found his mate and a plus-one.

I hang my head as jealousy invades my thoughts. Why can't I have this? Why did I get stuck with Brock? Then raped for days while he slowly cut through my soul and destroyed all of my happiness?

Someone squeezes my shoulder and I jump. I look up into Jackson's eyes. "He will be fine."

I nod to the beta, then I pivot back to my twin. I'll make sure my brother keeps his happily ever after, even if I never get my own.

"I'm sorry." I kiss Azure on the forehead, offering him my final farewell.

Jackson

Tracking

After dragging Azure's wounded ass into the room and standing by Lily as she cried at his bedside, I'm exhausted. I collapse on the couch in Celeste's cave. I lean my head back and rub the bridge of my nose. Today has been a shitshow, to say the least.

I'm glad the boys are staying the night with Ash's adoptive parents, because I'm going to pass the fuck out when I return home.

"This doesn't make sense." Frost flips through the folder Carly snatched from the office.

Curiosity gets the better of me. I lean towards him and scan the documents. "What's up?"

"They think Lily is the leader of a rogue pack that's been attacking government buildings."

I snort. "She's way too skittish for that." Then I cringe at my words. She has every right to be scared after the shit she's been through. "Her time has been accounted for, between our pack and the Pawson pack. Plus taking care of a child."

Frost wrinkles his brows at the paperwork as if he doesn't hear me. "They say that Hunter is government property, because his sire was an experiment conducted by them." He shakes his head. "This can't be true." He pivots to me. "Has she said anything to you about this Brock guy?"

Do I break her confidence and tell Frost what I know about her mate? Or keep it to myself?

I yawn and stretch out my arms, refusing to meet my alpha's gaze. "She doesn't talk much, does she? It's a miracle I even know her name."

Frost sighs and slams the folder closed. "We'll worry about this tomorrow." He stands and pats my shoulder. "Make sure you get some sleep."

"You too."

I blow out a breath. *Man, that was close.*

I scan the room and realize I'm the last one waiting in the living room. Carly and Sky are with Azure and Celeste, whose mate went to bed already. I rub the back of my neck and work out a kink. The Guardian is going to make a full recovery, but it'll take some time, especially with that serum in his blood, unless he decides to be a test subject for the vaccine.

I check my phone and sigh. Lily said she felt uncomfortable sleeping in my cave without the boys present. I have to admit I'm disappointed I won't have her all to myself.

A grin tugs at the corners of my mouth. The things I could do to make her howl. Then another yawn rips through my chest. Who am I kidding? I'd hold her close and just sleep deeply. But if she initiated a play session, I'd never turn her away. I drool at the thought of her dark skin pressed against mine. My tongue slipping into her folds, tasting her...

I stride into the night air. The cool breeze brushes over my heated frame. I take in my blood-crusted limbs, Azure's life force, before glancing towards Lily's cave and chewing my bottom lip.

Maybe I should check on his sister? That's what a friend should do, right? Cuddle up to her naked form and mouth-fuck her into a restful sleep...

I chuckle at the thought. Carly and Sky would approve. But their husband? I cringe. He'd fry me with his powers.

My lip twitches. Except he doesn't have access to them right now. I rub my palms together as I pivot on my heel and head towards Lily's den. My mind is made up. I'm going to rock her world, help her get out of her shell, and make her feel loved and safe.

But she wants something permanent...

I pause at her door. She's a single mother. She isn't like Bridgett, an unclaimed female content with having no strings attached. My mind continues to unravel the facts as my knuckle pauses an inch from making contact. We have a lot in common too. Lily had her mate and lost him, just like I did. We both love art, have one child, and know loss. Deeply.

I dip my chin with finality. I want Lily. As more than just a fuck toy, as someone more constant. What do they call those? Girlfriends? Or we could keep things totally casual like Carly and I did? Just scratch our itch and have fun.

I wrinkle my nose. No. I don't like the idea of her having another male. I want her all to myself. The resolution causes me to backpedal. My eyes widen as they land on Lily's welcome mat. What is wrong with me? This isn't Jackson, beta of the Tala pack and mate to Ashely Tala. My heart clenches. What has the Guardian's sister done to me? This is why I keep things casual.

But when my mind drifts to thoughts of what would happen if they pair Lily with another male, rage boils in my core. She's special, a gem amongst the pack. I want to be that man for her. To paint beside her. Attend art galleries together.

But what if she doesn't want to be with me?

My confidence falters. She might have sworn off males altogether. Do I really want to make an ass of myself?

I brush the thought aside with a smirk. She's worth it. I won't give up on her. Even if it takes years to wear down her barriers... And if she desires another male, I'll learn to deal with it because I only want to see her happy. That's all that matters. *Her* happily ever after.

I breathe in a lungful of confidence and rap my knuckles on her door. It echoes inside but I don't hear any movement. "Lily? It's Jackson." Shit. I don't even smell her. "I'm coming inside." I turn the knob and push through. Darkness encompasses the layout. "Lil?"

I check the rooms but no one has been here in days. Where is she? Fear creeps up my spine. Could the folder be right? Is Lily working with a rogue pack under our noses?

I turn the corner, leave the den, and double-check all of her normal spots. By the glistening lake, where she spends time contemplating life. My house, where she plays board games and Legos with the boys. I even glance inside the room where the boys are sleeping.

Fuck. This doesn't look good.

My phone vibrates in my pocket. I stare at the caller ID and breathe a sigh of relief. "Where are you?" Silence. The hairs on the back of my arm stand up. "Butterfly?"

"Take care of Hunter. Please."

My spine straightens. "Where are you?" I repeat.

"They won't let me live." She chokes on her words. "I can live with that if I know he's taken care of."

No... What is she talking about?

"Lily. Damn it. Tell me where the fuck you are right now."

"It's too late," she whispers before she gasps. "Nana! No!" Then the line goes dead. The silence slices through my lungs. What the fuck?

"Lil? Butterfly!" I attempt to call back, but it keeps going to voicemail.

Think. Think. She said something about Nana. She must be on Pawson territory, while the terror in her words means they must be in trouble. I step towards the woods but pause. She'll need more help than I can give her, especially if there's another group of shifters attacking. I pivot to the alpha's house and knock.

"Jackson?" Raven waves me inside. "What's wrong?"

I pass through the entryway as I rack my hair with my hands. "Lily is in trouble, and I need some shifters to travel to the Pawson pack to save her."

Frost leans on the wall. "How do you know this?"

"She called me."

"That can't be right. I saw Lily go to her den earlier. She's sleeping." Raven yawns.

"Trust me. That was the first place I checked," I huff. "Please, there's no time to waste."

Frost scratches his chin. "The Guardian is healing and won't be able to safeguard our pack, *and* our numbers are not enough to protect our family if we send some members that way," he says mostly to himself.

"Is Hunter safe?" Raven clutches her chest.

"Yes, he stayed with Ash."

"Thank Luna." She sighs.

"I can go to her myself, if we can't provide the manpower. But I can't abandon her."

"Are you sure she's actually in danger?" Frost raises a brow.

"What are you getting at?" Raven crosses her arms over her chest.

"The folder did indicate that Lily was destroying government facilities. She could be a double agent."

"You don't honestly believe that," I snarl. "She's been with us the whole time." When he cocks a brow in my direction, I continue, "And she's the Guardian's sister. If we don't rescue her, he'll be furious."

Frost pinches the bridge of his nose, his age shining through. I made a huge mistake coming here. I should have just left.

"Please trust me," I beg. "Lily is a good person. She'd never do what you're thinking."

"What I *think* is that your judgment is clouded," he accuses. "We've all noticed how she runs to you, even sleeps in your cave."

"Because she trusts me! And if you'd give her a real chance, you would too," I growl. "Never mind. I'm wasting precious time arguing with you. I'm leaving, and when the Guardian wakes up, let him know I'll be right back with his sister." I pivot and stomp towards the door.

"Jackson." Frost's alpha tone is thick. "You will not leave this territory."

My limbs become cold. I turn to him, mouth hanging open. "Why would you demand that of me? Have you lost your mind?"

"I'm the leader of the Tala pack and my word is law." He sighs. "Don't look at me like that. I'm doing this for the safety of our entire family."

My surrogate mother looks between me and her mate. "Honey, maybe you should reconsider?"

"No. I'll face the consequences with Azure when the time comes. But I can't risk it. Especially with the humans on the verge of war with us." Frost shakes his head. "I'm sorry, Jackson. I hope you're wrong and she's just overreacting. But my answer is no." He turns to his room and walks off, without a care in the world. "I'm going back to bed for a few hours. Are you coming, Raven?"

"I'm going to walk Jackson out first." She rubs my back. "I'll be right there."

He nods and disappears down the hallway.

How can he abandon one of his own kind? I storm outside and snarl. "How can you just sit here and let him do this? Lily needs our help now!"

Raven tugs on my elbow. "Follow me, dear. We don't have a lot of time."

I blink at her as she knocks on her daughter's front door. Why are we here?

The alpha's wife doesn't wait for an answer before pulling me into the dimly lit den. "Maya?"

"Mom?" The other shifter shuffles into the living room, tying a robe around her waist. "What's wrong?"

"Where's Sable?" Raven whispers.

"I was trying to sleep." The man in question rubs his eyes until they fall on me. "What the hell are you two up to?"

Raven waves off his question. "This is an emergency." Their eyes snap to hers. "I need you two to combine your alpha powers and tell Jackson he may leave the territory."

Hope rises in my chest. She's on my side, not her husband's. I wrap my arms around her and squeeze. "Thank you," I whisper into her neck.

"Don't thank me yet, son. This might not work."

Maya frowns. "I can't agree to go against Dad until I know what's going on."

I meet my adopted sister's eyes. "Lily called and she's in trouble, but Frost thinks she's not who she says she is."

The alpha-in-training appears to digest my statement before turning to her husband. They share a glance and then they nod in solidarity. "Lily is a good shifter. I'm sure of that. Even if she weren't, she's in trouble and we need to assist her."

"Plus, her brother will freak the fuck out if he finds out that we abandoned his only sibling... and probably electrocute us," Sable interjects. Maya elbows him and he shrugs. "That shit hurts, right, Jackson?"

I rub my arm and nod. "He has some strong powers."

"You two are big babies." Maya drops a hand to her belly. "We need to do this because it is the right thing to do, not because he might lose his temper." She looks between us. "So how does this work?"

"Just speak the command from your heart." Raven places a palm on her daughter's chest. "And pronounce each word meaningfully."

Maya's eyes water. "We can do that."

"I need to return to the cave and keep Frost occupied." She winks. "If your father asks, this was your idea." She embraces me, then she squeezes my hand. "May Luna grant you the peace you need, son, and direct your paws."

"Thanks, Mom. I owe you one."

"You owe me nothing. Just bring Hunter's mother home." She nods before exiting the room.

Once the front door closes, I arch a brow at the pair in front of me. "Well, hurry up." I wave them on.

Maya clears her throat. "I, Maya Tala, grant Jackson Tala permission to travel."

A beat of silence passes but nothing happens.

"Did it work?" Sable questions me. "Think about leaving and see what happens."

I step towards the door with every intention of leaving the territory, and my feet freeze to the spot. "Try again."

"Yeah, and make it sound less lawful," her mate whines.

"What?" She crosses her arms over her chest.

"Raven said it has to come from your heart, not your teacher's brain." He flicks her forehead.

"I'm going to kick your ass!" Maya snarls.

"Can we do this first?" I leap in her path. "Think about Lily! Come on!"

She closes her eyes and takes in a breath. "Jackson may leave the territory."

But the same coldness creeps in at the thought of traveling. "Fuck." I tug at my hair. "She could be dead! And I'm stuck here fucking around with this!" I pace back and forth across the room. "I know! I'll challenge Frost to a battle and take the alpha title, then I can leave."

"That would take too much time," Sable grunts.

"And cost too much blood." Maya jabs at her husband's chest.

"That too." He smirks.

"Damn it!" I snarl.

"You really love her, don't you?" The alpha-in-training tilts her head to look at me.

My heart skips a beat. *Do I?*

Lily's contagious smile flashes in my mind. Then her dazzling eyes. It's what I live for. And if I can't get to her soon, I'm going to lose it all. Again.

I kneel at Maya's feet, my head lowered in defeat. "I love her," I whisper to myself. "Please help me save her life."

Maya stands tall, grabs her husband's hand, and squeezes. "We can do this."

"We?" Sable questions. "Your dad really just wants you to lead, not me."

Her neck snaps to his. "Hey! It won't work if you don't believe in your powers."

He rolls his eyes. "Frost would rather have *Jackson* by your side than me."

They both pivot in my direction. I arch a brow. "Man. I just confessed my love for Lily. Catch back up."

"But you're always fucking someone. Bridgett. Carly. And you keep hitting on my mate." He holds the woman closer.

I bite my tongue. A metallic taste floods my mouth. He's right. But things have been different since Lily and Hunter joined the pack. "I'm done with all that. Well, except for messing with Maya." I wink her way. "Because I get to remind her mate how special she is."

"Aw, that's so sweet," Maya coos, stepping forward to give me a hug, until her husband tugs her back.

"Let's just channel this love into the command, shall we?" he grumbles.

"You're right! That's what we've been missing!" Maya clears her throat and places a palm on my head, nudging her mate to do the same thing. He begrudgingly complies. "Jackson, my brother, beta of the Tala pack. I entrust you with saving the life of another family member. We order you to travel to the ends of the world until you find Lily Pawson."

Her endearing words wash over me and warm my heart. *Please let this work.* I envision myself traveling and no bad feelings hold me back. I stand and stride to the exit with every intention of leaving our boundaries. Nothing.

"It worked!" I praise before smashing them to my chest. "I'll be back as soon as I can."

"Wait!" Maya shrieks. I pivot and worry she may be second-guessing her decision. "You're going by yourself?"

"I know the pack is large, but I'm pretty sure Frost will notice people are missing when he wakes up."

"I'll help you," Sable says, and Maya meets her husband's gaze. He shrugs. "Your dad hates me anyway. What's one more reason to add to his list?"

"Aw, sweetie!" Maya holds him tight. "I love you. Be safe and bring her home."

"I love you too." Sable melts in her arms and kisses her softly. "So, if I don't come back with Jackson…"

She smacks his arm, effectively ending their embrace. "Don't you dare leave him behind. I expect everyone to come back in one piece."

"Then let's get this over with," Sable demands.

Lily

Experiment 217

Earlier that night

After I say good night to the Tala pack, I slip into my cave. I take a few deep breaths. I have to do this on my own, to save them.

Sneaking out the back door, I stick to the shadows. I morph into four legs. My black fur helps me camouflage with the nightscape. The stars sparkle, the moon twinkles, and the insects serenade the world. Everything is as it should be. Except for the danger looming around Nana.

I cower in the brush and wait until the shifters change for border patrol, then I slip past during those precious seconds no one is guarding the territory line. Once I clear them, I gallop full force into the forest. Twigs tug at my legs, begging me to stay where it's safe. But I can't. I extend my limbs and contract them.

How could this have happened?

Hunter has always been my number one priority. I never thought

I'd have to abandon him to save his life. But sacrificing myself is the only way. The farther I get, the more my heart constricts. I'm also going to miss Jackson, but I know he'll take care of Hunter as his own. Plus, Azure will help him. Tears wet my pelt.

I shake my head. *Stop.* I must focus on the mission and saving what's left of my pack.

After hours of traveling, my legs tremble and I shift to my human skin. I cautiously glance around. The pack is just starting to wake up. Nothing seems amiss. Nana makes coffee. Jackie is stirring a fire.

What the heck? I push past the brush and my grandmother's eyes light up.

"Lily? Oh, my! What a wonderful surprise!" She rushes over and hugs me. "Are you feeling all right? You're shaking."

Words fail me. Did I imagine that disturbing text? I rub my forehead and sag my shoulders in relief. Thank Luna everyone is safe. Damn. I'm such a drama queen.

"Why don't you take a nap? You look like you've been awake for days," Nana says as she guides me to my old den and helps me sit on the bed. "Here we are." She clutches my wrist. "Where's Hunter?"

I blink through my confusion. "He's with Jackson and Azure."

"That's right! Azure got married! Tell me everything about his wife!"

"I... well..."

Where do I even begin?

Grandma, he has two spouses. One mate and one human wife.

No, I do not want to explain that to her.

Worry lines take over her face and she goes into mom mode.

"How about you rest, and we'll catch up soon?" She kisses my forehead. "It's great having you home. Thank you for visiting this old lady." Nana strides out into the early morning sun.

I should tell her why I'm really here, but I don't want to scare the shit out of her. I lay my head down and stare at the stone ceiling.

Rest. Yeah. That's what I need. Then I'll return to my son, and we'll all laugh about this one day. My lashes shutter closed.

A vision blossoms behind my lids. A large metal building with no windows and only one door appears in my mind's eye. I hear a rushing ravine close by. If I could paint this scene, it would be titled "Run." The atmosphere thrums with promises of pain and suffering. I sniff the breeze and gag on the bleach and blood as they burn my nose. Screams rip through the area, vibrating the dream until it's gone.

I jolt awake, rush to the window, and peek out. At first, nothing's amiss; then golden eyes glitter from the tree line. Fuck. I back up.

"No…" I whisper. Those eyes. They look like Brock's. My mind races. He said he was captured and tortured.

Are his abusers coming after me?

I take another look and squeal. They're almost here. I tug out my phone and my fingers automatically find the one person I know will come searching for me.

"Where are you?" His voice soothes my icy nerves. *Luna, take watch over him and my child.* I'll sacrifice everything for them to have happiness. "Butterfly?"

That nickname causes me to smirk. He's the biggest dork.

"Take care of Hunter. Please," I whisper.

"Where are you?" he asks again, and I hear the pain etched in his voice. I'm hurting him. I hope he'll forgive me someday.

"They won't let me live," I sob out the truth. "But I can live with that if I know my son is taken care of."

"Lily. Damn it. Tell me where the fuck you are right now," he yells down the phone.

"It's too late." I wish I could brush my hands through his hair and assure him it'll be okay. That this is my choice. My gaze snaps to the window. Men with guns are flanked by two massive beasts. They aim at their target. "Nana! No!" The phone slips from my fingertips and shatters into pieces as it crashes onto the stone floor. But I don't care. "Stop!" I scream as I burst out of the house.

"Lily, go. Run," Nana stutters as her hands shake.

One of the men nods, and the beast on his left snarls before it leaps forward. I shift and slam into its stomach, just before it lands on my grandmother. We tumble head over tail. My back slams into a tree and I crumble to the floor. My vision is blurred, but I hear boots stomping in my direction. Something jabs my arm and I slowly morph back to two legs.

"She's been dosed. Grab her." Someone snatches my elbow and pulls me up. "You were supposed to bring the child," a man shouts before a palm collides with my cheek. "Where is he?"

I spit blood. "Who are you talking about?"

"Don't play games! Where is the pup that Experiment 217 sired?"

"217?" I shake my aching head. "Do you mean Brock?"

The wolf standing guard whimpers his acknowledgement. I meet its gaze. Is it a sibling? Or maybe a parent?

The man grabs a fistful of my hair and forces my gaze on his. "You were instructed to bring the pup, or your pack would die." He assesses my jutted chin. "You didn't bring him, did you?"

"I decided to offer a trade instead." When he raises an eyebrow, I continue. "Leave the child and my pack alone and take me instead."

"Are you fucking kidding me?" he snarls. "You? You're not worth shit!"

No, this wasn't how it was supposed to go down!

"But… but… you can breed me," I sputter. "Make more pups."

"We don't want a worthless bitch!" He sprays spittle on my face. "We wanted 217 and his pup!"

"Why?"

"To continue our experiments!" He sends bits of pine through the air as he slams his fist through a tree

Damn. Is he a shifter too? Some sort of hybrid?

"Kill the pack!" He shoves my head into the dirt at his feet. "Add the bitch to the body count."

The wolves hesitate as they glance at each other, then back to the man. That's all the time I need to plead my case one more time. "My brother is a Guardian. He has powers, which means any pup of mine has the chance to have those same abilities," I lie through the skin of my teeth, but it's the last thing I have. "If you spare my pack, I'll go quietly and do as you say."

He pauses as if considering my compromise. Then he scratches his chin as he assesses my naked body. I have to sell this. I puff out my chest and saunter over to him, swaying my ample hips. His gaze smolders.

"Unless maybe you want to keep me for *yourself?*" I swallow bile at the thought.

He glances at the other man. "Lock her in the truck." Handcuffs are slapped on my wrists, and I'm tugged towards an idling vehicle. Once the door opens, the leader pats the wolves' shoulders. "Don't leave any witnesses." Then he strides to me, shoves me inside, and locks my only exit.

Snarls echo outside. "No!" I jam my shoulder against the wall. "Stop!"

"Let her go!" Nana yells. "Lily!"

"Nana!"

The engine revs and lurches forward. My temple slams into metal and my vision darkens. But before I pass out, screams and the sounds of shredding flesh echo in the distance. I open my mouth to beg them to spare my family, but nothing comes out.

I've failed them.

"You were supposed to bring the boy!"

My consciousness returns but not my vision.

"I don't know where he is."

"Fuck." Something slams onto a hard surface. "First they arrested the General, then they stormed the office building, and now this." Silence. "They'll have our heads for this shitshow, and I don't want to be the one hanging from the noose. Call in the General's kid. He'll be able to instruct us further and take the fall when they show up."

"What about *her*?"

"Keep her chained and drugged, and when he arrives, let him deal with her."

"Where are you going?"

"In case the rumors are true, I'm not staying around to see if the rebels show up to rescue their leader."

A male snorts. "This little thing is not the master planner of the rogue pack."

"Either way, I'm not waiting around to find out. I'm going to collect the beasts. They should have finished destroying the shifters by now."

"Don't forget this."

The other man sounds like he catches something. "After all this time, you doubt their loyalty to us? Do you really think I'll need to zap them?"

"Do you want to find out the hard way like Derrick did with 217?"

"Good call."

Footsteps pound away before a door is slammed and I'm left in silence. My vision is still gone, and I can't shift. The drug must be the serum Sable was talking about.

I hang my head. The Pawson pack is gone and it's all my fault. Tears kiss my cheeks. They died protecting Hunter. Their deaths will not be in vain. Even hearing it bounce around in my mind, I don't believe it. It hurts so much. My heart is broken. Luna has finally punished me for murdering Brock. Or Experiment 217. I shudder at the thought. He was one of those monsters forced to destroy his kind. And what about this rebel group they're talking about? Who's behind that?

I guess that's a tale for another day…

The door slams and I jolt to attention. Well, as much as I can while dangling from the ceiling by my wrists.

"Shit," the male voice curses under his breath. He rushes over and fiddles with the chains holding me in place. "This can't be happening," he says as I fall to the floor in a heap of useless limbs. "Sorry."

I must be losing my mind. Did a soldier just apologize to me? My arms are freed and then I feel myself being cradled.

"Lil, are you okay?" The man tugs off my blindfold.

The bright light draws a groan out of my chest. Once my vision returns, I gape up at the man hovering over me. I must be seeing things. "Jake?"

He strokes my cheek and gives me a boyish grin that shows his dimples. "You've gained some weight, my friend."

"After all this time, that's what you have to say for yourself?" I shuffle back, trying to put distance between us. How can this be? Jake was a kind soul. I guess *was* is the key word here. "You're the General's son?" I bark.

"I told you that my dad was in the military."

"But all this time, you've been assisting him in destroying shifters?" I screech.

"Hey! You never told me you could change into a monster!" he growls.

"Monster? Monster! How fucking dare you! You're murdering innocent lives and experimenting on others."

"They aren't human," he spits.

How can he say that? This man rescued a *spider* from my shower once and rehomed it outside.

"So what does that make you, Jake? Huh? A monster-fucker? What would Daddy say about that?"

"I didn't mean you," he attempts to clarify. "I meant the other ones."

"We are all the same!" I scream. "We are wolves!"

He pinches the bridge of his nose. "You are different. Special."

"Why? Because Experiment 217 bred with me and we had a

pup?" I snarl.

Then it's as if Jake suddenly remembers why he's here. "Do you know where the offspring is? Can you bring it to us?"

"You mean will I bring my son here so you can fuck him up like you did with his father?"

"Lily, you don't understand. If we don't turn it over, they will kill us for our failure." Jake clutches my hands, fear radiating off his frame. "I'm begging you."

This man is not the same kid I went to college with. His dad manipulated the sweet young boy I knew until there was no trace of him left.

"I'll never let any harm come to my pup. Do what you have to with me, but my child will remain safe, always."

Jake slams a fist into the wall. "Damn it, Lily! You don't realize what you're saying. You have no idea what they'll do to you."

"I do. But you see, I'm willing to sacrifice everything to protect the ones I love. Can you say the same thing for yourself, Jake?"

He meets my gaze. I can tell he's battling his demons. Fighting what his dad has taught him versus what we've known together.

The building shutters and the power flickers, drawing Jake from his thoughts. "Shit. They're here." He leaps to his feet and dashes to the door. "Sound the alarm," he blares at the guard outside. "Grab the weapons and hold them off as long as possible, while we destroy the evidence."

"What about her?" The burly man nods to me.

"Leave her here."

"She's a liability," he snarls.

Jake grabs my wrist and tugs me behind him. "I'll take care of it," he replies as he shoulder-checks the guard before running down a hallway. Alarms shrill and flash all around us.

"Jake, what's going on?"

He slams me against the wall and shoves his chest against mine. "You tell me. Who's attacking my facility?"

"*Your* facility?"

He grabs my shoulders and shakes me. "Who are they?"

"I don't know," I whimper as my neck screams.

An explosion goes off in the distance, and rubble sprinkles on top of us. "Fuck. They've breached the entrance." He pulls me behind him again. We stop in front of a door and he yanks it open. A young woman meets our eyes and hope rises in my chest. He's changed his mind and is releasing the other shifters.

"We're here to help," I promise my fellow wolf.

Jake's maniacal laughter sends a shiver up my spine. There's a click, followed by an ear-splitting boom as brain matter showers the walls and my chest. Before I can regain my sanity, he opens another door and aims.

"Jake…" I sputter past my hysteria. "Stop! You're better than this!"

He never lowers his weapon as he says, "Just tell me where the boy is." There's the warning *click*. "They all die, unless you tell me."

The weight of the world falls on my shoulders and crushes the oxygen out of my chest.

The girl drops to her knees as she sobs. "Please," she pleads with him. "I don't want to die."

My heart explodes as I imagine Hunter taking her place in this dungeon, chained to the wall unable to move, filth decorating his slim frame while he's forced to beg for his next meal.

"I can't," I whisper. "I have to protect my son."

The woman trembles but nods in understanding. I open my mouth to apologize, but her head shatters into a million gory pieces.

"Her death is on your hands," Jake growls, tugging me farther down the hallway to the next prisoner's cell.

I can't do this anymore. *Luna, save me from this nightmare.* I dig my feet into the ground.

"Well, well, well. If it isn't the General's spawn." A blonde shifter steps into our path. Blood drips from her fingertips.

Jake shoves me in front of him like a shield. "Back the fuck up." Cold steel kisses my temple.

The woman leans against the wall and picks her fangs like she has all the time in the world. "Using a defenseless woman as body armor is a dick move. You're a pussy just like your worthless father."

He ignores her taunts. "Let me leave safely and I'll release her."

Her shoulders rise and fall. "I've saved most of the shifters here. One life for the General's pussy-ass son's blood is well worth it," she snarls, talons extending from her fingertips.

"Aw, did Daddy leave a nasty taste in your mouth, bitch?" Jake cackles. "He did enjoy fucking his hostages." He tilts his head. "Tell me. Did he cut into your skin while he rode you? Dad loves to hear his woman scream while he slams home."

"You little…" She lunges at us. "How dare you!" She collides with me first, knocking Jake off balance. When he wavers, she throws my body out of her way. I roll until my shoulder hits a corner. I scream at the blinding pain. But the two are too busy tearing at each other's throats to notice.

Who is this shifter? Is she the leader of the rogue pack?

"Over here!" a female yells from the dark hallway.

275

I look towards the pair on the floor, then over to the mystery voice. *Shit. Should I save Jake?*

I focus on the crimson decorating his military uniform. No. His soul has been drenched in poisonous lies from his father. I run towards the shadow. Once I'm close enough, they pull me to safety.

"It's okay." They guide me to a ravine and set me on the sandy beach. "Here's some water."

I chug the cool liquid until I choke and cough.

"Easy. Try to take smaller sips."

I observe the area and the other freed shifters. The rogue pack was only able to rescue three females from the facility. I swallow the bile in my throat. I wonder how many are dead...

"Wolves incoming!" a voice warns, and the group circles us in a protective barrier. Two shadows slide to a stop at the edge of the woods. They cower and snarl. "Announce your intentions or face the consequences."

My maternal instincts kick in and I hug the other victims as they whimper and cover their ears. "It's okay." I try my best to soothe them. "You'll be all right."

The newcomers sniff the air and their gazes attempt to look past our guards before they land on us. The fur beast on the left shifts to two legs, and my eyes widen.

Am I seeing things?

Battle of the Beasts

Earlier…

Once we sneak past the sentries, Sable and I gallop through the woods, refusing to stop for anything. We are determined to get to the Pawson pack as quickly as possible. I know I'm going to get an earful from Frost when I return. That's if I make it back. But my main priority is to grab Lily and get her and Sable home, even if I have to sacrifice myself in the process.

The trees pass in a blur of green and brown. We're almost there, but it still feels like I'm not moving fast enough.

"What happens when Azure finds out his sister is gone?" I send down the mental pathway.

"My mom is covering for us. She's telling Azure that Lily isn't

sleeping well and that she prescribed her some medications to knock her out."

That won't buy us much time. Plus, if we don't make it back, we're now dragging Celeste down with us under this mountain of deceit.

Sable whimpers as the territory comes into view. My nose twitches with the acidic scent of blood. I force my limbs to extend farther as adrenaline courses through me. I can't lose Lily. I emerge from the bushes and stumble. Chaos encompasses the area. Smoke billows from homes. Chairs are overturned and broken. Panic increases with the thundering of my heartbeat.

Where is the Pawson pack?

I pop into the caves, only to find that mangled bodies litter the stone floors. This can't be happening. This family was full of elders. They were no threat to anyone. Who would inflict such a senseless act of violence?

Sable's snarl catches my attention. Two beasts exit Lily's old home. Blood drips from their dark fur. Did they hurt her? I join my fur brother's side, my hackles rising. They are going to pay for what they've taken from us. We circle the enemy. These creatures are unique. They don't smell like ordinary shifters, and they wear metal collars. They lunge for us, but we dodge their attack at the last second. They are quick to recover and charge forward again. Just as they leap into the air, they wince and crumble in a heap at our feet.

"Is this a trick?" I send down the wolf telepathy to Sable.

He tilts his head as the pair convulses. *"It looks like those collars are shocking them."*

Just as suddenly as it started, the strange wolves shake off their discomfort and limp away, appearing to track some tire prints embedded in the mud.

"We have to follow them!" Sable trots after the duo.

I take one last look at the destruction. There's no reason to linger here when there's nothing we can do for the dead. I gallop after Sable but falter when my nose twitches.

Is that Lily's scent? Could the beasts be guiding us to her?

There don't seem to be any survivors of the Pawson pack, but I also don't have time to identify the bodies. I sniff the air. Lily's scent is faint in this area. She may have been taken. But why?

Only one way to find out…

If the wolves leading the way know we're following them, they never let on to it. Once they slow to a walking pace, we fall back and watch from a distance, in case it's a trap. Sable finds tall brush to stand behind. We peek through the leaves and see the duo pause and howl. The ground vibrates until dirt clears and a hatch opens. A heavily armored man appears in front of them.

"What the fuck took you idiots so long?" he snarls. "Is the job done? No survivors?" The pair nods. "Good. Now get inside."

My heart sputters. *No* survivors. The word echoes in my head. Fuck.

Sable nudges my shoulder. *"Don't lose hope."*

"You heard them! What hope is there?"

"Hey! You all thought I was dead when I was kidnapped," he growls.

A twig snaps in the distance, cutting our argument short. And we watch as a group of shifters stride to the hidden door from across a field. Some of them shift and place devices in the ground. Then they move back and press a button, which seems to detonate the bombs, shaking the ground beneath our paws.

I squint. Some of the shifters look familiar. Where have I seen them before?

I step forward, but Sable shakes his head. *"Let them smoke out the enemy. If we need to interfere, we will. Right now, we're severely outnumbered."*

Alarms blare in the clearing and men scatter from underground. The wolves attack them without mercy. The rogue pack only pauses when the beasts from earlier return to the fight. An arrow soars from the tree line. It impales one in the shoulder. It winces, sways, then crumbles. Then the other one gets hit.

Are they dead? I lean forward to get a better look.

No. Their chests rise and fall. I raise my brow. So, they are murdering the soldiers, but not the wolves. Interesting.

My spine tingles as ragged females are guided out of the hidden bunker. They are seated by a lake and guarded by the pack.

"Is that Lily?" I whimper when her scent hits my nostrils.

"Can we risk rescuing her?" Sable winces. *"They took down an entire squad of trained soldiers."*

"We came here for her! I'm not backing down now!"

We stick to the shadows and attempt to sneak up on the group that appears to be recovering at the water's edge.

"Shifters incoming!" a voice calls out.

We freeze and curse as the group circles around the wounded. "Announce your intentions or face the consequences."

I share a look with Sable and he sighs. We morph into two feet with our hands raised. "We come in peace."

Dark hair pokes up from the crowd. "Jackson?"

That voice! "Lily!"

She steps through the barrier, but they grab her elbow. "It's not safe," they warn her.

I grind my jaw and step forward. "Let her go!"

Sable tugs at my wrist. "They're only trying to protect her. They don't know who we are."

Footsteps approach from the hidden door. A blonde strides over, dragging a limp soldier behind her. She tosses the body at the feet of the rogue pack. "Get him ready for transport."

The human moans as he comes to. "Let me go!"

The woman kneels and grabs his chin. "You don't get to tell me what the fuck to do." She nods to the others. "When I'm done with your sorry ass, I'm feeding you to the wolves. These defenseless women have been abducted, abused, and raped by your men and they aren't happy about it." Snarls echo off the trees. "I'll enjoy watching them rip you to shreds."

"You all don't know who I am," he stutters to the wounded women. "Who my father is."

She slaps him. "I know exactly who your father is, you little prick." She fists his torn uniform and lifts him into the air. "That fucker tortured me and stole my child from me."

"Wait, please!" Lily pleads.

The woman doesn't even look back. "Why?"

"I need to know if he hurt my Nana." Her lip quivers. "Please."

My face falls. She doesn't know yet.

The shifter holding the man growls. "Did you hurt her family?"

He swallows until she shakes him so hard his head bobs from side to side. "Yes!"

"How could you?" Tears stream down Lily's dirty face.

"Get him out of my sight." The blonde shoves the soldier to a waiting group of shifters.

"What about these two?" one of the women standing between me and Lily asks.

"What do we have here?" The blonde smirks as she saunters over to us. "Now that's a face I haven't seen in a while." She assesses Sable's naked body. "I would say it's nice to see you again, but the last time we were in a room together, you murdered my alpha."

I cringe at her deadly tone.

Sable tilts his head, seemingly unfazed. "Seeing as your mate sold me to the General and marked me for dead, we're even."

She shrugs. "I haven't seen Freddy in a long time, so you can't blame me for his life choices." She picks at her nail. "Last I heard, he was fucking your sister. How's that bitch doing?"

Sable snarls and leaps forward, but I hold him back. "Keep Sky out of this! Freddy ruined her and I'm happy to report he's dead!"

My head is spinning as I try to keep up. I know Freddy and Sky were seeing each other for years. Even after Sable killed Freddy's alpha, Spike, in a battle. But I don't recognize the blonde woman. Yet she claims to be Freddy's mate.

"Did you see Freddy's body? Because he seems to be more feline than canine with his nine lives. I doubt he's six feet under." The blonde arches a brow, daring us to prove her wrong.

"We need to move out, Angelica," another woman interjects.

Oh! That name rings a bell!

"What am I going to do with you two?" Angelica watches Sable. "Why are you even here?"

"We came to rescue a fellow pack member," I explain.

"And who are you?"

"Jackson. Beta of the Tala pack." I cringe. "Or at least I was. I disobeyed a direct order to save her."

The blonde nods approvingly. "Frost is a jackass. I don't think his reign will last long." She pivots towards the rescued females. "You have two choices, ladies. Join my cause and help others who are trapped like you were, or return to your packs. Either way, you are free to do as you please."

Once the guards step aside, I rush to Lily. I pick her up and she sobs into my neck. *Thank Luna she's all right.* I bury my nose in her hair. "I'm here," I soothe her.

"So, you're the alpha of the rebels," Sable blurts out to Angelica. "*Your* pack is murdering humans."

Her eyes are ablaze. "I'm releasing shifters who were stolen from their families to be bred like animals... *and* preventing their offspring from being turned into trained weapons."

"Angelica. I get it." Sable steps towards her. "They did the same thing to me. But we can't retaliate like this. We have to find peace."

"Fuck you and your fictitious ideals of peace." She waves him off. "We are moving out," she shouts at her pack before glaring at us. "You are not welcome to follow us. I'll only warn you once."

Sable joins me and Lily. "We need to get out of here before reinforcements arrive and we are blamed for the carnage."

I scan the bodies littering the perimeter. The rebels are leaving behind a message. Loud and clear. They're done being chained and forced to do their masters' biddings. I cling to Lily's shuddering frame. And she was almost added to that list.

"I'll carry her for as long as I can." I nod to Sable. "We can switch off until she can walk on her own, or until we make it back to the Tala pack."

He sighs. "Then we better get going."

We set a brisk pace, sticking to the shadows and heavily leaved areas to hide our footprints. My mind whirls. We've become prey. It's impossible to tell how far back this war has gone. The young man Angelica took hostage was at least a few decades old and his father was leading the abductions. The Guardians are going to have their paws full.

Lily whimpers in my arms and I kiss her head. I'm glad she's alive. I shudder at the reminder of the carnage left behind in the Pawson territory.

"We need to go back," she whispers.

"What?"

"Jackson." When I meet her tear-stained eyes, she continues, "We need to give my family a proper farewell." Her lip quivers. "They deserve that."

I brush a loose strand of hair from her brow. "Should we call Azure?"

She leans into my chest. "No. He should concentrate on healing. Plus, his wives will want to spend alone time with him afterwards."

"But don't you want him for support?"

Her fingertips dance over my stubble. "You're all I'll ever need." I press my forehead on hers and we share a breath. "Thank you for rescuing me."

"I'm sorry I couldn't save them too," I admit, then quickly return my attention to the task at hand.

We are blanketed by silence again. So much has happened in a short amount of time. It feels like a nightmare. All those shifters who've lost their lives…

Soon, we stumble upon the Pawson boundary and Lily tenses in my hold.

Now we have to say our goodbyes.

Lily

Burning Bright

Jackson came for me.

That thought hums softly in my chest as he carries me away from that horrible place. I shiver as my mind wanders from relief, to wondering what Angelica will do with Jake. I wish he could have tried to change his ways. But then the screams of the girls as they begged for their lives before he shot them causes chills to rack my body, and I'm not sure change was ever an option for the man I once considered a friend.

Jackson kisses my head and whispers to me. I snuggle into his neck. He disobeyed a direct order from Frost and risked everything to be here. Even with all the loss surrounding me, this glimmer of loyalty strains while holding my broken pieces together. I am wanted and worth being rescued.

I peek over at the alpha-in-training, Sable. He left his pregnant mate to assist the beta. My heart swells with pride. I'm lucky to call the Tala pack my family. Their love has no bounds.

Only when Jackson's arms spasm uncontrollably does he ask if he can pass me to Sable. After the events of today, the thought of another man's hands on me makes my skin crawl. Instead, I tell them that my legs are cramping and I walk between the two males. Jackson holds my hand as we push through the tall grass. The afternoon sun glimmers through the canopy of trees. It sparkles as it dances at our feet.

"We won't get there before nightfall if we don't shift," Sable groans.

Jackson side-eyes me. "Do you think you're feeling up to it?" His fingertips graze over the bump on my forehead before trailing down to my swollen elbow. "It might aggravate your wounds."

"But the sooner we get there, the quicker we can rest and let them heal properly," Sable interjects. "Stop babying her." He nudges the beta. "She's tougher than she looks."

"I know she is!" Jackson snarls. "But she deserves the choice, doesn't she?"

The corner of my lip twitches. They believe in me. More than I believe in myself, honestly. Exhaustion hums in my bones. But they've been running and fighting. I sigh. I can do this. For them, I'll dig deep for additional strength.

"Let's shift," I push out.

"Are you sure?" Jackson asks.

Sable smacks him. "What did I say about babying her? Damn, man. How she even looks your way is beyond me." He puffs out his chest. "Women love confidence."

"Fuck you." Jackson jabs the inflated male in the stomach. "Lily knows a real catch when she sees it." He winks at me. "Right?"

This conversation has taken a weird turn. But I laugh. They're ridiculous but it's nice that they're able to lighten the mood. So I play along. "I don't know. Sable does have a point."

"What?" Jackson frowns. "I'm the one who dragged his sorry ass to come and get you."

"If I remember correctly, I volunteered," Sable counters.

I love the way these two bicker. It reminds me of my brother. I swallow hard. I'm not looking forward to telling him what's been going on.

"Hurry up, slowpokes!" I shout before turning into fur and paws and bulleting through the forest with renewed confidence.

In order to make it to Tala territory, we are forced to trudge through what remains of the Pawson pack. It's a massacre. Limbs litter the picnic tables. Fur and flesh decorate the walking path. I pinch my eyes closed. This is my fault. If I would have just...

A head rubs against my chest, and I meet Jackson's canine gaze. *"They did this. It's not right, but it's done. Now let's give them a respectable farewell."*

My legs shake before I shift and run to a pine tree, towards Nana's prone form. She could be sleeping, if her neck wasn't at an odd angle. I cradle her cold body like she's done to me so many times before.

"Oh, Nana." I remain by her side as the boys continue to clean the area of debris. The smell is rancid, even with us wrapping discarded shirts around our noses. It's too much. We agree it'll be best to cremate the pack in the open field. Soon, the fire burns bright, the resulting heat warming my hands.

"We can do this if you want to go wash up." Jackson rubs my back. "The scent of burning flesh isn't great."

"There's a cave at the end of the mountain that's untouched," Sable offers. "And we can watch the door from here."

"Thank you," I whisper to the flames as they lick the darkening sky.

"Do you want me to walk you over there?" Jackson asks, ignoring Sable's groan of annoyance.

"No. I'll be all right." Although I'm not sure if I will be. I've lost so much.

"I'll watch over the process until the flames die down," Sable adds. "After the heavy lifting is done, Jackson can nap for a few hours with you. Then he can relieve me so I can get a few hours in too."

My eyes water before I throw my arms around them. What more can I do? They've both given up a lot to be here for me. "I'm grateful to have you guys in my life."

We separate and I head towards the empty den. I pause to look over my shoulder. Jackson's watching me with a twinkle in his gaze. He nods, encouraging me to place one foot in front of the other. And I do.

I viciously scrub the day off in the shower as quickly as I can manage. I don't want to linger too long because I'm sure the boys want some hot water too. I slip under the covers of the queen bed and stare at the ceiling.

I can't believe the government is training shifters to destroy their own kind. I nibble my lip. But it seems like Angelica isn't making it easy on them. From what I've heard, she's been demolishing every facility she can get her paws on. She rescues the wolves, murders the soldiers, and sets the buildings on fire after she raids them for information. Rumor has it she also has a sizeable army at her disposal.

"Lily?" Jackson whispers from the door.

I sit up on the pillow. "What's wrong?"

"I didn't want to wake you up when I took a shower."

"I'm so wired from today's events, I don't think I'll fall asleep anytime soon."

He steps towards the bathroom and pauses. "Should I find somewhere else to rest?"

It takes me a minute to understand what he's asking me. There aren't many habitable places free of gore.

I move to one side of the bed. "You can sleep here if you want."

"Are you sure?"

"Of course."

His face lights up before he ducks into the other room and starts the water. I smirk as I lean against the headboard. It's nice to make him smile like that. If I painted the scene, I'd call it "Wolf Love." The background would be a soft gray and Jackson's naked torso would be front and center.

I shake the image away. No. I'm not going back to that.

Why not? A tiny voice questions in the back of my head. And I begin to wonder that myself.

The mattress sinks down and startles me out of my internal dialogue. "I'm sorry. I thought you heard me leave the bathroom," Jackson says.

"It's not your fault." I pat the empty side. "I was lost in my head."

He burrows beside me, then wraps an arm around my shoulder before tugging me to his sculpted chest. The steam from the shower warms my back. He glides his hand over my arm. "Do you want to talk about it?"

I shake my head. "I can't. I'm afraid I'll have nightmares."

"I'll protect you, even from those."

I turn to face him. "I believe that." My fingertips trail his chiseled jaw. He leans into my touch and kisses my palm. Sparks shoot to my toes and I shiver. He drags his lips down my arm. I moan softly as they graze my collarbone.

"Do you want me to help you tire yourself out so you can rest?" he whispers against my neck.

I squeeze my thighs together as my core ignites. It'd be easy to fall into a sexual relationship with Jackson. But I have a son I have to think about. Whatever relationship I choose to jump into should start with the intention of being permanent, and I know that's not how the beta sees it.

"Jackson, I'm not sure if that's a good idea."

"Are you afraid I might hurt you?"

"No," I say more forcefully than I mean to. "I trust you."

"Good." He dips below the covers. "If I trigger any painful memories, just warn me and I'll stop."

I open my mouth to protest until he cups my breast with his warm palm. He tweaks my nipples until I'm arching my back off the bed.

"Jackson," I breathe out, not sure if I'm asking him to stop or continue lower. There are so many mixed emotions, and my brain is short-circuiting.

"Shh. Let me take care of you." He eases between my legs before resting my thighs on his shoulders. He dips to my waist, then pauses. I'm panting, waiting for the blissful full contact, but he starts *laughing* instead.

What's going on? I attempt to put distance between us but Jackson holds me in place.

"Why didn't you tell me you had another tattoo?" He smirks.

It takes me a minute to process what he's saying. Then I chuckle. "You mean the one that says *if you can read it, eat it*? I got that while I was away at college."

"Lily, what did they teach you in college?" Jackson taunts.

"To be myself and have no shame in my talents or sexuality."

"That sounds like a damn good time."

"It was." I wring the sheet between my fingers. "You know the man Angelica took as a hostage today?"

Jackson tilts his head. "The military guy? What about him?"

"His name is Jake and we kind of dated casually throughout college."

He arches a brow. "Isn't he younger than you?"

"So what?"

"You do realize I'm younger than you too, right?"

"What are you insinuating?"

"That you're a bit of a cougar."

"Jackson! It's not my fault if I attract younger men."

"Was he even a *man* when you had sex with him?" The beta cackles as I smack him. "I'm just saying."

"He was of legal age, jerk." After a few more chuckles at my expense, I turn the conversation around. "What about you and Ashely?"

"We were the same age."

"I saw the pictures of her in your home. She's beautiful."

"Beautiful and stubborn." Jackson snorts. "She always had to have it her way."

"I guess that's the kind of woman you fall for."

"Why do you say that?"

"Uh, hello. You and Carly."

"She's a pain in my ass. But now she's Sky and Azure's emotional complication."

It seems like everyone has found their mates around here. Even Jackson and me… at one point.

"Do you ever think how cruel it was that our relationships with our mates didn't work out? I mean, I know our reasons were different. Mine was abusive and yours died during childbirth," I whisper into the darkness.

"Yeah." Jackson sighs as he considers my words. "But maybe it was supposed to be this way, so we could find each other in the end." He traces the scar on my neck. "I miss Ashely, and I know you regret meeting Brock but I'm happy to be where I am."

"And where are you?" I arch a brow.

He offers me a mischievous grin. "About to *eat it* because I can *read it*."

"You're never going to let me live that down, are you?"

"Are you kidding me? It's an open invitation to make you howl. I love it."

"Well, maybe we should get you one too?"

"And what would mine say?"

"Lick it before you stick it."

Jackson bursts into a fit of laughter. "I think you missed your calling as a comedian." He wipes the sides of his eyes.

"We should try to get some sleep," I remind him. "I'm sure Sable will want to rest soon too."

"But I didn't show you my secret way to help you exhaust yourself."

The playful smile curling Jackson's lips tells me he isn't talking about a cup of warm milk. I bite my lip as I zero in on his mouth.

How long has it been?

His fingertips dance over my arms and desire pools at my core. "Am I making you feel uncomfortable?" He watches my chest rise and fall in rapid succession.

"No," I breathe out.

He runs his tongue over the soft spot of my neck. I moan and arch my back, allowing him full access. I cringe. Fuck me. I shouldn't be this horny, considering the day I've had.

Jackson ceases his caress, misinterpreting my hesitation.

"Do you trust that I won't hurt you?" Jackson meets my heated gaze. "Because I can wait, as long as you need, and I don't mind proving to you that I'm safe."

I close the distance between us and kiss him gently. I pull back, but he groans and yanks me to him again. He devours my mouth, leaving me breathless.

"Answer me." His chest heaves like he's hanging on by a thread. One word and he'll snap the tethered leash and ruin me in the most delicious way.

I lean into the pillows, Jackson's gaze never leaving mine. Then I spread my legs with a wicked grin. He's reawakened that crazy sex ninja in me who's been dormant for so long. Too long. Jackson practically drools as he recognizes my submission.

"I trust you, Jackson," I purr. "Now show me what that magical tongue can do."

Jackson

Connections

There's something truly magical about hearing the woman you've had a boner for, for months, give you permission to service her. It's freeing. Mind-blowing. I don't wait a single second to allow her to question her decision. I soak in her glorious mom bod. I trace her stretch marks. They reiterate how she's a badass having carried and given life. My knuckle pinches her nipple and I'm rewarded with a moan. The same breasts that once offered sustenance to her pup. She's amazing.

"I'm going to mouth-fuck you until you pass out." She shivers at my dirty talk, and I lift a brow in question. "Is that what you want?"

"Yes." Her hips wiggle, begging me to follow through on my promise.

I'm the predator and she's my next meal. I spread her legs. Her glistening center drips with her eagerness. My gaze gets caught on her tattoo again. I fight the urge to growl.

How many men have seen this before me?

I shake the thought from my head. Why am I getting possessive? I'm the one-night stand wolf, who helps out unclaimed females in the area. This shouldn't bother me. But it does. The last time I was like this was with my mate.

"Jackson," Lily whimpers. "Please."

My spine tingles. I love hearing my name on her lips. I never want that to change.

"I want all of you, Butterfly." I rub my calloused palm over her sensitive bud. "You're *mine* and I'm yours."

Lily jolts up and pulls away from me like I've burned her, which was not the reaction I was hoping for.

"Actually, I'm really tired." Her voice cracks. "I'm just going to go to sleep." She's pale and her skin is ice cold.

Shit. What the fuck did I do wrong? I replay the conversation in my head. Everything was going so great. Does she *not* want a permanent relationship with me?

The problem is I know that once I get a taste of her, I'll be drowning and never want to leave.

I settle behind her, pressing my chest to her back. "Hey. Talk to me." I place soft kisses on her shoulder. "Tell me what triggered you?"

The silence is suffocating. I want to shake her and demand to know what I did. To remind her that I'm always going to be here for her, no matter what. Her body shakes as she sobs into her hands.

I stroke her hair. "It's been a long, emotional day. Just close your eyes and rest. I'll be here when you wake up." I pull the comforter over us as I continue to hold her. I yawn and that's when the exhaustion finally hits me. I can't keep my eyes open. I'm so damn tired.

"He used to call me that," Lily whispers so quietly I think she's talking in her sleep. "When he raped me."

My heart splinters and my jaw ticks. No shifter should take advantage of the sacred mating bond like that. No means no. I kiss her neck so she knows I'm still listening.

"The military fucked him up." She sniffles. "They broke him. Then he broke me."

"You're not broken. You're just in the process of healing. It hurts like a bitch, but it's what we have to do. Do you remember what Nana told me all those years ago? We can't run from our pain."

"I miss her."

"I know you do, Lil. But we'll get through this. I promise."

"How?"

"Through our art," I say, and her body goes rigid again. "Don't tell me he ruined that for you too?"

"Yes," she whispers.

"You have to stop letting him run your life. Do what you want and move through the trauma."

"That's easier said than done," she huffs but relaxes into my hold.

"Nothing in life is ever easy. But with the right support system, you can accomplish anything."

Lily turns to face me, eyes assessing mine. "Do you really believe that?"

I run a hand down her face. "Absolutely."

"What if I want to go to the moon?"

I chuckle and shake my head. "I guess we need to buy spacesuits then."

She caresses my arm while appearing lost in thought. "I do want to paint again."

I kiss her nose. "I think that's a great idea. Plus, it's a good way for you to remember your old pack." She arches a brow. "I've seen artists sprinkle their loved one's ashes into their pigment before creating masterpieces. Then they hang them in the house. It makes the deceased feel closer."

"I like that idea." She nibbles her bottom lip. "But it's been so long. Will I even remember how to hold a paintbrush?"

"I'll teach you how to handle it." I wink.

She blinks a few times, until she realizes my double meaning. Her fingertips slither to my manhood before wrapping around it and giving me a good tug. I hiss and thrust into her palm. "How's this, teacher?"

She's a tease. I love it. "That's good, but if you use your mouth, I'll give you extra credit."

Lily laughs and the sound lights up the room. "You're so bad."

"You're the one grabbing my dick."

"But you suggested I pop it into my mouth." She wipes the corners of her eyes. "We are the perfect pair."

"I agree." My thumb lifts her chin. "And whenever you're ready, I want to date you."

"Well, you do realize what that means, right?"

"That we can fuck whenever we want."

"Jackson…" she whines.

"Oh, I can watch you shower and offer to help you with all those hard-to-reach areas." I grab a fistful of her ass.

She smacks my chest. "We have to tell Hunter and Azure."

She just had to bring up her blue idiot of a brother. He warned me to be a gentleman around her, so he'd probably frown at the fact I want to feast on her pussy while she screams my name.

"I'll tell Hunter and Ash. You tell your brother."

"We should tell them together."

"But he'll zap me again," I groan.

She grabs my wrist and places it on her breast. "I think I'm worth a tiny zap."

I massage her flesh, tweaking her nipple to a peak. "You think very highly of yourself." She moans and her head falls back. I take the opportunity to place kisses down her body. She's delectable. "I'm going to need a sample before I agree to dying at your brother's hands."

"I'm yours," she announces breathlessly. "Do what you must."

I spread her legs and begin feasting like a starving man. She gasps with the ferocity of my nips. My tongue slips into her folds and her nectar coats it before I swallow her down.

Luna save me. She's right. Lily's definitely worth the painful death Azure is sure to sentence me to when he finds out what I've done.

She drags her hands through my hair and tugs, creating delicious pain on my scalp. My palms slide under her ass before pressing her core as close as possible to my lips. I could die like this. With her thighs squeezing my face.

She quivers and digs her claws into my skin before exploding in my mouth. She rides the waves of pleasure, then hums softly into the pillow. I peek up at her, ready to give her another orgasm. But she's fast asleep. I pull the covers over us and hold her close. Then I join her in dreamland.

A few hours later, Sable wakes me to take over the night watch.

"Is the fire out?" I ask, rubbing the sleep from my tired eyes.

He nods. "It's been quiet, but I'll feel better when the sun rises, and we get back home." He sniffs the air before sending me a glare. "You're an idiot."

"What else is new?" I smirk, knowing he likely smells Lily's scent on me.

He pinches the bridge of his nose. "Are you trying to die?"

"Nope."

"Why can't you think with more than just your dick?" he snarls. "Don't you think our pack has enough bullshit to deal with without you fucking the Guardian's sister?"

I narrow my eyes at him. "Since when did you become a fan of Azure's? If I recall correctly, he ignored your plea to help you find Maya when she was abducted. Then you almost became the General's pet when he couldn't locate you properly." I jab a finger into Sable's chest. "Lily deserves to be happy too."

"And you think you'll make her happy, Mr. I'll-Sleep-With-Anyone."

"Where I stick my dick is none of your concern," I snap back.

"Except it is, since I'm next in line to become alpha and have to deal with the consequences of said dick-sticking."

We stare each other down. We're both tired and should let this go. But not until I make him see reason.

"I want to be with Lily and *only* Lily. I want her to move into my den so I can hear her laugh when she paints again. Damn it. I deserve to be happy just as much as everyone else does!"

The demand simmers around us before he nods. "Whatever, man. Just stay the hell away from Maya."

I smirk as he pivots towards the shower. I'm never going to stop poking the beast when it comes to his wife. It's just too easy to get a rise out of him.

Soon, the sun kisses the world with orange and red hues, warming the air around me.

"Mind if I join you?" Lily sits next to me on the log overlooking the lake. The same spot where we met all those years ago.

"How did you sleep?" I can't withhold my grin as she blushes.

"Sable snores. I don't know how Maya puts up with it."

I smirk. "She's stuck with him, especially with a pup on the way."

The light twinkles in Lily's eyes. Even with all the lingering death surrounding her, she looks happy. Or maybe that's the post-orgasm glow talking?

"We should probably hunt for breakfast. It's been a while since we've had a good meal." Lily nods to the lake. "We could catch some fish. Or there are usually some rabbits scurrying around the meadow."

Honestly, it'd be more logical to hunt small game. But to see Lily naked and dripping wet is a far more enjoyable idea. I stand and stretch my sore limbs. I glance back at the cave. "Do you think Sable will be safe while we fish?"

She ignores me and dives into the calm surface. When she reemerges, she already has a scaley meal in her palm. "Hurry up, slowpoke."

I take the bait and cannonball beside her.

"Hey! You're scaring away the fish!" She splashes my face. We make it a competition and soon have eight flopping trout on the shore, ready to be cooked. "I'll race you to the other side of the lake," Lily challenges. Her smile is contagious.

"We really should fry these up before Mr. Sourpuss wakes up."

"You're just afraid you'll lose." She paddles off.

I grunt but follow behind her. Lily looks back and winks. It does amazing things to my man bits. By the time she pivots from the other end, I'm right beside her. Before she can gloat about her win, I crush my lips to hers. Lily wraps her arms around my neck and opens wide for my tongue to explore. I groan against her teeth. She rubs against my erection, and I almost combust. After everything that's happened between us over the last few hours, I'm on the verge of blue balls.

"Lily," I warn as I steady her hips.

Her heated gaze meets mine. The early sun's rays glimmer and dance around us. It's a perfect moment. "I want this," she whispers.

My heart pounds. *Is she saying what I think she's saying?*

"What exactly do you want, Butterfly?"

"I want you to make love to me, right now."

The demand slams into my chest. *Well, shit. Don't have to tell me twice.*

I tease her entrance with my tip. "Is this what you want?"

She eases against me, pushing my length a little more into her channel. "Yes."

I hiss at the sudden tightness. My cock throbs, weeping to go deeper. "We're taking it slow. I don't want to hurt you." I'm not sure if I'm telling her or my overly eager dick.

"That's not how I like to fuck," is my only warning before Lily takes charge. She pierces herself on my rod and gasps. Then she rolls her hips to a steady tempo. "It's been so long," she says to herself. "Too *long*."

"I know. He's quite impressive, isn't he?" I dig my fingers into her ass. "But, sweetheart, you haven't seen nothing yet." I take over the motions and ride her hard.

Her moans are the only things I hear and they make a beautiful symphony. She clenches around me and screams her release. The pressure sets off my own orgasm and I see stars. I hold Lily to my chest as we share breaths.

Once my heart stops pounding, I stroke her hair. "Is that what you wanted?"

She purrs against me. Her fingertip traces my bicep. "Thank you."

Well, that's a first. No one has ever thanked me for getting them off. I shrug. But I'll take it.

She meets my gaze. "Thank you for everything," she clarifies. "Especially for proving that I'm worth saving."

"I'll always come to your rescue." I hug her tight. "Now, let's eat so we can return home."

We make it ashore, and I toss together a fire while Lily cleans the fish. Once the fresh meat sizzles in the pan, Sable stirs from the cave and joins us. He arches a brow as Lily and I hold hands but is smart enough to keep his mouth shut about it.

"Good morning, Sleeping Beauty," I tease him. He bites into his breakfast and gives me a grunt in response.

"Sable, can you grab some of the ashes from the funeral pyre for me? That way, I can bring some back to the Tala pack?" Lily asks.

He meets her sad eyes and nods. "No problem."

"Thank you." She brushes dirt off her knees. "I'm going to see if there's anything salvageable to give to Hunter to remind him of our family."

"Do you want me to come with you?" I step towards her.

"No, I'll be okay." She pecks me on the cheek, then she walks to the caves.

When she's out of earshot, Sable gives me a pointed stare. I glare back. "What?"

"You know damn well what," he grumbles. "You're seriously going to travel back home with her scent on you and yours on her?"

"Why? Should I mix yours in too? I bet Maya would love that."

He growls. "Leave her out of this."

"Calm down." I pat his shoulder but he brushes me off. "We're planning on explaining everything to Azure anyway. Why not leave him a few hints?"

"If he tears you to pieces…" Sable warns.

"Then you won't have to worry about me stealing Maya." I pause for dramatic effect. "Again." The alpha-in-training leaps from his spot and tackles me. "Careful, Sable. Or you might get Lily's scent on you too."

We wrestle in the grassy field until Lily scolds us. "You two are no better than a couple of pups! Stop bickering like children."

I separate from my fellow shifter and shake off the dead leaves littering my body. That's when I notice what Lily's holding. "Is that a photo album?"

She clutches the book to her chest. "It was in Nana's room. It has pictures of my mom and dad and my brother and me."

I wrap an arm around her waist. "I bet Hunter will love to have it."

"Let's get going. I don't want to spend any more time with *you*."

Sable shoulder-checks me. "I'd rather be with my mate. No offense, Lily," he adds.

"None taken. I'm pretty sick of him too."

I clutch my chest. "Ouch."

Her smile is bright as she presses her lips over mine to ease the sting of her words. "I'm joking."

"Bad joke," I mumble.

"I'll make it up to you when we're alone." She wags her eyebrows.

My dick stirs at all the possibilities. "Oh, really? Dare I ask how you plan on making it up to me?"

"What do you want, Stinky?"

That fucking nickname!

Sable's booming belly laugh shakes the ground. "Stinky?" He slaps my back. "I can't wait to tell everyone your pet name."

My harsh reply is on the tip of my tongue but dies there at the sound of Lily's soft giggles. Her joy warms my heart. I tug her to my chest. "You're going to pay for that later."

She purrs against my neck. "I look forward to it."

Lily

New Beginnings

The trip to the Tala pack is slow. Not only are we tired, but the emotional drain of the last few days weighs heavily around us. Every now and then, the soreness between my legs reminds me that it wasn't the *worst* week of my life. Jackson risked everything to rescue me. He even challenged the alpha's command because he believed that I was worth saving. I let a smile spread over my muzzle. It feels amazing to have someone put me first.

"Whatcha thinking about over there?" the man in question teases.

"Nothing," I fib and pick up the pace.

"Well, that nothing needs to stop," Sable grumbles. *"Because we can smell what you're not thinking about."*

I cringe. It's been so long I'd forgotten how wolves can detect your arousal. I decide to shift my thoughts to what masterpiece I'm going to create with the ashes Sable gave me. It should be colorful but also meaningful. Maybe Hunter will want to help me? Speaking of the pup, I miss him. I've never been away from him this long before.

We crest the top of a wide hill and take in the grassy meadow. Sable lifts his nose into the air before he howls from the depths of his throat. Jackson and I join in on the welcome, alerting the pack that we are on our way. Jackson nuzzles my neck while the orange and red hues touch the rest of the world. The sun warms my heart, and for once, I'm optimistic about my future. It won't be perfect. We still need to figure out how to deal with the government and the rebels. But for now, peace settles in my soul.

"This is Willow Hill," Jackson says as I gaze into the vast area. I never realized how much land the Tala pack guarded. *"We share the property with the natives, and the reservation is home to many protected plants and animals."*

There's a whirlwind of vibrant colors swaying in the breeze from the array of flowers. Between the stems, rabbits leap in search of clovers, and mice scurry with nuts in their mouths. It's dazzling, a painting waiting to be splashed onto a canvas.

A deep howl echoes in the valley, reminding us of our waiting relatives. It's time to face the consequences of our actions. We trudge towards the caves. I left the territory with no plans to return. Sable and Jackson snuck out in the dead of night and against Frost's orders. This should be interesting.

As we turn the corner, a crowd of shifters emerges, and I pray no blood is shed.

"Mom!" Hunter chokes me with his death grip. I guess he missed me too. What I didn't expect was the huge alligator tears wetting my fur. He never cries.

I shift to two legs and cradle my son in my arms. "It's okay, baby. I'm here."

"You left without saying goodbye," he wails.

I rock him back and forth. "I'll never leave without telling you again."

"You promise?" He pulls back to meet my gaze.

I swipe his wet cheeks. "I promise."

"Sable!" Maya squeals as he twirls her around. When he sets her on the ground, he devours her mouth and I look away to give them their well-deserved moment.

I pivot and see Ash and Jackson embracing too. This is going a lot better than I hoped.

"There are steaks on the grill." Raven hugs us. "While they're cooking, why doesn't everyone come inside so we can discuss how your impromptu trip went?" The alpha's wife guides us into her home.

Jackson pats the kids' shoulders. "Why don't you help set up the barbecue while the adults talk?"

Hunter looks to me and I give him an encouraging nod. He follows Ash to the picnic tables as we enter Raven's den. Sable and Maya snuggle together on the love seat while Jackson and I take the couch. Frost paces the living room, anger radiating off his tense shoulders. Once we settle into the plush cushions, his rage erupts.

"What the fuck were you thinking?" he snarls in my direction.

"It's a long story," I squeak.

"And you didn't think to share it with me before shit hit the fan and shifters lost their lives?" he roars. "You placed our packs in danger because you were selfishly withholding information."

My throat constricts and I focus on my feet. He's right. I'm so

313

foolish.

"Frost..." Jackson starts. "Lily had no idea how far this operation went."

"And you." Frost points at his beta. "I gave you a direct order to stand down."

"Well, *we* didn't agree with your choice." Maya leaps to her feet. "Dad, how could you allow Lily to go on her own like that? She's one of us and was begging for help."

"It was too dangerous," he yells. "And that was not your call to make. You are the alpha-in-training, emphasis on *training*."

"Honey, I think we all need to just take a breath," Raven coos. "What's done is done. Now is the time to catch up on what has transpired and move on."

We hold our breath as the alpha grinds his molars, his gaze bouncing from one shifter to the other.

"There will be consequences." Frost glares at us. "You four will have extra guard duty, pup patrol, and are prohibited from leaving the territory until I say otherwise. Do I make myself clear?" We nod. "Now tell me what the hell happened."

Jackson squeezes my hand, encouraging me to answer.

Here goes nothing.

I retell my tale. Every heart-breaking moment. And when my sobs choke the air from my lungs and tears drown out my voice, Jackson holds me until I regain enough composure to continue. Until all of my pitifully broken shards lay at the alpha's paws.

"I'm sorry I didn't tell you sooner," I breathe out my conclusion.

To my surprise, Maya squeezes me into a hug. "You were forced to be strong for so long, Lily. But now's your time to let someone else take that burden for a while." She dabs a tissue on my cheek. "Let us support and provide that for you."

Her words are a magnet for my shattered parts. I meet her gaze. She's speaking from experience. I tilt my head, and Maya gives me a knowing smile.

"One day, I'll share my tale with you," she promises.

"I look forward to that."

The door slams open, causing us to jump. "Lily?" Azure runs over and smashes my face to his chest.

I rub his back. "How are you healing, brother?"

"Celeste gave me the vaccine and I'll be able to shift soon."

"That's wonderful news."

He pulls away and looks me over. His gaze lingers on the bump on my forehead and the various bruises on my arms. "What happened?"

In the corner of my eye, I see everyone around us share a look of concern before they all turn to Jackson. "How about we go for a walk, and I'll tell you?" I grab my brother's wrist and tug him towards the exit.

The others follow us outside but quickly detour to the food. Carly and Sky step towards Azure but he shakes his head, and they too join the growing crowd around the picnic tables.

"How bad is it?" he asks me.

I stop in front of the large oak tree with those haunting tics marking our lost loved ones. I'll soon be adding more to its trunk.

"It's soul-crushing." I let out a breath. "But it's nothing we can't handle, together, as a pack." Azure tenses but lets me continue. I offer him my palm. "I want you to witness everything through my memories."

"Are you sure?"

I can only nod. He doesn't know I just told the others what happened and that I have no energy to verbalize it again. My brother offers me a comforting smile before he closes his eyes and inhales. I watch as the blue lines adorning his body shimmer, and a warmth travels up my arm, to my neck, and then spreads across my head. The mystical force sucks me into my memories as if I am reliving them. My brother sees everything, from Brock's abuse to my recent trip to the Pawson pack, and finally their devastating end.

When the reel of events concludes on itself, Azure stumbles and clutches the sides of his head. "No… How could this have happened?"

"I'm sorry," I whisper before wiping my cheeks. "I went there to save them, not destroy the family."

Laughter breezes over from the barbecue and my brother locks eyes with the beta. He shifts and gallops towards him. "Azure! Stop!"

My warning shout gives Jackson a second to shred to fur before he's hit full-force by my twin. They tumble head over tail until my brother has my boyfriend pinned to the ground. He snarls and snaps at the other wolf's neck. Anger builds in the back of my throat. I stomp to the dog pile.

After reviewing all those memories, does Azure comfort me or even apologize for being a shitty brother?

Nope. Instead, he attacks the only man to stand up for me.

I shift to fur before I headbutt my dumbass brother with all my might, my actions fueled by rage. He jolts to the side, freeing Jackson.

"What the fuck is wrong with you?" I mentally roar at Azure.

"I warned Jackson that if he tried anything with you…"

I snap at his muzzle. *"Shut up! Who told you that you had a say in my love life?"*

"Lil…"

"Don't Lily me! Instead of judging me, how about you offer condolences for my lost mate?"

As my words hit him, he lowers his head. *"I'm sorry."*

I sigh my rage out through my nose, then rub my forehead over his shoulder. *"Don't be sorry. Just be there for me. I need my big brother, especially right now."*

Azure takes in the crowd building around us. He pauses on Hunter's tear-stained face. *"You're right. I'll be a better sibling and uncle."*

"And you owe Jackson an apology," I add. Azure narrows his eyes at the beta. *"He saved my life."*

My brother shakes the dirt from his dark fur. *"I'll consider apologizing."*

I roll my eyes but stride towards Jackson and nuzzle the cuts on his neck. *"Are you okay?"*

"Yeah. He's just a big puppy." He smirks at Azure's back.

"If everyone is done trying to kill each other, we can eat." Raven uses her mom tone to get us back in line.

We morph to two feet and settle in with Hunter and Ash, eager to dig into the buffet. Azure scrapes his plate with his fork, his mood clearly still soured. He hasn't even looked my way since I separated him and Jackson. I peek over at the beta, who is acting normal, shoveling beans into his mouth as his son warns him about the gas it'll cause later.

"I'm sorry for your loss," Sky offers from beside her husband. "I know the Pawson pack was filled with many compassionate shifters who will all be greatly missed."

"Thank you, Sky." I nibble my dinner roll. "The food is amazing. Did it come from your restaurant?"

"Yes, it did!" Carly sings. "You should try the gluten-free, double-fudge brownies. They're my favorite."

"Don't lie," Jackson teases. "Your favorites were those *fun*-shaped cookies you made for Valentine's Day." He wiggles his brows, until she throws a spoon at him.

"You're just jealous that I could deep throat 'em and you couldn't." She sticks out her tongue.

"Mom, what's *deep throat* mean?"

"It's when—" Carly starts to say, and I quickly cut her off.

"I'll explain it when you're older." I give my sister-in-law a pointed stare.

"Can we go play freeze tag with my friends?" Ash asks Jackson.

"It's okay with me. What about you?" He elbows my side.

"Just don't be too rough with the other pups. Most of them are younger than you are."

They run towards a small group of fur children. Once the boys are close, they turn around, aim their rears, and fart at their friends. There are shouts of shock, followed by roars of laughter.

"Charming." Skylar smirks.

"So, boss man." Carly nods towards Frost. "What are we going to do about this rebel group?"

"Don't call me that," the alpha snips.

"We can't let them continue to attack the humans," she urges.

I share a look with Jackson. I hate to think about it, but those humans deserve what's coming to them. Even if my college bestie is included in the mix. Especially after experimenting and breeding shifters.

Jackson clears his throat. "Carly, this really isn't the time to discuss that."

"What has your underwear in a bunch? You got the girl, and you can have your second-chance romance." She jabs at him.

Azure bristles before glaring at his wife. "Lily is not an object to be owned."

"Ha! That's hilarious coming from you, husband. You're always grunting about how I'm *your* wife. Blah, blah, blah."

"Those are completely different circumstances," my brother grumbles.

"Why?" She pokes him.

"Because they'll never marry." He gestures a thumb in my direction.

My hackles rise. "And who the hell are you to say we won't marry?"

Carly snickers into her napkin.

"If we decide to tie the knot, it'll be a choice *we* make, not you."

"Lily," my brother whines. "You can't honestly say you'd choose him."

I smirk at Jackson's barbeque-sauce-stained grin. "Only time will tell."

After dinner, the pack gathers around the towering oak tree as Frost adds more tic marks to its bark. Tears blur my vision as each one indents into the wood. I can't believe they're gone.

The candles flicker and a violinist strums in the distance. Hunter leans into me and I rub his back. Nana and Jackie helped me give birth to him, aided me in teaching him how to shift, and they never missed a single moment in his young life. Until now.

I dab the corners of my eyes. They are with Mom and Dad, enjoying a pain-free retirement. My fingertips glide over the rough surface. I wonder if Brock is there too? I know what he did to me was unkind but maybe, deep down, he was a good guy? I steal a glance at my son. I think he had to be, considering how his genes created an amazing pup.

I wrinkle my nose when a stench wafts my way. Hunter grins, owning up to the toxic toot in question. Really? This child. His smile reminds me of Azure and the many Dutch ovens my brother gave me growing up. I nod towards my twin and elbow Hunter to hint that he should let one rip around his favorite uncle.

"That was mean." Jackson chuckles against my neck as Hunter sits next to Azure.

"Hey, my brother deserves that and so much more."

"He loves you. You know that, right?"

"I know." I sigh. "He just doesn't always show it."

"No one is perfect. Not even one of Luna's Guardians." Jackson leads me to the area where everyone is swaying to the soft music. He wraps his arms around my waist. "So, what's next for us?"

"More sex?" I smirk.

He brushes his lips over mine. "Sounds good to me." He moves to the beat. "We should probably go on a date too."

"Where did you have in mind?"

"My bedroom." He grins.

"That's not a good spot for a first date."

"Well, can it conclude in my room?"

"Sure, and I'll have Carly bring some cookies by, to deep throat for dessert." I wink at him.

He groans and adjusts himself. "Stop teasing. Your brother already hates me."

"He'll warm up to you. He has no choice."

We glance towards Azure as he laughs with Carly and Sky. He pauses as if he knows we're watching him and meets my gaze. He smiles and waves.

"See? He's already starting to accept you."

Jackson grabs a fistful of my ass and I squeal. Azure glares daggers at him. "I like it better *this* way."

"You're impossible."

Lily

First Date

A few days later, I finally begin a new routine. The loss of my pack is still heavy on my heart, but the grief comes in waves.

I sip my coffee. *Damn, it's good.* Jackson knows how to make an amazing cup of joe. I breathe in his fading musky scent. A ripple of pleasure tingles my spine. Ever since we returned to the Tala pack, he's been busier than ever. Especially with the extra chores the alpha has thrown at him. Jackson has been gone from sunrise to past sunset for the last two days. Poor guy is exhausted.

"Good morning, wolf-in-law." Carly dances through the front door. She kisses my cheek. "Did you sleep better last night?" She nibbles her lips. "If not, I can give you some more alcohol."

Even after revealing all my secrets, I still have lingering nightmares. But when I wake up, Jackson always helps settle me with his magical tongue.

I hold up a palm. "No, thank you. I think I've drunk enough alcoholic beverages in my day to know how to stay away from *that* poison for a while."

"Whatever you want, sweets." She rustles through the kitchen cabinets. "Do you have any honey?"

"Why do you want *honey*?"

She twirls around and a grin brightens her face. "It makes giving a blow job a lot tastier."

Coffee spittle drips past my lips. "What?"

"It's where you take the guy's penis and…"

"I know what *it* is." I wave my hands around. "Shh… my child may be listening."

Carly shrugs. "He has this magical thing called the internet. If he doesn't know by now, he'll know soon enough."

I mentally check *a phone* off the list of things I was planning on buying him when he turned ten. No way is he going to know what *that* is before he's in college.

"You don't have any honey. Bummer. Can I borrow your strawberry syrup instead?" She shakes the item in question in my direction.

"Uh, sure. But you can keep that bottle and I'll buy Hunter another *untainted* one." I cringe at the thought of what they will do with that.

"Thanks, chica." Carly pauses at my side. "You know, if you ever need to talk about anything, I'm here for you."

Our eyes meet. I've heard she has abandonment issues. Her parents died and she lived in the foster care system all her life until college, where she met Sky. Her beginning was rough, but she now has her wife and husband keeping her busy with *syrups* and *blow jobs* apparently.

"Thank you."

"Even though Jackson is a furry pain in the ass, he is also a great listener." Her fingertips glide through my hair. "Just don't keep it locked up inside that pretty head of yours, babe." Carly slides over the bottle of syrup. "I bet Jackson would love some mouth action too."

"What's *mouth action* mean?" Hunter decides to materialize in the kitchen.

"That's my cue to leave." Carly snatches her goods and ruffles the boy's hair. "Bye, fam!"

"Where are you going with my strawberry syrup?" He pouts.

I cringe and plead with Carly to not explain what she's actually planning on doing with it.

My sister-in-law reaches into her cleavage and tugs out a wad of cash. She hands him a few bills. His eyes grow wide. I'm not sure if it's because of her boob trick or the amount she handed him. "I'm going to flavor some *milk* of my own, little man. Is that okay?" He nods and she continues, "Now you can buy a case of syrup."

"Thanks, Aunt Carly." He skips out the door while waving his prize in the air. "I'm going to show the guys! They won't believe it!"

"I think I'm going to make a pretty awesome mom." Carly brushes lint off her shoulder.

"You're pregnant?" I zoom in on her flat, stretch mark *free* stomach.

"Not *yet*." She shimmies the bottle in my face. "Do you think if I swallow every drop, it'll make it to my eggs?"

I meet her grin. She's amazing. No wonder Azure married her and Skylar. "It's worth a shot."

"Hopefully a money shot." Carly winks. "I'll give you all the details tomorrow, *sister*."

"Oh, Luna. Please don't." I cover my ears for good measure. "That's my brother."

I block out enough to not hear her sarcastic remark as she sashays past the exit. I relax in my chair and rub my temples of the images it's shoving into my consciousness. But then those pictures morph into Jackson. The beta leaning against the doorframe… Me on my knees… His rod dripping with precum, begging for my warm mouth… Oh, the artwork I could conjure up. There'd be white and tan hues with a splash of black as I stroke him.

"Mom! Can you take me to the store! I want to buy tons of snacks for me and my friends!" Hunter's smile tugs me out of my daydream. I should say no, but he's so damn happy. And it's been a while since he's succumbed to a massive sugar coma.

Oh, boy. Our new packmates are going to hate me for sugaring up their pups.

"We can go, but first I want a hug."

"Can some of the guys come with us?" Hunter mumbles into my chest as we embrace.

"If it's okay with their parents."

He jumps up and down as he does his signature happy dance. "I'm sure Ash can go! His adoptive parents are so cool." Then my son dashes back outside and shreds to fur.

"Hey!" A voice startles me, and I have to throw a hand over my heart to settle the beating. "Sorry. The door was open."

A blush creeps up my neck as I recall what I was just imagining. "Hi, Jackson."

"Are you okay?" he asks slowly.

"Perfect. I'm about to take our little fur monsters to the store to rot their fangs out."

Jackson's frame takes up the entire doorway. He crosses his arms over his chest as his eyes sweep over my mom bod and messy bun. "Do you think that's a good idea?"

My hackles rise. "What's that supposed to mean?"

"Only that you're in a delicate state." His eyebrow rises, hinting at something that I'm obviously missing. "Your heat cycle is approaching. I'll take the pups to the candy store for you."

"No." I stand up and place my mug in the sink.

"No?" He steps farther into the house.

I pivot to him and lift my chin. "I'm perfectly fine walking with my son and his friends."

He steps forward, causing me to backpedal. "Are you now?"

That musky scent is rolling off him in waves. My libido is firing on all cylinders. "Yes," I whisper. My back meets the counter and I swallow. "Why wouldn't I be?"

His lip twitches and that predatorial gaze of his makes me all but combust. It's the thrill of the hunt, and I'm the prey. He traps me between his arms. "I can't believe I get to wake up to this every morning." He clutches my hips, and in one swift movement, he sits me on top of the counter.

Well, hot damn! Before I can collect my jaw from the floor, Jackson grabs my knees and separates my thighs. I only have a second to release a squeak before he smells my arousal at its source. I melt against the cabinets. *Oh, my Luna. What is this beast doing to me?*

"You're lucky I'm a gentleman."

Wait. What? My lids flutter open and I see him standing in front of me with a cocky grin on his face. When did he get off the floor? Did I imagine everything? Maybe I should stay behind...

"Besides, Frost is gearing up the boys to go camping in the woods and he won't allow *sweets*." Jackson winks at me. "They attract nosey ants, and while most are harmless, some bite *hard*."

Why does everything he says sound so sexual?

I clear my throat. "We wouldn't want *pests* lingering where they shouldn't be." I lock on to his gaze. "Right?"

"Of course not." Jackson smirks before he strolls towards the door. "But…" He pauses. "If they're wanted, all you'd have to do is spread that *sweetness* and they'll come howling," he says, then laughs at the redness creeping up my cheeks before leaving me in a puddle of my own arousal.

Stupid *ants*.

Later that night, Jackson returns to his den. I look up when he enters the room. "Are you sure about this?"

"Yes. Sable and Maya are watching the pups for the night and getting some practice parenting in."

I tug the wrinkles out of my sundress. It's the only semi-decent piece of clothing I have for a date. "Where are we going?"

"Not far." Jackson lifts my chin. "You look beautiful." He kisses me softly.

"Thank you." I lay my hand flat on his black button-up shirt. "Do you have any more hints for the night?"

His dimple pokes through as he grins. "You can leave this pesky barrier behind." His fingertips glide up my thighs. When he notices I've gone commando, he purrs, "Who's my naughty girl?" His nose brushes my ear before he nips it. "Are you planning on getting lucky tonight?" He tempts my opening with his knuckle. "Fuck," he groans. "You're already dripping wet."

"Only for you." I grind against him, until he's grazing my sensitive bits.

He growls. "The things you do to me." His erection begs to be released from its zippered cage. "But it'll have to wait." I whimper as he moves his wrist. Then he pauses. "Does my girl want to chase her release?"

I hum in response as he returns his attention to my swollen clit.

"I should leave you a simpering mess," he threatens against my lips. He pinches my soft spot and stars burst behind my eyes. I ride the pleasure waves, until my knees buckle and I melt in his arms. "That's my girl." He sucks my nectar from his hand. "Delicious as always."

I'm a puddle of happiness as my body thrums with orgasmic vibrations. This is why we can't have our date. We get distracted too easily. Jackson's awoken my inner sex kitten and I plan on making up for lost time.

"Can you stand?" he whispers as his lip twitches. "Or should I carry you bridal-style?"

I tilt my head. "If you did that, I'd drip all over your arms."

He blinks for a second, letting my words sink in. "It'll be worth the risk."

The things he says aren't what make my heart skip a beat. It's the *way* he says them. Watching me with admiration and desire, like I'm the only woman in his world… That's what does *it* for me.

"Where are we going?" I nudge him towards the door.

"Our first stop is the Wolves' Den steakhouse for an amazing dinner." He twirls me around. "Then dancing with Carly and Sky."

My pulse thrums. It's been so long since I've done that. Plus, my sisters-in-law know how to have a good time. Especially when their husband is away on business. "Well, it's a good thing Azure is out of town."

My brother and the other Guardians are meeting with government officials to remind them of our treaty of peace, in hopes of keeping war off our heels. But this is our last attempt. If they cross the line again, the gloves are off and there'll be consequences. The shifter community has lost too much.

I shiver at the thought of the Pawson pack, Brock, and those kidnapped women...

Jackson wraps an arm around my waist. "Don't worry. Mr. Judgey will be back soon." His thumb rubs over my belly button. "But not before we can cause some trouble."

"I look forward to it." I lean into him. "Hopefully he's home for Lunamas. It'll be Hunter's first one without Nana."

"Either way, you'll have me by your side. Plus the rest of the pack." He kisses the top of my head. "Just you wait. When you wake up, I'll have a bright-red bow tied to the biggest, *longest* gift."

I cackle at the thought. "You really think highly of your dick."

"Lily. I'm astonished. I was talking about a paintbrush." He tsks his tongue at me. "You have a dirty mind."

"Whatever." I roll my eyes. "We both know you were not talking about that."

"The present I'm getting you is life-changing." He nods as if convincing himself. "Hunter thinks so too."

"You told Hunter what it is?"

"Yes, I did." Jackson straightens his spine, very proud of his accomplishment.

I worry my lip. The only thing I was planning on giving Jackson was a key to my den. He gave me his because we're basically living with him already. But I've been rearranging things at my place so we can have a shared art studio. I wring my hands together. Slowly, I've been gaining the courage to play with pigment again. It's progress.

Jackson grabs my wrist and kisses my palm. "Are you ready for a night out?"

I catch his double meaning. He knows I've been locked in my head lately, but tonight we are letting loose and having fun. Not worrying about the future or the past.

"As long as you're by my side, always."

I lean back and pat my lips with a napkin. I'm so full. But I couldn't help myself. The girls know how to please the shifter community with their prey of the day, and their succulent meat options are heavenly. My waistline thanks them. Phase one of the date has been great. We've talked about the boys, beta duties, and my hopes to start volunteering to teach another youth painting course.

"Do you want any more children?" I rub Jackson's arm.

"Other than Ash and Hunter?" He lifts a brow, then shrugs. "To be honest, I'm pretty traumatized by the whole child-birthing experience."

"Then your sister being pregnant must be killing you." I frown.

"It is. But she agreed to actually *go* to the hospital, unlike Ashely. So, I'm more confident that she'll be okay." He gulps down his rum and coke. "What about you?"

"I don't think I'll ever be blessed with another one."

"Why not?"

"Because I slaughtered my mate."

"In self-defense." Jackson squeezes my leg under the table. "I'm sure Luna has forgiven you." He lifts my chin. "You just need to learn to forgive yourself." His thumb brushes my lips. "I mean, if you're looking for some rough play, I can punish you." He grins.

I'm a puddle again. *Oh, this man.*

"Here's dessert," Carly sings.

"Please, no more," I beg her. "I'm so stuffed."

"We'll save it for later, then." The she-devil winks as she passes me a plate.

I burst into a fit of giggles. It's the penis-shaped cookies they were talking about. "You shouldn't have."

"I just wanted to watch you deep throat it." She leans towards me with her elbows firmly planted on the table.

I grin as I wrap my fingers around the delicate treat. Her eyes widen. I tip my head back and shove the cookie inside my mouth until even the sugar testicles have passed my lips.

"Marry me," the golden goddess pleads. "Or just let me fuck you. I'm not picky."

"Hey! No stealing my date!" Jackson smacks her arm. "I saw her first and I do not share well with others."

"Since when?" Carly arches a questioning brow.

Jackson tugs me to his side. "Since now. Lily is too special to me."

I pull back the dessert and smirk. "Carly, you're already married. To not one person, but two."

"There's always room for another." Her evil grin spreads.

"You're with my brother," I remind her.

"So you can keep it in the family." She shrugs.

"Ew. No thanks."

"Fine, but at least let me have a dance?"

"Are you guys coming with us tonight?" I ask.

"Yup. I'm dragging Sky there and we are letting loose!" Carly sashays her hips, catching a college boy's attention midbite.

"Are you meeting us there?" Jackson ignores the drooling man across the restaurant. "Or do you want to drive together?"

"Rethinking the whole sharing thing?" Carly taunts him.

"On second thought, you can walk."

"You're no fun anymore." Carly sighs. "Lily has tamed the beast."

He rolls his eyes. "Jealousy doesn't look good on you."

She slaps her chest. "I'm not jealous. Let me make out with Lily and prove it."

"Keep me out of this." I raise a hand, then sip my wine as they continue to bicker.

Thank Luna Sky walks over and spanks her wife's ass before crossing her arms over her chest. "Causing trouble, love?"

I love the couple's dynamic. Sky seems to keep Carly in line.

"No. Never." The blonde grins before she taps her chin. "Lily, have you ever heard of the salt-tasting trick?"

"The what?" Jackson and I say in unison.

"Well, they say if you pretend to sprinkle a saltshaker on your tongue, you'll actually taste the saltiness."

"That's the dumbest thing I've ever heard." Jackson throws his head back and opens his mouth wide as he jerks a hand towards his face. We burst into laughter as the gesture mimics giving a guy head. "What's so funny?" He narrows his eyes at us.

Carly pivots her phone in his direction and taps play, so the beta can watch himself in action. "I'm submitting this to Pornhub."

"No, you aren't!" He leaps forward, attempting to snatch the device from her hands.

Sky rolls her eyes and sighs. "I thought you said you weren't causing trouble?"

Jackson

New Love

The red neon sign welcomes us to *Prey & Predator*. I crane my neck at the shifter-exclusive nightclub in front of us. It's been ages since I've been out here.

"If it's wolves only, how does Carly get in?" Lily whispers into my ear.

I side-glance the wives as they bounce past the doorman. "When your husband is the Guardian, you get perks everywhere."

"What if she gets hurt?" Lily squeaks.

And she has good reason to ask, because unrestricted violence is all too common, just another reason why this club makes the big bucks. It's safe to shift and start a bar fight without murdering a fragile human who accidentally got caught in the crosshairs.

"Trust me. No one is going to mess with her."

"Because Azure is her partner?"

"Because Carly has proven she can handle herself, without claws or fangs." I tug Lily inside the establishment, and we make our way to the bar. "Hey, Steven," I greet the young bartender.

"Jackson! Long time, no see. Where have you been?" He slides over my usual whiskey on the rocks.

"Pack duties," I mumble into the glass. Then I nod to Lily. "What do you want?"

She wrenches her eyes away from the strobing lights and lands them on Steven. "A strawberry margarita with a sugar rim please."

"You got it." He winks before tending to her cocktail.

I tug Lily closer, staking my claim so no one gets any ideas. I make eye contact with the unclaimed males sitting around us, reminding them to keep their paws off. I know Lily can handle herself, but I don't want to trigger her if some sleazeball gets a little too handsy. She's been doing so well with getting out of her comfort zone. I don't want to jinx it and have her clam up. But if she does, I'll be right here by her side.

"Here you go." Steven hands Lily the frozen drink. "Enjoy."

"Thank you." She wraps her tongue around the straw and I about lose my shit, wondering what it would be like to have my dick in its place instead.

I clear my throat. "How does it taste?"

She nods and swallows before she answers, "It's perfect."

"Come on!" Carly reaches out a hand and tugs on Lily's arm. "Gulp it down so we can play!"

I fight the urge to remind the blonde that this is my date, not hers. But the smile on Lily's face has my mouth snapping shut, while the way her throat works to chug the drink sends jolts to my dick.

Luna help me. I already want to bend her over and fuck her brains out.

The music thumps all around us. The lights flash off our sweaty bodies. It's chaotic madness. And my girl is loving every single minute of it. She sways her hips against mine, flips her hair as I suck on her neck, and moans when my erection pokes into her backside.

This was a great idea.

"I have to go to the ladies' room," Lily yells over the bass.

"I can show you where it is, then buy you a drink on the way back," Sky offers.

I kiss Lily's hand and play bow. "I'll be waiting until you return."

"I'll keep my feet warm out here." Carly smacks Sky's ass. "Hurry up."

I lean on the wall and watch the girls prance to the back of the building. I'm glad everyone is getting along, but I can't wait to have some alone time with my girl when we return to our bedroom.

"There you are!" That's my only warning before a feminine frame leaps into my arms.

I stumble back and frown at the woman in question. "Bridgett?"

"Has it been so long that you've forgotten *my* pack owns this establishment?" She bats her lashes. "Or are you playing hard to get?" Then she lowers her lips towards mine.

I dodge her ruby red lipstick and set her on the ground. "It's nice to see you again, but I'm dating someone."

She throws her head back and cackles. "Stop."

I arch a brow and smell her breath. Nope, not drunk yet. "I'm being serious."

"Jackson, you're never serious when it comes to relationships." Bridgett runs a claw over my chest. "Now, how about I let you tie me up and fuck me into tomorrow?"

Glass shatters and we pivot to see Lily gawking at our close encounter. "I…" She swallows her shock. "I brought you a drink, but it looks like someone got to you first," she chokes out before she turns on her heels and attempts to walk away.

"Lily! Wait!" I shout, but Bridgett jumps in my path.

"You can do better than *that*, Jackson," she coos.

I narrow my eyes at the shifter in front of me. "Don't judge her. You don't even know her."

"I don't need to know her to know that you can do better than that," Bridgett hisses.

I go to step around her again, but she continues to block me. I run a hand through my hair to keep it off the twit in front of me. "Don't do this."

"Do what?"

"Act like you're better than everyone else."

"Jackson." Bridgett inches closer, but I step back. "What happened to you?"

"I'm a one-woman man now. Get over it." I shove past her, but she snatches my wrist.

"How dare you defile Ashely's memory like this!"

I freeze. *What the fuck?*

"Don't you ever say that again," I snarl. "Or you'll never be welcomed to visit the Tala pack to see your self-proclaimed nephew."

My cheek burns as her claws slash at my face. Shock racks my frame. Did she seriously just slap me?

"Ashely loved you with all of her heart and this is how you repay her?"

I open my mouth to respond but a blur of color tackles Bridgett to the floor. The two figures wrestle at my feet. I don't realize who jumped to my rescue until she speaks.

"Don't you ever talk to Jackson like that again!" Lily pins Bridgett's arms and legs. "His loyalty to Ashely speaks volumes!"

Bridgett thrashes on the floor but is stuck in place. Carly and Sky flank my sides. Both of them cross their arms over their chests.

"Shouldn't you help your sister-in-law?" I blurt out.

"She's fucking up the trash pretty well on her own." Carly smirks, before turning to Lily and shouting, "Go for the hair!"

Lily freezes as she slowly tilts her face to ours. When she notices that she has an audience, she backs off.

Bridgett smooths out her clothes and tips her chin to me. "We're over."

I wrap an arm around Lily and shrug. "I wish you nothing but happiness." My former lover storms off in to the crowd. I pivot to Lily and run my hands over her. "Are you okay?"

She reaches for my wrists to still me before her palms warm my cheeks. Her gaze burns into mine. "You are not disloyal."

"I know."

"I would never try to replace your mate. I respect Ashely's role in your life. You know that, right?"

I mimic her actions as I place my hands on Lily's face. "I love you, Butterfly."

Damn. It feels good to finally let those words fly free. I know she's not there yet, but ever since she was attacked, I knew how much she meant to me.

"What?" she whispers.

I press my lips to hers and show her how much I adore everything about her, flaws and all, until she's left breathless. "I fucking love

341

you, Lilith Cassandra Pawson."

She blinks at me. "That's not fair. I don't know your full name."

I chuckle and shake my head. "I'll tell you later, so others don't hear and use it against me."

She peeks over my shoulder at Carly and smirks. "I don't blame you."

"Hey! Stop talking shit about me!" Carly hollers at my back.

"Are you ready for phase three of our date?" I squeeze Lily's hand.

"Will it be less dramatic?"

"Maybe." I tug her under my arm and stride towards the exit. "It's definitely more messy."

Lily

Painting Perfection

I don't know what the fuck came over me. I rack a hand through my hair. But with the way Bridgett was speaking to Jackson… I just leaped at her. The things she said were fallacious. He valued his mate above all else.

I glance at the shifter in question. He loved her until her dying breath. I sigh, my shoulders slumping. Jackson's nothing like me. I had my mate and I slaughtered him in his sleep. I know Jackson would give anything to have Ashely back.

But not me when it comes to mine. Brock can continue to rot in the ground.

Jackson pulls me out of my despair as he cups my face. "I love you, Butterfly."

I attempt to back away, but he keeps me close. No. He loves *Ashely*. His wife. Not a worthless shifter damned to meet her mate in hell. I heard him wrong. "What?"

He smirks before lowering his lips to mine. The way he slowly touches every part of my being with his kiss warms my toes.

Luna, he's amazing. How could he care for me? *Me!* A single mother. Damaged goods.

"I fucking love you, Lilith Cassandra Pawson," he tells me.

Who told him my middle name?

I tilt my head. There's so much we don't know about each other, and yet he's declaring that he favors me above all other females.

"Are you ready for phase three of our date?" He grabs my hand and leads us to the parking lot.

My heart jolts. I can't wait to see what Jackson has planned. He drives us to a small office, then guides me to a side door and flicks on the lights.

I gasp. It's a tiny art studio. Canvases surround a platform and paint decorates the tarp protecting the tile floor.

"Raven taught me and hundreds of other kids the ways of the artistic mind. *Here.* In this very spot." He waves me forward. "And tonight, I get the honor of teaching you."

My fingertips dance over the instruments. The ache to sit and conquer the white burns bright, urging me to give it a second chance. I pick up a charcoal pencil and examine it. The usual flashback to the cabin doesn't come. Nor does the fragmented body of the delivery boy.

Shuffling in the corner causes my neck to snap in that direction, my eyes landing on the platform in the center of the room and a very naked Jackson. I gawk at his toned abs and take note of how the light glimmers off his sweaty forehead.

I clear my throat. "Your surrogate mother will probably frown at you for doing *this*."

"I told her I was modeling for you."

"Did you also explain that you were going to be nude?"

"It must have slipped my mind." He shrugs. "Now that I think about it, *we* could do nude body art together and create an optical illusion. You know, by painting streaks of color on each other's frames, then combining our bodies to form one image."

I ignore his suggestion as I quickly glance around the room. "What if someone walks in and sees you without your clothes on?"

Jackson leaps off the platform, strides to the back door, and locks it. "Problem solved."

"I'm sorry. I was too distracted by your ass. Can you repeat that?" I smirk at him as I match his sarcasm.

"Well, grab your canvas and begin sketching this fine ass," he says, resuming his model stance.

"Are you serious?"

He arches a brow. "No. I'm just standing here, freezing my balls off for nothing. Now hurry up."

"Yes, sir." I sketch the outline of his muscular frame, then pause. "Where are we going to put this when we're done?"

"In the front entryway, so everyone can adore me as much as you do." He winks.

I wrinkle my nose at the thought. "What about the children? You'll scare them off."

A piece of chalk thumps me on the head. "No, it won't. Now focus."

I return to the canvas but it's so quiet. I can hear every breath. Feel it on my skin. I shiver. Why is this such a turn on?

Concentrate, Lily.

After some time and a lot of doodling, I turn the easel back towards my man. "Well, what do you think?"

347

He steps forward and grins. "I'm pretty well-endowed."

I glance at the beast between his legs. "You're right. It's unrealistic."

"What's next?" he asks, clearly ignoring my jab.

"I would love to add some color."

"There's paint in the corner." He points to a table.

I grab a few bottles and get to work mixing until I have the perfect golden hue that matches Jackson's skin tone. I brush it between the lines I sketched and get lost in the image. It's a great feeling, to create something from nothing again.

"That's amazing." Jackson's breath tickles my neck.

When did he move behind me?

"If you use shorter strokes." He guides my wrist. "You can amplify your lines and form shadows." I shiver and the paint brush slips from my grasp. "Pick it up," he whispers as the heat rolls off his chest.

I bend at the waist, pressing my ass into his groin. He grunts and clutches my hips. I peek over my shoulder and bat my lashes. His eyes widen as he realizes that I'm intentionally taunting him.

Jackson spins me until we are chest to chest while sharing the same breath. "Do you want me to fuck you, Lily?"

"Do I?"

He arches a brow. "Yes or no."

"Maybe."

"Why are you testing my patience?"

"I'm not testing you." I reach behind my back, dipping my fingers into the bottle. "You brought me here to paint." I smear a few strokes across his abs. "So, that's what I'm doing." I tilt my head at his wide gaze. "Teasing you is just a bonus."

The force of his kiss has me stumbling back. I wrap my arms around his shoulders to deepen it. He slips on the tarp and we crash to the floor. My dress is yanked off me and discarded in a heap. His hands roam my frame, causing goose bumps to rise along the surface of my skin. I moan and arch my back. Jackson sucks my nipple between his teeth.

The things this man does to me…

I hiss when he nips, then quickly follows it up with a long stroke of his tongue to ease the pain.

"Jackson…" I beg as my core throbs.

He lines up his erection and teases my entrance. "My turn to test *your* patience."

He enters slowly, filling me to the hilt before pulling back again. He continues this torturous rhythm, even as I dig my nails into his arms and plead for him to pick up the pace. He chuckles but doesn't obey.

That's it…

I grind my jaw and shove at his chest, forcing him rearward so I can leap on him and pierce myself on his weeping rod. I ride him hard, until stars burst behind my eyes. Jackson rocks my hips and helps me extend the waves of pleasure. As I clench around him again, he roars his release and pours into me.

I trace circles over his corded biceps as I catch my breath. "Your mom is going to be mad." My teeth graze his chest.

He moans and arches forward before he takes in our colorful mess. And winces. "Shit. What did you do?" He tickles my sides.

I swat him. "Me?"

"Yes, *you*. I was innocently modeling for you when, suddenly, you jumped me."

"You're too cocky for your own good."

"Do you blame me?"

"Yes. It's your fault!"

"You're the one who shoved your ass into my dick." He slaps the limb in question.

"You ordered me to grab the paintbrush."

"Because you dropped it." Jackson gives me a pointed stare. "And it's still on the floor, by the way."

I roll off him and take a closer look at the studio. Most of the destruction is localized. I hold up my canvas. "It's perfect."

Jackson joins my side and laughs. In the heat of our impassioned tumbling, my breasts must have left an imprint on his nude silhouette, giving him a broader chest. He massages my sensitive skin, smearing more paint across me. "I like the upgrade."

My nipples harden and I lean into his touch. "Me too."

"We should probably clean up." He rubs his erection against my ass. "Unless you want to bend over again?" He lifts a questioning brow.

A rainbow of pigment decorates our sweaty bodies. *We* are masterpieces. Gone are our plain canvases. Replaced by perfection… with a touch of the flaws that make us who we are.

Jackson

Pack Dynamics

*L*ater that night, after we've cleaned up our mess, Lily lifts on her tippytoes and hangs the new piece of artwork in our bedroom. It's not my naked body, but still amazing. Her eyes shimmer with unshed tears as she glides her fingertips over the canvas. The picturesque lake landscape is identical to the ravine in the Pawson's territory. If you look closely, you can see the ashes of her pack speckled in the lush grass as if they are still out there running between the blades.

Lily swipes at her cheeks. "Is the frame even?"

"A little to the left."

She lifts the side and adjusts it. "How's this?"

My eyes lock onto her. "Perfection."

She pivots and her soft smile lightens the atmosphere.

"I wish Ash could play with us tonight," Hunter grumbles from the doorframe. "I miss him."

"Sorry, pal." I ruffle his mane. "He's spending time with his adoptive parents."

The disgruntled pup crosses his arms over his chest. "Can they adopt me too?"

Lily guides her son into the kitchen. "Why don't I make you some hot chocolate?" She rustles around the cabinets. "Where did I stick those packets of cocoa and marshmallows?"

I smirk as she struggles. I like to move shit around the kitchen just to aggravate her. The angry sex is worth every glare she throws my way.

"Jackson?" Hunter tugs my shirt. "When can I start calling you *Dad*?"

Lily sways, and I steady her hips before she can tumble from the shock. She blinks at her child. "Why would you ask that?"

Hunter shrugs. "Ash calls Jackson and his adoptive father *Dad*."

I chuckle. The logic makes sense. But that's not my decision to make. Hunter can call me anything he'd like unless it's disrespectful.

"What happened to my dad anyway?" Hunter demands.

Lily pales. I help her onto the chair next to her son before she passes out.

"Hunter, what's up with all these questions?" I ask, giving his mom a break.

He fixes us with a stare. "Lunamas is coming," he says, as if that somehow explains everything.

"And?" I press him.

"The guys are excited to get toys and movies, but I don't want that."

I share a look with Lily. We already bought him a gaming system. Hopefully that wasn't the wrong gift. "What is it you want, bud?"

"A little brother." He watches us expectantly as if we can materialize one from midair. When we don't, he adds, "Or sister."

Now it's my turn to pale. I rub my forehead. No way on Luna's green earth is *that* happening.

The front door slams open and causes our trio to jump at the sudden noise.

"We're pregnant!" Carly waves a stick in the air.

"That's not fair," Hunter grumbles.

Carly arches a brow at the pup. "You do know boys can't get pregnant, right?"

"Duh. I wanted Mom to give me a brother or sister."

Carly glances between me and Lily, then drapes an arm over Hunter's shoulder. "You can be an honorary brother to our children."

"Really?" He perks up.

"Sure thing, little man."

"Awesome!"

They share a hug before Hunter skips into the living room. "I'm going to pick the card game we're going to play tonight."

The quick change in conversation makes my temple throb.

Lily bangs her head on the table, and I pat her back. "Are you okay?" She only nods as she rubs her neck. I kiss her cheek. "One day at a time."

Lily blinks at Carly, then leaps into the blonde's arms as she catches on to the announcement. "You're pregnant? Congratulations!"

"I helped too," Azure says, squeezing into the house.

"Azure!" His sister embraces him. "I can't wait to become an aunt."

"You should really knock." I point out. "We could have been having sex."

The Guardian narrows his eyes in my direction. "With my nephew in the same room?"

"He's not here. He's in the living room." I throw a thumb behind me. "Speaking of which, why don't you say hi to him?"

Azure bumps chests with me. He still hates the fact that Lily and I are together, but he's going to have to get over it. Because I'm not going anywhere. Lily tugs her brother towards her son, leaving me with Carly.

I elbow the blonde. "How does Sky feel about you getting pregnant first?"

She shrugs. "Considering she doesn't have to deal with the sore breasts or the morning sickness, she's content to let me go first."

"You do realize that the child won't be able to shift, right?" I blurt out. "And when Skylar has her pups, you will have to be very careful no one gets hurt from their claws or fangs."

"Hey. Don't ruin this moment for me." She glares. "Everything will be fine."

"You're right. I'm happy for you guys, and I'll always be here to help when you need it."

She rests her head on my shoulder and rubs her belly. "I can't believe I finally have a family and it's a bunch of crazy wolves."

I chuckle and lean my cheek on hers. "Just don't die during childbirth. We'd miss that loudmouth of yours."

She smacks me. "Rude." But she knows my fears are legitimate.

"I thought you were supposed to talk to Azure and get me in his good graces?" I change the subject.

"If you would stop fucking his sister, it'd help your case." She elbows me.

"Nope. Never."

We watch the trio as they laugh and set up a game of Uno. Lily peeks over the couch and our eyes meet. I'm the luckiest wolf alive.

"Are you coming, Dad?" Hunter yells.

Azure's neck snaps to his nephew, then to me. I shrug. What's another rugrat to add to the mix? I'm already planning on asking Lily if I can adopt him, so I can surprise the boy with the certificate on Lunamas. "I'll be right there, son."

The pure delight in Hunter's gaze is one in a million. He dashes over, slams into my legs, and squeezes. "Can I go first?" He gestures to the coffee table. "Please."

I lift him up until he rests on my shoulders. "Sure thing, big guy, as long as your uncle goes last."

"That's not fair," the Guardian growls.

"Life never is." I smirk at him.

We settle into the other room to play the card game that always ends in full-on family destruction. I wrap an arm around Lily and Hunter. I'm glad we can have our second chance at a happily ever after.

Lily

Epilogue

Five years later...

"Thank you all for coming today." Jackson's voice booms as his eyes scan the gathering crowd, lingering on me for a moment before he winks.

I smirk and nod at him to continue.

Jackson lifts a worn paintbrush into the air. "My journey began with this gift from my adopted mother, Raven." He swallows, faltering in his speech. Maya gives him an encouraging pat on his back. "This simple instrument changed my life. Even led me to my mate." He smiles at Ash as the boy stands next to Cynthia and Frank. "And today I invite you all to enter the same walls of healing that mean so much to me and my partner." He waves me forward.

A blush creeps up my neck. This was not what we rehearsed for the reopening of his mom's old studio. Carly shoves me towards the front of the group, while Azure squeezes Hunter's hand. I stumble on my feet, but Jackson steadies my waist before he tucks me under his arm in a protective stance.

"Although our pasts were traumatic, we overcame the haunting memories through creative outlets, and we wanted to provide that same opportunity for our community." He nods at Sable, who cuts the red ribbon adorning the entrance.

Shouts of joy echo around us.

"As part of this amazing institute," Maya booms with her alpha tone. "All packs are welcome to enroll in any of the workshops and counseling sessions. No one will be turned away." Claps resonate around the room before she continues, "Let's take a peek inside and see all the amazing work Lily and Jackson have completed."

Maya leads the way. She should have mentioned all the hard work she put into this project too, like the program she's directing for the foster children she busses in from Carson City.

"Also, please enjoy a buffet of the best barbeque in town, provided by the Wolves' Den steakhouse," Jackson adds with a smile towards Sky and Carly.

The crowd moves into the building, and my lip quivers. We're going to change the lives of so many people. The clouds part in the sky and the sun's brilliant rays spotlight our efforts. Nana is smiling down at us. I know she is. My hand glides over Jackson's. Along with the many other shifters we've lost too.

Jackson kisses the top of my head. "We did it."

We watch as, one by one, everyone pushes through the entrance. Even Bridgett and her family. She nods at us in acknowledgment. We return the gesture, a silent promise to catch up with them before they leave. I lean my cheek on Jackson's shoulder and enjoy his warmth. Life hasn't been easy. But we've made it through.

"Dad!" Hunter waves at a goodie bag. "Can I have one?"

Jackson rolls his eyes. "Don't you have enough paintbrushes at home, son?"

"But this one has the studio's name etched on it!" Pride pours from his statement. "Please?"

"Let the guests grab them first and if we have any extra, you may have one." Jackson gives the boy a pointed stare, letting the kid know that he means business.

We put those together for our customers, so they remember to return. But if Hunter wants one…

"I can always order more if we run out," I remind our pup.

"Can I have one too, Mom?" Ash shouts from beside his brother.

I smirk. After Jackson adopted Hunter, Ash insisted on calling me *Mom*. I thought Cynthia or Jackson might have discouraged him, but they foster the free-flowing love and admiration Ash extends to me.

"I'll make sure to set *two* aside," I yell over the noise.

The boys run off towards the plates, ready to fill their bellies with the delicious grub.

"You spoil them," Jackson grumbles as he leads me towards the open door.

I elbow him. "Who was the one who bought them that new gaming system?"

He rubs his stomach. "They are excelling in their academics and pack duties. That was a reward for a job well done." He pauses at the threshold and sighs. "I miss them."

I follow his gaze to the portrait of Raven and Frost hanging under the company's name. "I know, honey." I kiss his cheek. "But they are so proud of everything you've done in their honor."

"I hope so," he whispers.

Then Jackson wraps an arm around my waist. We pivot towards the shifters and examine the brightly lit space that Raven left for

Jackson and Maya. At one point, it was a simple painting studio, but after a few renovations, it now offers mixed media areas too, including: drawing, collage, and sculpting. Sable's brother Aspen has even volunteered to add a writing class to the ever-growing list of activities.

"Welcome to Healing Creations." Jackson raises a glass to the group. "May it bring you peace in troubling times."

Once the crowd thins and empties into the parking lot, I sigh and lean my head on Jackson's shoulders. I still can't believe we organized all this.

"I love you, Stinky," I tease my man.

He brings his lips to mine, stealing my breath away. "I love you too, Butterfly."

Thank You

This book baby never would have been born without the many individuals who breathed life into its pages.

A huge shout-out to my editor, Kat Pagan! She is a mighty word witch, and without her incredible techniques, this book wouldn't be as amazing as it is!

Thank you, Frankie Page, for the incredible formatting on all my books! I hate all the technical stuff with paperback layouts, but she makes it look so easy and beautiful!

Also, a super-sized thank you to all my beta readers: Jennifer, B.L., Heather, and Hannah. You guys are amazing! The fact that you took time out of your already crazy schedules to read and answer feedback blows me away! I couldn't have done it without you!

Finally, thank **YOU**! Without readers, I couldn't continue my writing dreams. You make my world a brighter place.

Scan my QR code to chat with me on social media, **review** my books, and join my exclusive newsletter that includes freebies and sneak peeks.

Additional Titles by the Author

Wolves of Cold Creek (18+, paranormal romance):

The Cold Creek packs are loyal—while bursting with mouthwatering, unclaimed shifters—all just waiting for their mates. Why not drop in and enjoy the picturesque views by day and scorching fires at night? Don't be shy. They don't bite… hard.

Suggested Reading Order:

Scarlett's Tail

Sky's Tail

Lily's Tail

Rebel's Revenge (release date TBA)

Cooking Up Disaster (slow-burn romance):

Step into the Decadent Cup and grab something hot! In the small town of Jasper, this café offers handcrafted coffee and killer banana nut muffins while stirring up the most unlikely couples. Read their journeys as they cook up disaster and create new blends of mischief. Season 1 with Blake and Amy: Ep 1-69. Season 2 with Kay and Jason: Ep 69+.

(Episodes available now only on Kindle Vella.)

Feathered Dreams, completed series (a rags-to-riches, clean romance):

Join Ann and be swept into a world of swoon-worthy characters, glittering gowns, and unrelenting intrigue.

Ann is beginning to see how naïve she has been, though by no fault of her own. Farming side by side with her father, away from the drama of the outside world, is what she has always loved most. But now that she is at the Palace, she is forced to focus on other people and their daily struggles. In the midst of her personal growth, she starts to realize how cruel the world can be. Will she shy away and run back to the familiarity of her old life? Or can she share her unique sense of compassion and fierce loyalty to help those in need?

Feathered Dreams (Book 1)

Plucked (Book 2)

Molting (Book 3)

Split Feather (Book 4)

Final Flock (Book 5)

www.ingramcontent.com/pod-product-compliance
Lightning Source LLC
Chambersburg PA
CBHW071507260626
47170CB00002B/295